Hyde Park Adventures

The Colonel's Lost Vault

TS WIELAND

Written by:
TS Wieland
Text Copyright (c) 2021 TS Wieland
Photos Copyright (c) 2022

This novel's story and characters are fictitious. Certain long-standing institutions, agencies, and public offices are mentioned, but the characters involved are wholly imaginary. The opinions expressed are those of the characters, and should not be confused with the author's.

First Edition, English: May, 2022.

Hardback ISBN 978-0-9991941-8-8
Paperback ISBN 978-0-9991941-9-5

Lead Editor: Rebecca Tyler
Associate Editor: Tammie Wieland
Assisant Editor: Brooke Benedict
Paperback Artwork by Samuel Bourguignon
Hardcover Artwork by Rebecca Tyler

Direct Inquiries to:
Tammie@WieRok.com

Visit TSWieland.com for more adventures!

Hyde Park Adventures

The Colonel's Lost Vault

TS WIELAND

Prologue
Nazi-occupied Athens, Greece
1943

The Colonel used the early morning darkness to his advantage, repacking the last crate—one among twenty-seven—with that which he had collected from all across Greece. His day had been preoccupied by inspections and meetings, leaving him a short window to do what now had to be done. He held his lighter in his hand, standing before the crate, surrounded by the large airfield hanger, making sure the contents were secure before hammering the wooden lid closed. He scanned the empty hanger nervously, checking to make sure the coast was clear. He held the lighter with one hand and tried to close the lid with his other. The wail of the air raid siren outside caused him to jump, dropping his lighter. The Colonel picked his lighter back up and, still lit, and finished hammering the lid over the crate in a hurry. Placing the hammer down on the crate beside him, he straightened out his uniform and fixed his hair, then proceeded out onto the tarmac to see what all the fuss was about.

Placing his cap back on, he looked up towards the half-moon sky to see a squadron of British Lancaster bombers on the verge of passing overhead. He ran towards the officers' quarters, fearing for his guest's safety. Opening the door to his quarters, he found his room vacant with no sign of her. He checked under the bed and behind the desk only to discover they were both clear. He called out, "Oliwia!"

There was no reply.

Hearing the air siren grow louder, the Colonel ran to the airmen's barracks and threw the door open to see half of the platoon still sleeping in their cots while the rest slowly awoke and put on their uniforms.

"Wake up!" the Colonel shouted in his native German. He proceeded around the barracks, hitting each one of the privates with his cap. "Up! Up! To your stations! Get up, now!"

The Colonel watched as a young private with oiled blonde hair—no older than eighteen—stood before his cot putting his jacket on like a sloth. He grabbed a clipboard from off the wall beside him and threw it at the young private, striking him in the back. The young man reached for his back, wincing in pain as he faced the Colonel. "Move or I'll see that you're all shot for your incompetence!"

The young private hurried his pace.

"Sergeant Boden!" the Colonel called throughout the barracks.

"Sir!" replied Boden, approaching him as he tucked his shirt into his trousers.

The thunder of the anti-air guns shook the barracks from outside. The Colonel remained focused on his orders as Boden looked towards the window.

"See to it my cargo from hanger 6 is loaded onto a cargo plane for Munich," the Colonel ordered, reclaiming Boden's attention.

"Yes, sir," Boden replied, throwing on his coat. "I'll have my men tend to it after the raid—"

"Now, Sergeant! Any later and I'll have you transferred to the eastern front."

Boden nodded fearfully.

The Colonel turned back and stepped out onto the airfield. He scanned the sky once more to see the bombers now directly overhead with the tracer rounds from the cannons cutting through the sky like shooting stars. The quake of a British bomb pounded into his chest as the first hit pummeled the nearby hillside, continuing in a chain of explosions which lit up the airfield. The Colonel marched towards the Heinkler parked along the runway. He began shouting at the two pilots, running for cover beside one of the anti-air cannons at the sight of the first wave.

"No! No! Get up! Get that plane moving!" he shouted at them, waving them back to their post. "Get that plane over to hangar 6, now!"

The pilots nodded and hurried back to their plane.

The Colonel proceeded to the command post with his back to them. His heart was racing with fear for his daughter, yet he refused to show it. A blast of heat and a shockwave rolled up the tarmac from behind him as he stumbled forward. The Colonel recoiled and looked back from his hands and knees to see the Heinkler now consumed in a billowing inferno—along with the two pilots. He rose to his feet and ran towards the command building. Swinging the door open, the men all saluted him.

"Colonel Wagner," said Lieutenant Schäfer.

"Lieutenant," the Colonel replied, calmly, "where's my daughter?"

"I had her moved to the bunker when I found you missing from your quarters, sir. I came looking to inform you of the raid."

The Colonel sighed with relief.

"Colonel, I must speak with you regarding these papers. I have no account of the flight mentioned baring her arri—"

"Another time, Lieutenant! Send a message to Major Fischer and inform him that I'll be sending another plane full of crates to Munich that'll need to be escorted to the vault."

"Yes, sir!" Schäfer replied, picking up the phone.

"And ready a transport for me and my daughter for Florence."

"Perhaps she would be safer back in Munich, sir."

"No!" The Colonel shouted back. "She's my responsibility!" He turned back to the door. "Just get it done, Lieutenant!"

The men all stood and raised their hands, proclaiming their loyalty to the Führer as the Colonel lazily raised his right hand before heading back outside.

Hearing the explosions continue to beat down upon the surrounding Greek coast, the Colonel marched back towards his hangar to see Boden and his men opening the double doors.

The Colonel approached him. "Sergeant! Find us another cargo plane!"

"Yes, sir," Boden replied, hurrying with four of his men away towards the nearby hangars, leaving behind the other four to tend to the crates.

The Colonel stopped before the hanger and pulled his lighter and cigarettes out from his pocket. He lit one as he watched the Heinkler continue to burn. He heard the scrapping of wood from one of the crates as the four young privates moved them by hand towards the doorway. "Careful!" he shouted at them.

The Colonel shook his head in annoyance, turning his attention back to the raid. He spotted the young eighteen-year-old private he had struck back in the barracks making his way over to the hanger across the tarmac, late to his duty. The young man ran over to Boden before heeding his instructions to help with the crates.

The young private ran towards the hanger as he locked eyes with the Colonel. The Colonel cast a tense glare at him, making sure the private knew he was not in the mood for incompetence. The private looked away and ran into the hanger.

Smoking his cigarette, the Colonel watched the airfield and surrounding hillside be bombarded by the British offensive. His fears for his daughter remained ever-present but were settled for the moment. The Nazi war machine had finally reached its limit, rupturing at the seams by the strain of two fronts, and now both in retreat.

The Colonel reached into his pocket, continuing to watch the privates out of the corner of his eye. He pulled out his leather-bound journal, flipping back through the pages, trying to recount his journey in full while also ensuring he hadn't made any mistakes; its pages tailored only to what he wanted his associates to know. He finally reached the newest page, separated by a that which was now missing—and would hopefully forever remain missing.

In a blast of heat and an ear-splitting roar, a Focke-Wulf exploded as it was hit by the raid. The Colonel turned away from the explosion, feeling the chunks of tarmac pelt his coat as he stuffed his journal back into his pocket. He looked back to see the men who had been prepping the Focke-Wulf for takeoff now either dead on the tarmac or yelling out for help. The four of the privates loading his cargo set his crates down and hurried to help.

The Colonel chased after them, only to be forced to stop by the sound of a wood crate clattering to the ground inside the hanger. He looked to his left.

The young private with blonde hair stood before the crate he had packed only minutes prior. The crate now rested on its side, fallen as he undoubtedly and foolishly tried to move it by himself. The lid was open, exposing its contents.

The private stood staring down into the crate in stunned silence.

The Colonel slowly approached the private's back as he continued to stare. He grabbed the hammer from off the crate beside him.

The young private turned back to face him; his eyes were wide, and the color was drained from his face.

The Colonel bared his teeth. He swung only once with all his wrath.

One
NEWARK, SCOTLAND
PRESENT DAY

THE SOUND OF metal clashing against stone echoed off the vacant crumbling halls of Newark Castle, awakening the stronghold from its nine hundred years of slumber.

Sophie took another swing with the sledgehammer in her hands at the inner left wall of the grand fireplace before her. She stopped and took a breath, seeing the softball sized hole she had now made; little remained of the stone mosaic which once was laid into the wall, as she had now finished what time had already started.

Sophie rested the hammer against the wall beside her and pulled a flashlight out from her trusty field backpack, decorated with her Marine Raider service patch. She brushed her black bangs away from her eyes and gazed into the hole with her flashlight.

Inside was a palm sized stone with finger grooves cut into the outer edges. Sophie reached into the hole and turned the stone clockwise, feeling the stone resist with age. The sound of rock grinding against rock came from beyond the back wall of the fireplace, followed by the slow trickling sound of sand falling away.

The back wall of the fireplace began to slowly sink as the tightly packed sand beneath it fell away unveiling a dark hidden passage beyond it. The wall finally dropped into a secret stone cutout below the floor with a heavy thud. Sophie pointed her flashlight towards the opening she had uncovered. At her feet was a rotted, wooden rope ladder leading down a shaft to the castle's lowest foundation. "Found you..." Sophie muttered to herself with a sense of satisfaction.

"Young lady! Young lady!" shouted the elderly castle curator from beyond the great hall's doorway.

Sophie hurried towards the open doorway, ducking down under the yellow caution tape strung across the entryway to keep visitors out. She tucked her flashlight away, doing her best to not seem suspicious. Beyond the castle's main entrance, she could see the curator making his way towards her from the visitors building.

The curator, with his combed grey hair and mustache, shuffled with age towards her as he spoke with a thick Scottish accent. "Thought I heard a boom comin' from ya direction! Ye awright, lass?" asked the curator.

"Splendid actually," replied Sophie, stepping out of the castle into the drizzling rain in an attempt to keep the curator away. "It may have just been a crack of thunder. I heard it out here as well."

The curator stopped beside the stone grave marker and expressed an unconvincing look. "Are you sure yer' from the Museum's Association?"

"Yes, sir! Just doing my annual report for the community records, as mentioned. Few stone shaving and soil samples here and there. Some photos of the structure. Honestly, nothing too adventurous," Sophie replied as she withdrew her camera and a plastic zip bag from her backpack and held them up for the curator to see.

The curator continued to stare at her with uncertainty before nodding in agreement. "Very well. Just keep yer distance from the great hall, if ye please. That floor has been looking to give way' any day now. We had to block it off tae visitors. Might put that in to the report as well. A plea to the Association for funds to have it repaired would be a treat, if ye'd be so kind of course?"

"Absolutely! Will do, sir!" Sophie replied, once again lying through her smile.

The curator turned back around and made his way into the main office, casting a suspicious glance towards her. Sophie let out a sigh of relief and returned to the castle. She ducked under the caution tape once more and crossed into the great hall to return to the fireplace. She took a series of photos of the secret passageway, then swapped her camera out for her flashlight once more.

Sophie peered down the old ladder to the floor below with her flashlight, seeing the long drop. The lower floor remained sunken beneath several inches of water, brought in from the river which guarded the castle's flank. She put one foot on the rung of the ladder, feeling the wet and aged wood sink under her weight. The rung snapped. Sophie climbed back up onto the main floor, relieved. "Don't know why I thought that would hold me. Might wanna find another way down, Broadway."

Sophie removed her backpack, withdrew her climbing rope, and tied it off around the railing across the hall. Grabbing her backpack, she tied the rope around her waist, and then rappelled down into the depths of the castle.

Slowly descending the rope into the damp and molded chamber, she could feel her left hand struggling to hold on to her lead rope without the aid of the tips of her pinky and ring fingers. She swapped hands with her right, using her left to hold on to the guide rope as she continued to lower herself down.

Splashing into the shallow water below, Sophie pulled her flashlight from her pocket and scanned the surrounding chamber. Before her was another musty hall of stone, supported by rotting wooden beams meant to hold up the floor of the great hall above. A lone coffin rested at the center of the sunken chamber, its lid carved with the likeness of a man dressed in Catholic robes, cradling a bible in one hand. The walls of the chamber were engraved with names of those who had protected the chamber's secret, now washed away from the trickling rainwater seeping through the cracked stone from outside.

As she circled the chamber, she pointed her flashlight towards the back corner to see one of the wooden support beams was split down the middle, barely holding and on the verge of collapsing. To the right of it was the secret pathway leading to the river; just as the old friar's writings had described, a hidden passageway reserved only for times of siege.

Sophie approached the lone coffin and pointed her flashlight at the man depicted on the lid. "Found you," she said with a grin.

She fastened the flashlight to the shoulder of her tan button shirt and began pushing on the lid. She grunted, feeling the heavy lid starting to slowly give way, inch by inch. The lid finally fell away from her and splashed down into the shallow water. She wiped her hands clean using the shemagh[1] wrapped around her neck before pointing the flashlight down into the open coffin. All that remained was the skeleton of the once-holy member of the Catholic church and court priest, Father Nicholas; still clutching onto his trusted bible with his right hand while holding something hidden away in his left.

"Forgive me, Father, for I am about to sin," Sophie said, making the sign of the cross. She reached into the coffin and lifted the Father's boney hand away to find a small, glazed, clay pot underneath. She gently picked the pot up and replaced the hand.

She held the pot out before her and examined it with the flashlight; painted across its surface was the illustration of the most hated king of England, King John the First. On his head was her prized story, the lost crown jewels of England.

"Miss Sophie Lions," said a heavy, Scandinavian voice from the entrance to the chamber. "You are forgiven,"

Sophie pointed her flashlight in the direction of the voice, startled. Her nervousness settled to a feeling of disdain.

---

[1] A square cotton scarf, also known as a 'keffiyeh'

"Just Miss Lions, if you'd please, Bjorn. And I didn't know you were a priest," she said to him, playing coy.

Bjorn stood shoulder to shoulder with two of his hired bodyguards. He was a man known for embracing his Viking heritage, dating back to Harald Hardrada, the last Viking King, in all its forms. From his rugged beard and partially-shaved hairstyle to his plunderer's appetite. All but his clean-cut attire and wealthy lifestyle; a modern Viking if there ever was one.

"I'm not," replied Bjorn. "But I still forgive you for our unfortunate parting in Marrakesh. I've been trying to unravel the riddle that is you since we went our separate ways, yet I always come to two conclusions. What are you: a journalist, or a treasure hunter, Miss Lions? Looks to me like the term 'grave robber' would be more fitting in this light."

"Perhaps if everyone stopped burying their shiny things with them it wouldn't be grave robbing. They have it, and I need the story that goes with it," Sophie replied.

"You're a fortune seeker, then."

"No," Sophie chuckled, amused by the term. "Unless by fortune you mean fame. I'm just a woman looking to make a name for herself. The value of money is lost with each civilization that rises and falls but finding that which was never meant to be found and the story that goes with it means gaining something far more valuable: immortality. Like the heroes of old, I seek the chance to pass my name from history into legend. So, call me… a dreamer. As for you, though, I dub thee a fortune seeker and criminal. You shouldn't have turned on me in Marrakesh."

Bjorn began to pace around the coffin. Sophie kept a close eye on him and his goons, refusing to be caught off guard.

"You talk too much, Miss Lions."

"So I've been told, yeah."

"You revealed to me the true value of the Heritage Knife in Marrakesh, and so I saw an opportunity to claim a prize."

"You're shit out of luck in that case, 'cause I never found it. Was a dead end; one of the many downsides to the job. So, you can go ahead and go now, before we have another 'unfortunate departure.'"

"I heard you came up empty-handed, both with your story and prize. That's why I followed you here. We parted ways so quickly, our business was never concluded. Treasure or not, I still want my portion. Our agreement isn't finished."

"You mean the agreement you rewrote on me without consent? Apologies, Bjorn, but once you tried to kill me, you forfeited your portion. I should have seen it more clearly. You and your security company are just a cover for being a mercenary. You've proven that you have a tendency to go back on your word along with being a liar."

"We are one in the same, Miss Lions. Historians on the road to truth. Braving great dangers to get what it is we seek. Our only difference is that you lie to get what you want, while I—" the two bodyguards unslung their assault rifles from their shoulders and took aim at her— "prefer to take things by force."

Sophie remained calm, putting faith in the fact that Bjorn would rather conduct business before bloodshed.

"If we were to work together again," said Bjorn, "then perhaps we could both get what we want."

"Hm... Not really a fan of sharing," Sophie replied in a smug tone.

Bjorn made his way back over to his bodyguards. "Another thing we have in common, then. A shame. I had high hopes for you."

Bjorn's men took aim.

"Wait!" said Sophie, extending her free hand out in a plea, offering Bjorn one last chance for his own sake. "You're a gentleman, Bjorn. You wouldn't shoot an unarmed woman in the middle of a cold, wet, abandoned crypt before a man of the cloth?" Sophie gestured to the skeleton. "I mean... Come on... You know you're better than that."

Bjorn nodded in agreement. "Indeed. You're right. I wouldn't. But then again, as you said, I have a tendency to go back on my word," he replied, gesturing to his men.

"Aww, shit..." Sophie grumbled in disappointment.

The two bodyguards opened fire on her as she ducked down behind the coffin, cradling the clay pot in her hand. She hastily unslung her backpack and removed one of her shemaghs from the bag. She wrapped the pot with the scarf and placed it in her bag as the gunfire stopped.

"Give it up, Miss Lions. This is another dead end for you. Hand over the prize and I'll make sure you live to write another one of your articles," said Bjorn.

Sophie drew her Glock[2] from her bag. She loaded a magazine in the bottom and pulled the slide back to load it. "All right, Bjorn! It's all

---

2   A German made 9mm handgun, favored for its design and safety.

yours…"

Sophie rose to one knee and fired two shots at one of the bodyguards. Both shots landed in the bodyguard's chest, dropping him to the water with a splash. The other bodyguard returned fire as Bjorn picked up the fallen man's rifle and began firing back at her. Sophie ducked back down behind the coffin as the shots pulverized the stone.

The firing stopped. She could see Bjorn moving to flank her on her left side in the reflection off the water. Meanwhile, the other bodyguard was advancing on her to her right. She removed the flashlight from her shoulder strap, and then leaned to her right side, pointing it into the bodyguard's eyes. The guard squinted in surprise as she made her move, firing a shot at both his head and chest.

The guard fell backwards, floating lifeless as she heard Bjorn's heavy steps trudge through the water, advancing behind her. She scurried around the other side of the coffin as Bjorn fired another round of shots towards the water at where she had been.

"Just you and me now, Bjorn!"

"Shakspearian, wouldn't you agree?" replied Bjorn. "A man and a woman, destined for death in a tomb by their own hands."

Sophie noticed him moving back around the other way on the opposite side. She looked over at the fractured wooden beam ahead of her, holding up the ceiling. "I couldn't agree more. I shall kill you with much cherishing in that case."

She began firing the remainder of her clip towards the beam. The hollow points splintered the rotting wood, spitting wooden chunks as it creaked. The great hall above them began to quake as slabs of stone began to fall in the water from above.

Sophie stood up to see Bjorn staring up at the ceiling in panic.

"Parting is such sweet sorrow, Bjorn!" she shouted with a feeling of satisfaction.

Bjorn aimed at her only to realize he was out of shots. He scowled at her as he threw the rifle down into the water before turning and running towards the rope leading out. Sophie tucked her pistol away and grabbed her bag before hurrying in the opposite direction towards the hidden passageway as the chamber continued to collapse.

Sophie dove into the passageway with her backpack on, catching on the narrow opening. She continued to try and claw her way inside, the castle shaking around her. She took a step back and removed her bag, tossing it in through the passageway ahead of her. She climbed inside just in time to see the light from the great hall entrance disappear into darkness.

The stone walls of the passageway around her continued to quake as she crawled through the darkness. The dust and rocks inside the three-foot-wide passageway continued to fall as it began to rob her of each breath. She felt her bag sink into a hole ahead of her as she held onto it by the strap, sensing a drop ahead. She heard the sound of water sloshing in the hole ahead over the quaking.

Sophie took a deep breath and dove in through the opening, allowing her bag to fall ahead of her. With a short drop, she felt the cold-water from the river pass over her head as her knees bounced against the rocky riverbed. A light appeared ahead of her, shifting with the movement of the water.

    Sophie swam towards the light, holding her breath with ease. The passage carried on for forty yards before she saw sunlight glimmer over her head. Sophie swam for the surface. Her head finally emerged from the water as the sound of the rushing river passed over her ear drums. She shook the water from her eyes and gazed back in the direction of the castle.

    A plume of dust rose up from the top of the castle as the north tower collapsed with a sweeping crash across the riverside.

    Sophie swam towards the shore and made her way up the slopped bank, keeping her head low and out of sight. She could see Bjorn emerge from the castle, yelling at another one of his hired bodyguards as he jumped into a parked SUV, and drove off.

    She smiled with a grin of self-satisfaction at the sight of Bjorn being forced to turn tail and flee. "As we say in the Raiders, Bjorn: Gung-ho."

    Sophie looked towards the visitors building of the castle to see the curator laying on the gravel outside, replacing her amusement with worry. She ran towards him, fearing Bjorn had done his worst. Kneeling down at his side, she was relieved to see only a bloodied mark on his forehead from where Bjorn or one of his goons had struck him. The curator laid unconscious with his head in Sophie's lap as she pulled an aid kit from her backpack and offered him her best field training. She could already hear the sirens of the local police on their way, forcing her to hurry as she cleaned the wound and wrapped a bandage around his head.

Hyde Park Adventures

Seeing the flashing lights over the hill, she fled from the scene herself, leaving the curator in a better state than Bjorn had left him.

Two

LONDON, ENGLAND

SOPHIE STEPPED OFF the train at King's Cross station, welcomed home by the bustling atmosphere of London's busiest train station. She stepped out into the damp and drizzling rain of the evening air, enjoying the short walk to the nearby Underground at Angel Station. She boarded the train and rode through the steel underbelly of the city towards Saint James Park, emerging once more among the clouded skies as she made the walk towards STORY Magazine's head office, only a stone's throw from Buckingham Palace.

Sophie stepped into the lobby and rode the elevator up to the second floor, then wove through the maze of editor cubicles. She entered her shared desk space in Oz's cubicle and dropped her bag down on the floor. Sophie noticed Oz's skinny shoulders jump as her bag hit the floor.

Oz turned to face her in his office chair, seeing it was her with a look of relief laced with annoyance. "Do you Americans enjoy destroying our history? Perhaps out of spite that you don't have your own history?" he said to her in his native English accent, pointing to an article on his computer screen.

Sophie removed her shemagh and threw it down on her chair and looked at the screen; there was an article already posted online about the north tower collapsing at Newark Castle due to "structural damage." She leaned over Oz's shoulder and read the article closer, seeing no mention of her or the two mercenaries she had left slain in the castle's lost undercroft. She only wished Bjorn were among them. Sophie removed her jacket as she offered her own defense. "We've got the old west. The golden age of Hollywood. My own people predate yours, you know."

Oz pointed at her accusatively. "You're only half Native American, Broadway. So don't get ahead of yourself. The other half is pasty English, same as the rest of us. Your father's English so if you had any decency about you, you'd remember that and try to treat the part that's English with the similar respect—"

"Half your family's from New Delhi. You're just as mixed as I am."

"Ah! Don't interrupt. The American half of you is still eight hundred years behind the curve from the rest of the world. Your mother's Native ancestors spent those eight hundred years hunting and gathering in peace before we, the white men of my family and yours mind you, arrived, ready to show the rest of the world how to have a bloody good time."

Sophie sat down in her chair and opened her backpack, shaking her head at Oz's ranting. "You mean imperialize us like so many others?"

"As I said: a bloody good time! Though maybe it may've been

one-sided," replied Oz, jokingly.

Sophie snickered and shook her head, ready to change the subject to more pressing matters aside from Oz's banter. "Bjorn showed up."

Oz turned his attention back towards his computer. "Ah! I figured you ran into someone from your past after reading this morning's snitch sheet. What's the old 'prat been up to these days? Killing? Stealing? Still sore about you stabbing him in the back in Marrakesh?"

"He stabbed me in the back first; and he got away, sadly."

"You got what you wanted though, right?" asked Oz, turning around to face her again.

Sophie pulled the glazed pot from the castle out of her bag and tossed it over to him. Oz caught the pot and inspected it with an unenthusiastic expression. "Ooh!" he said with sarcasm. He sniffed the pot. "Ugh! Blimey! An old pot that smells of still water and bird feed!"

"Was buried with our friend, Father Nicholas," Sophie replied.

Oz immediately held the pot with a disgusted expression. "Glad I only smelled it and didn't lick it."

"It's not the pot I was looking for," Sophie replied, standing up from her chair.

"How do you open it, then?" asked Oz, "I don't see a lid on it."

Sophie took the pot from his hand and raised it up over her head.

"Wait!" shouted Oz, trying to stop her.

Sophie smashed the pot on the empty space among the desk to Oz's right. Grainy white particles mixed with grains of rice scattered across the desk amidst the pieces of broken pottery.

Oz sighed as the sound of rolling chairs filled the office, accompanied by the curious eyes of his coworkers all glancing over the walls of their cubicles towards them.

"Again! Do you just love breaking history for your own amusement? Perhaps we should get you a club to help maximize the damage. You're the reason we keep stolen history in the British Museum behind panes of glass."

Sophie paid no mind to the eyes watching her. She pointed down at the grains, waiting for Oz to finally stop talking and see what had been inside the pot.

Oz picked up a small pinch of the white substance on his desk. "What's this?" He sniffed it with hesitation. "Salt?"

"Salt and rice used to preserve what's hidden away inside." Sophie grabbed hold of the small corner of the folded piece of parchment paper that had been stashed away in the pot, buried under the salt and rice. She unfolded it and examined it, seeing the eight-hundred-year-old Latin script written in ink upon it.

"'Guess there was a good reason to break it. What is it?" said Oz, straightening his back to see the page from his chair.

Sophie handed the page to him. "The final will and testament of King John the First[3], written by Father Nicholas of Newark Castle on his deathbed, chronicling who he really entrusted the Crown Jewels[4] to,

---

3 King John I (24 December 1166 CE - 19 October 1216 CE) was a tyrannical king of England, deposed by his subjects in 1215.

4 The crown upon which the ruling monarch of England (now the United Kingdom)

before he died."

Oz sat the page down on his keyboard and grabbed his glasses from off the desk. He examined the page with his young eyes, squinting behind his glasses like an old man. "I thought the Crown Jewels were in the Tower of London? I've seen them myself, riding along a moving walkway so you Americans don't rub your dirty noses on the glass."

Sophie sat down on the desk and pointed at the page. "Those are the replacements for these. These are the original Crown Jewels. The ones King John lost while crossing the English countryside after being defeated by his own barons.[5] If I'm right, this page proves he lied about losing them."

Oz leaned back and gasped at her with a shocked expression. "No! Say it ain't so! One of our kings of English history told everyone a lie?! Shall wonders ever cease?"

Sophie shot him an unamused expression, wishing he would hurry up and get to work. "Oz..."

Oz waved his hand at her and turned his attention back towards the page. "All right, all right. I'll get to work translating it. I was never good with Latin, though I can probably do some freshening up." He removed his glasses and put them in his vest pocket. "In the meantime, you need to pursue a more proactive story."

Sophie sat back down in her chair again and leaned with her head back against the padded wall, expressing a heavy sigh. "I just got back,

---

wears to represent their rulership over Britannia.

5   Following King John's deposition, he began a campaign against his own subjects to reclaim England which ultimately cost him his life when he died of dysentery along the journey.

Wizard," she replied, calling him by his nickname. "I haven't even been home yet."

"And you did the right thing by coming to see me first. But you came back with more clues and no story for the magazine and after running into a dead end in Marrakesh, you still owe Maple a new story. She even called for you this morning, wanting to discuss the renewal of your publishing contract by the way."

"She what?" Sophie quickly rose upright in her chair in a panic, scanning the office out of paranoia. "Is it the first already?"

"Clock's about to strike midnight, Cinderella, and you've already started off on the wrong foot."

Sophie buried her head in her hands and expressed her own personal agony. "Shit…" She returned her focus to the objective at hand: finding a new and exciting story worthy of discovery. "All right. Show me what you've got for me? Maybe if I show up at her office with a promising lead, she'll give me more time."

Oz grabbed a stack of folders from the shelf on his desk. He opened the top one and began reading through them one after the other. "Uhh, let's see… A man over in Northampton claims he has an old cup that's the 'Holy Grail.'"

Sophie scowled at him.

"All right. That's a no. Uh… Here's one about a bloke in Glasgow who speaks to the ghost of St. Peter every night."

"Oz…" Sophie replied, in no mood for his jokes.

"A woman from Cardiff says she's married to the reincarnation of Napoleon."

"Oz!"

"What?!" Oz replied, looking back up at her. He held the two folders in each hand with an appalled look. "You asked for me to do research for you, this is what I found! Everything so far has been bullocks and bird droppings. Stories of legends and treasures are always full of muddled rumors and nutters."

"Do you have *anything* worthwhile?"

Oz fell silent before expressing a grin at her. "I do have *one*…"

Oz turned around and grabbed another folder he had hidden away beside the shelf. He opened it and held up a black-and-white photograph. On it was a middle-aged man with pale skin and dark hair, dressed in a Nazi officer's uniform; he carried with him a deep scowl.

"Sophie, I'd like you to meet Colonel Peter Wagner. The Nazi's private curator and Director of Art during the war," Oz said with delight.

"The pleasure's mine, Colonel," Sophie replied, talking to the photo. She rested her elbow on the chair arm to prop up her head, expressing her lack of enthusiasm. "What about him?"

"Seems the Colonel here was in charge of stealing works of art specifically suited for Hitler's own private museum during World War II. Of course, the thankfully-departed Führer never succeeded, and his museum was never built."

"And?"

Oz put the photo back in the folder. He pulled out another typed page and read it. "*And* legend says he hid all the prized works he stole in a vault somewhere." He pulled out a series of photos and began handing them to her. Each one was a printed version of various works of popular oil paintings, some of which Sophie had seen before in the London Art Museum.

"Monet's, Rembrandt's, Raphael's, you name it," Oz replied. "Hundreds of works across Europe, all the great masters, stolen."

Sophie flipped through the photos, her curiosity now intrigued. "I've seen some of these already in person. I thought all the art that the Nazis stole was accounted for?"

Oz continued to speak with growing enthusiasm and interest in the mystery. "Most of it has been. But have you ever really seen the back of the Grand Odalisque? Or carbon dated the Mona Lisa? Supposedly, when the war broke out, replicas were being made all over Europe intended to fool the Nazis and save the originals. One story I found out of France even confirmed it. However, it seems our friend, the Colonel, wasn't fooled; he found the originals and hid them away in a vault. However, after the war was over, they never managed to find his stash and the unaccounted-for works remained missing. With no other choice, the museums decided to hang the duplicates, and they wrote them off as recovered."

"You mean to tell me there's an undiscovered vault out there somewhere with the world's most cherished original artworks still locked away inside?"

"Yes. Of which the current price has even been estimated at

nearly three hundred *million* pounds. The best part is, I just so happened to even track down the Colonel's only living relative: his one and only daughter. And it just so happens she lives right here in London."

The two of them sat in silence for a moment.

"Damn it, Oz! I need a story, not a conspiracy theory!" said Sophie, breaking the silence. "Legends and myths won't cut it this time!"

Oz threw his hands up as he spoke with an annoyed tone. "All you ever chase is legends and myths, Broadway! Think about it: a whole bank-sized vault filled with history's greatest works, lost for the last eighty years! You want your name in the history books alongside all those dead priests you rob, don't you?"

Sophie tossed the papers on the desk in frustration. "Yes, but not when my career is on the line! I'm looking for something less ambitious! One bad apple and I'm back in the basket with all the others!"

Oz placed the photos back in the folder and closed it with annoyance. "You asked me to find you a story, and this is what I found. Not like you've come through on most of your previous promises to Maple, anyway. Just follow the story for as far as it goes, and write about that, same as always. They've even got the Nazi Prime Minister, Heinrich Himmler's, key to this legendary vault on display at the British Museum if you want proof. The more I dug, the more facts I found over fiction. Worst case scenario, at least there will be some truth to the story. It's got more weight behind it than your old parchment from our dearly-departed Father Nicholas here," said Oz, holding up the old page.

The phone on Oz's desk rang. Oz and Sophie both looked at it with hesitation. Oz turned his chair around and answered it. "Wizard… Yeah…" Oz expressed a side glance towards Sophie that left her anxious.

"What if I said I'm looking at her right now?" said Oz.

Sophie scowled at him with wide eyes.

Oz turned around and continued to talk on the phone. "… All right. I'll send her your way right now."

Oz hung up the phone. He held the folder out to her. "Maple wants to see you."

She sat for a moment, staring at the folder in horror. She took a deep breath and stood up from her chair, yanking the folder from him. "I'd rather be shot than walk through that door right now."

◆ ◆ ◆

SOPHIE KNOCKED ON the glass door before her. She could see the editor-and-chief for the magazine—her boss, Maple Beckette—staring down at her computer screen as she typed without pause. Maple glanced up at her from under her bangs, the hair color matching her name. Maple waved her in with one hand as she continued to type.

She stood idle for a moment, weighing the repercussions and how long it would take before Maple looked back again to see she made a tactical retreat towards the elevator. Sophie took a deep breath, knowing her own morals and fighting spirit wouldn't permit her to walk away.

"Gung-ho," she said to herself, finding comfort in the Marine Raiders' old motto meant to uphold the new; always faithful, always forward, always with enthusiasm.

THE COLONEL'S LOST VAULT

She opened the door as Maple continued to type at her computer.

"Close the door," Maple muttered from behind the screen without looking up.

Sophie continued to stand with her hand clutching the door handle, as Maple's first three words had left her rethinking her retreat. "You sure, Chief? The fresh air of the office is—"

"Now."

Sophie closed the door, feeling as though she had sealed herself in her own prison cell. Sophie waited patiently in the middle of the office, as always admiring Maple's collection of Wonder Woman comic book posters and figurines in her office.

Maple hit the enter key on her keyboard firmly, presumably sealing the fate of another unfortunate member of her staff. She stood up from her desk and grabbed a stack of papers resting beside the signed photo of herself with original Wonder Woman, Lynda Carter.

"What are these?" asked Maple, holding the stack of papers out.

Sophie stood at attention before Maple's desk, preferring to take her punishment and banishment with dignity and pride. "Uh… Papers, Chief? All with information I'm sure I'm about to regret hearing out loud?"

"Why were you in Scotland? Did you enjoy yourself? Bring back anything for me? No, wait… I know the answer. You were following a clue. Which led to another clue." Maple threw the stack of papers down on her desk, expressing a disheartened look. "This is the second set of train ticket receipts I've received from you claiming they're work-related in the past four days. Behind that, I have six flights between Turkey, Yugoslavia, and Morocco, all in the past month."

"The Alvarado story kind of ran into a dead end. You'll laugh at this, Chief: turns out, Alvarado never *did* steal the Heritage Knife from the sultan. He just made the whole thing up looking to gain favor with the Spanish Monarchy. A servant girl was the one who actually stole it, so the trail went cold when the sultan finally caught up with Alvarado and killed him. So, rather than the story Alvarado boasted about, the knife probably just ended up in a pawn shop!" Sophie laughed. "Funny, right?"

Maple continued to stand behind her desk, expressionless and void of all sympathy.

Sophie's own laughter petered out. "You… not… laughing…"

Maple's appearance took on that of a disappointed parent. "You have no story? You mean to tell me all these—" she held up the papers—"were for nothing?"

Sophie thought for a moment, trying to rethink her strategy, preferably one with a better explanation. "I mean, it wasn't completely for nothing. I managed to find a lead on another story I've been chasing for a while. One of my contacts turned up with some new info which kind of complicated the situation in Morocco even more."

Maple threw the pages back down and crossed her arms. "So, you *do* have a story…?"

Sophie thought for a moment. Her words on the page had always spoken louder than her own voice, but she didn't have the convenience of time on her side.

Maple sat down at her desk and buried her head in her hands as she spoke. "Mother bless me, for I lack the strength to endure…"

Maple seemingly attempted to cast out all her frustration in order to speak with reason. She took a deep breath and looked at Sophie directly. "Broadway… You know I like you, right?"

"Aww, I like you too, Chief."

"Shut up," Maple replied, clearly not in the mood for Sophie's humor. "But I also despise you in so many ways."

"Ouch…"

"You are kind at heart. Hardworking. You respect leadership."

"Of course, I do. Especially towards those who deserve it. Such as you, Chief."

"Cut the flattery, Broadway."

"Sorry…" Sophie replied, not wishing to prod Maple any further.

Maple thought for a moment in silence, presumably trying to choose her words carefully. "I like your style of journalism, Sophie. I admire it, as much as I shouldn't. You're ambitious, and don't take no for an answer. When you walked in with Oz, I think those qualities were what I saw within you that prompted me to give you a chance. That, and I have even more respect for Oz."

Sophie grinned and flexed her eyebrows. "We all know you like him, Chief."

Maple's sympathetic stare vanished. Sophie's heart seized for a millisecond, realizing her mouth seemed to have a mind of its own. Maple's cheeks turned red as she continued to glare at her.

Maple took in a deep breath before continuing. "Yet, even as Oz's longtime friend, I have to admit that my favor to him has now been paid in full, and even more so with interest. You made a solid run with your first story, and the few you wrote after." Maple picked up a blue paper on her desk and held it in silence. The paper left Sophie feeling uneasy, believing it to be her contract. Maple readied herself to make her final statement. "But—"

"I have another lead!" Sophie interjected, trying to avoid her sentencing.

Maple scoffed and set the paper back down. "You *always* have a lead. You promised me one story, only to throw another on my desk that's not what you had promised originally."

Sophie approached Maple's desk and leaned over, expressing her sincerest passion and ambition through her voice. "But they *are* extraordinary stories, right?"

"You're all out of shots, Broadway. I'm sorry... We had our monthly meeting yesterday. Your contract renewal was—"

Sophie placed the folder from Oz in front of Maple. "This one is solid, Chief! Best part is, I don't even have to travel."

Maple froze, looking as though she could be swayed in either direction on her decision like a ship at sea waiting for a breeze.

Sophie offered her last gust of wind hoping to steer Maple her way. "Chief, please… Just take a look."

Maple sighed and rubbed her forehead. She opened the folder and began sorting through the pages, reading through Oz's notes.

Sophie sat down in Maple's office chair before her, with apprehension. "A treasure worth uncovering. For the world's sake..."

Maple examined the pages with a faint look of intrigue. "Is this another quail hunt Oz dug up for you...?"

"Yes! No...? If by quail hunt you mean easy? That is the exact reason why it's so solid! Oz gave it his full endorsement! Easy, interesting, and it won't cost you a pound."

Maple read Oz's report in silence. "A vault filled with missing artwork. Hard to believe."

"But there's a chance," Sophie replied, trying to embellish the story. "Think about it, Chief. A whole vault stacked with priceless artwork, lost since the forties, still out there. And if there's any truth to the matter, I'll find it. With it would be a story that'll have the click counter rolling like a snowball."

"Or like a rolling stone gathering moss..."

Sophie could sense she had her hooked. All she had to do now was make the final blow. "One last ride, Chief. One final assault. Please, for me. Let me go out with one final story. If it's good, you renew my contract; if it's mediocre or even gets one negative vote, at least you can send me packing from here with my head high still doing what I love. You have nothing to lose."

Maple clasped her hands together and raised them to her mouth in thought. She sighed heavily. "Get out of my chair."

Sophie hurried out of Maple's seat, and then stood at her desk in apprehension.

Maple sat down, then pointed a finger at her. "You have till the end of the month. You come up short again and you'll find yourself writing web articles about do-it-yourself make-up techniques. I'll take the heat one last time for you. One. Last. Time."

Sophie smiled in relief as she picked up the folder. "Thank you, Chief."

"When I first agreed to hire you, I figured a woman who had nine years in the US Marines would know more about obeying orders."

"Ten, actually… As we Raiders always say, gung-ho for life."

Maple's eyes narrowed with annoyance as she tilted her head to one side, as though she was reconsidering her proposal.

Sophie cleared her throat in an attempt to retract her own statement. "I mean… Damn right. Solid copy."

Maple shook her head at her and waved her towards the door. "Just… have that story written and on my desk by the end of the month." Maple pointed at her once again, as though issuing her one final order. "And I expect calls every step of the way! I get any more of these," she held the receipts up again, "and you had better enjoy wherever you are visiting, because it'll become your new permanent residence."

"Copy that. Not a single receipt," Sophie replied, backing out the door. She closed the door behind her watching Maple continue to glare at her. Maple pointed at her again with force.

Sophie nodded in understanding, and then hurried off towards the elevator in a sprint, refusing to waste any more time.

Three

SOPHIE FOLLOWED THE map on her phone as she walked under London's grey-capped skies overhead, surrounded by two-story homes stacked one next to the other with their own Victorian-colored doors. She rounded the corner, following the directions given to her by Oz further along the winding streets of Chelsea. She stopped before a home that resembled all the others, decorated with a cherry-red front door.

Sophie lingered in front of the home for a moment, contemplating how to approach her arrival. A woman dressed in a mail carrier shirt, carrying a side bag, approached the front door from around the corner. Sophie stepped out of the way offering her a polite smile. The woman smiled back and pulled a stack of letters from her shoulder bag. Sophie watched the woman, sprouting an idea.

"Pardon me!" Sophie said to the mail carrier.

The woman looked back at her, just as she was about to slip the letters into the mail slot.

"I can take those inside for her."

"Apologies, Miss," replied the mail carrier, "but I'm really not supposed to hand these off to anyone else."

"Oh, it's all right. I'm her granddaughter. I just got in from New York and wanted to surprise her, anyway."

"Oh! That's so sweet," the woman replied. "Very well. I would hate to ruin the surprise." She handed the bundle of letters to Sophie. "Enjoy your time in London." The mail carrier offered Sophie a warm smile, then continued on down the street delivering mail at each of the doors.

Sophie continued to stand at the door, waiting nervously for the mail carrier to pass out of sight. Sophie began flipping through the letters, finally finding a clear moment. Mixed in with the stack was a letter marked with the logo of a blue home, labeled C&C, Court and Castle, Insurance underneath. Sophie opened the letter and began reading its contents, taking note of the names written on it and the elderly woman's request to update her insurance policy. She folded up the letter and slipped it into her back pocket, then pulled her tablet computer out from her backpack.

Sophie checked the street once more, only seeing a man wearing a red-and-black plaid shirt and full beard making his way across the street, facing the opposite direction.

She quietly hid her backpack in the bushes outside the home, then buttoned up her red collared shirt over her t-shirt before tying her hair back into a ponytail. She delicately slipped the rest of the mail into the mail slot, then took a deep breath, adopting her new role as Hannah Strong, insurance agent for Court and Castle Insurance.

Sophie knocked on the door politely, feeling calm and prepared. She heard the sound of creaking floorboards from beyond the doorway, followed by a subtle turn of the knob.

A small, elderly woman with curly, grey hair appeared through the small opening. Her skin was wrinkled and weathered with liver spots over a set of amber eyes that held their own history. The elderly woman's head shook slightly as her hands trembled.

"Hello, ma'am. Are you..." Sophie looked down at the blank screen on her tablet, "Oliwia Wagner?"

"Yes?" the elderly woman cleared her throat and replied, with a surprisingly-clear voice. She spoke with no hint to her German heritage, leaving Sophie questioning whether Oz had the wrong person.

"Hi. I'm Hannah Strong with C&C Insurance. We got a notice about you looking to update your home insurance policy?"

"They told me over the phone you'd be here next week."

"Yes, ma'am. I actually came across your notice on my list this morning and happened to be in the neighborhood. So, I figured I'd drop by and see if now would be a good time to have a walk around your home, and make sure your policy is fully updated? As they say, no time like the present."

"Oh!" Oliwia replied with enthusiasm, clearly glad to have company. "Yes, yes. Please, come in." She opened the door the rest of the way.

Sophie looked down at her to see she walked with a walker,

resting behind the door. Oliwia took hold of her walker again and shuffled her way inside the home with the wheels softly squeaking across the floor.

"Thank you so much for coming," said Oliwia.

Sophie closed the door behind her, smelling the sweet scent of chestnut in the air filling the home. "My pleasure. I assume you've already had someone come in before?" asked Sophie, scanning the interior of the home. It was small and yet well-kept, decorated with a lifetime's worth of belongings. Every wall was covered with paintings and photographs, none of them depicting the man Sophie had set out to find.

"Oh, yes. Many times," Oliwia replied, turning back to face her.

"Would you mind if I just went ahead and had a look around? Mark down anything I see that needs added to the registry?" said Sophie, pointing up towards the stairs, preferring to start her search in private.

"Of course! Help yourself," Oliwia replied.

Sophie made her way over towards the wooden staircase lined with a chair lift to aid the elderly woman up and down. She looked down at her tablet, typing on a blank page as she made her own personal notes for her story.

Oliwia continued to stand at the base of the stairs, watching Sophie with a sweet smile. "Can I get you anything? I was about to put the kettle on for tea."

"Tea would be lovely," Sophie replied, ready to agree to anything that would keep the elderly woman busy while she searched for any of the Colonel's personal belongings.

Sophie continued up the steps, seeing several photos along the wall to her left of Oliwia over the years, surrounded by family members and grandchildren. She passed out of Oliwia's sight, reaching the top of the steps. At the top was a photo of the very man she had come to see: a young Colonel Wagner stood at attention, wearing an old uniform from the Great War, with his hat tucked under his arm.

Sophie cast a judging side glance at the photo as she entered into the one of two rooms at the top of the steps.

"I prefer to use heavy cream and a drop of butterscotch syrup! A tradition in my family from my home country! Can I tempt you with some?" shouted Oliwia from downstairs.

"Yes, ma'am! That sounds wonderful!" Sophie shouted back down to her, feeling genuinely curious about the taste.

Entering the room before her, Sophie saw a well-made bed in the center, decorated with more photos around the room and old furniture. She backed out of the room, stopping for a moment with curiosity as she stared at the nightstand. A wax candle twisted with blue and white coloring sat partially burned; under it was a white cloth with gold lettering embroidered into it.

Sophie stepped out into the hall and searched the opposite room. Inside were several cardboard boxes, stacked head high among old furnishings. She read each of the labels, all marked as clothing or legal documents.

"Is that an American accent I hear?" shouted Oliwia from downstairs.

Hyde Park Adventures

Sophie stepped away from the room and walked back towards the stairs, casting one last look towards the photo of the Colonel with scorn. She spoke out, telling the truth as she made her way back down the steps. "Yes, ma'am. My mother was Native American. My father is English. I was born in DC but grew up here in London with my father for a short time when I was little. When I was thirteen, I was sent back to the States with my sister to finish my education."

Sophie rounded the base of the steps to see Oliwia standing at the counter in her kitchen.

"Ah! You were in the military, too?" said Oliwia, dipping a spoon of butterscotch syrup into two pink and white teacups.

Sophie stood in the entryway, perplexed by Oliwia's insight into the truth. "Yes ma'am… I served ten years with the US Marines. Six of which as a Marine Raider."

Oliwia looked back over her shoulder at her. "I thought so. I'm sure you have lots of stories to tell then."

Sophie nodded in agreement as she entered the kitchen, pretending to take notes of the home. "More than most… How could you tell?"

Oliwia chuckled. She attempted to pick up the teapot on the stove, struggling as she shook.

Sophie approached her and aided her in pouring the hot water into the teapot.

"Oh," said Oliwia, allowing Sophie to take over, "thank you. My father was a military man himself. He walked with the same strong stride, same towering stance, same look about him; he was a Colonel in the

German military. Fought for the wrong side, sadly, but he was a kind man who loved art as much as life itself."

Sophie placed the pot back down on the stove top and helped carry the tea pot over to the table.

"Thank you," said Oliwia, handing the teacups and cream to her.

Sophie placed the cups down on the table, and then pretended to continue taking notes as Oliwia slowly sat down. The elderly woman sighed with relief. She pointed over towards the painting on the wall near the doorway. "Speaking of which, that was one of his pieces."

Sophie looked over at the painting. It was of an oil painting of a lakeside, blended in short, elegant, green and blue brush strokes among yellow reeds that permanently swayed with the breeze.

"I had it appraised recently. The young man told me it was only worth three hundred pounds. Can you believe that?"

Sophie continued to stare at the painting, unable to see the steel-forged man she imagined Wagner to be though the colors. "Outrageous," she replied, pretending to be surprised.

"I told him, it's not what's on the surface that counts, but what's underneath. Though, I can't find the will to sell it, and none of my family cares for it."

"Can't imagine why," muttered Sophie sarcastically, hearing Oliwia pour the tea into the cups behind her.

"What did you say, dear?"

Sophie turned around to address her. "Oh, I was just curious about your father. It's not every day I get to walk through a home with such history. Where was he stationed?"

Oliwia placed the teapot back down on the table, reminiscing in thought. "A great many places… He looked after artwork during the war. He worked as a museum curator in Munich before, painting on his free days. Before that, he fought in the Great War. I think he saw painting as a way of helping him forget all that he had seen."

Sophie sat down at the table. She set her tablet aside and stirred her tea with a spoon. "Wow! That *is* a life well lived."

Sophie took a sip of her tea, smelling the sweet butterscotch blended in, finding the taste surprisingly soothing. She glanced up at the elderly woman, seeing she was waiting with anticipation for her reaction. "That *is* good, actually."

"My mother used to make it that way when I was little. She would always serve it in my favorite pink and white tea set, just like this one. It's my oldest and sweetest memory of her," Oliwia replied.

Sophie took another sip of her tea, then picked her tablet back up off the table while looking at the blank screen as she spoke. "Seems everything is in order. Quick and easy. Though, I am curious now, did you inherit this home from your father? I'm an astute student of history and it's not every day you get to hear about a fellow military member from the opposing side during the war."

Oliwia nodded as she sipped her tea carefully. "Yes. As a matter of fact…" She stood up from the table, shuffling her way over to the bookshelf in the living room behind Sophie without the aid of her walker. She emerged from the living area holding a crimson and maple-brown, leather-bound book in her hands. "I still own his writings during the war. He used to scribble in this journal when I was a little girl. He'd stay up late some nights, putting his mind to paper. Another item my children have shown no interest in, I'm afraid."

Sophie took another sip of tea, trying to smother her sudden desire and need to read the book. "Really? Well, that *is* something special."

Oliwia stood in the doorway and held the book with a look of nostalgia. "I've had one or two offers for it. All tabloid journalists, seeking to blacken his name." She shook her head with disapproval. "Some folks just have no decency... He was a very sweet man, despite his faults."

Sophie watched as Oliwia returned to the living area and placed the book back on the shelf beside the only chair in the living room. "Couldn't agree more with you, ma'am. Some folks just don't know how to let the past lie. You said he raised you, though? Alone or...?" questioned Sophie, finishing the rest of her tea.

"Yes," Oliwia replied, walking back into the kitchen. "By himself, the poor man. My mother passed away during the war due to illness. He was forced to raise me by his lonesome. I grew up in Paderborn, north of Berlin for a time. Then we moved to London here in '52, where he sadly lived out the remainder of his years as an outcast."

Sophie offered her best look of sadness—saddened only that Wagner wasn't still alive himself to confess his secrets to her.

"I have some of his medals in the back, if you'd like to see?" offered Oliwia. "I've arranged to have them donated to a museum, but you can have a look first."

Sophie smiled at her. "That'd be quite the privilege. Thank you."

Oliwia stepped out of sight through the living area, passing out of sight for a moment. She reemerged in the entryway and sat down on her chair lift along the stairs. She slowly began ascending the stairs with the sound of her chair buzzing throughout the small home.

Sophie waited, refilling her teacup until she heard the sound of the chair stop at the top of the stair. She immediately jumped up from her seat at the table and hurried into the living area, over to the bookshelf. She pulled the journal from the shelf and began thumbing through the old pages, trying to scan its contents.

As she flipped to one of the middle pages, she read the last paragraph at the bottom of the page.

A vault. *One built to protect the world's most valued visual wonders from the conflict which was looming in secrecy. A vault with only three keys: one for Himmler; one I gifted to Fischer; and the last in my care.*

Heil Hitler.

Colonel Peter Wagner

Sophie held the journal idly in a trance, now no doubt in her mind. "Oz was right…" she whispered to herself in shock.

The sound of the chair lift beginning to descend snapped Sophie out of her trance. Her heart rate quickened as she tucked the journal into the rear lining of her pants, using her shirt to conceal its location before scurrying back to the table to sit down.

She heard Oliwia shuffling her way through the entryway behind her. "Here they are," Oliwia said. "I recently had them polished by the young man next door."

Sophie pulled her phone from her pocket, seeing only one message from Oz wishing to know where she went. "Shoot… No rest for the weary soul, as they say."

"Something the matter?" asked Oliwia, entering the kitchen, cradling a small wooden box in her hands.

Sophie stood up from her place at the table and picked up her tablet. "I apologize. It seems I've overstayed my welcome. I've just been asked to go see another client a few blocks away before the day is out. Though I truly appreciate your hospitality."

"Oh! The pleasure was all mine. Was nice to have tea with someone else for a change. Especially with a remarkable young woman sharing such an exciting background," Oliwia replied.

"I'll be sure to get these updates added and submitted for you, and you'll probably receive a new notice via phone call or by mail next week."

Oliwia sat the wooden box down on the kitchen table. "Excellent. And feel free to drop by anytime, Miss Strong. I'll keep these downstairs for you in case you come by again. I'd be honored to share more history with you."

Sophie politely shook her hand with a false smile, her heart still racing ahead of her feet, eager to walk out the door. "I just might. Thank you again."

Sophie stepped past Oliwia, presumably none the wiser as to what Sophie now kept hidden under her shirt. Sophie opened the front door as she noticed a mezuzah hanging on the wall beside the door. She glanced back over her shoulder to see Oliwia carrying the tea pot over to the sink, her back turned to her.

Sophie shook her head, perplexed, as the clues scattered around the home didn't add up. She stepped out of the home and closed the door softly. She let out a deep sigh of relief as she felt the journal still tucked away in her waistband. Grabbing her bag from the bushes, Sophie started her way back down the street.

Her phone rang as she pulled the journal out and answered her phone. Oz appeared on the screen via video. "Where'd you go, Broadway? You went to meet with Wonder Woman, then took off, saying you had to hurry."

Sophie held the phone out ahead of her so Oz could see her as she walked. "Maple gave me another shot. I didn't wanna waste time."

"So, where are you now?" asked Oz, eating a bag of popcorn.

"Just met with the Colonel's daughter."

"Well, that was quick. Was her home filled with Nazi flags and old propaganda posters?"

Sophie shook her head at him. "No. As it so happens, she's surprisingly sweet and enjoys butterscotch in her tea."

Oz stopped eating his popcorn with a disgusted expression. "That's... sinful."

"Look what I got, though." Sophie held the journal up in front of the camera for Oz to see.

Oz leaned in closer to his computer. "Oh! More smelly paper?"

"It's Wagner's personal journal; one he wrote during the war. You were right. He did have a vault."

Oz's eyes widened with a grin. "I bloody knew it! Well... me along with the rest of the internet."

"Bet you twenty quid[6] if the location is anywhere, it's written in here," Sophie replied.

Oz sat back in his chair, picking the popcorn from his teeth, expressing his suspicion. "You stole it, didn't you?"

Sophie scoffed, offended that Oz would use such harsh words. "I fully intend to give it back once I'm finished. I always return my library books."

"If you treat your library books the same way you do old pots, I can only assume they return burned and covered in coffee stains. Fine, but if anyone asks, I don't know anything. Where are you off to now, then?"

"Home to read. Clock's ticking," Sophie replied, hanging up the call. As the screen of her phone fell dark, she noticed a figure behind her in the reflection. She drifted her gaze over her shoulder to see who it was more clearly.

The same man with the full beard, dressed in a red-and-black

---

6   English slang for a British Pound.

plaid shirt from earlier was now behind her. He stared down at his phone, acting as though he was listening to the headphones in his ears. He turned the corner suddenly as she looked further back, avoiding her attention while still pretending to be focused on his phone.

Sophie directed her attention back to the sidewalk ahead of her. She crossed the street and down into the Underground station at Sloane Square. She checked behind her once more as she descended the tile-covered tunnel steps to see her stalker was still behind her.

Hoping to lose him at the turnstiles, she hurried and swiped her pass, and then headed down the next set of stairs. She saw her stalker swipe his own pass and continue after her with a quickened pace.

Sophie reached the bottom of the stairs to see a young man playing a violin among the acoustic tunnels for the passing crowd. She pulled out her wallet and dropped twenty pounds in his violin case before approaching him and whispering into his ear, asking to distract the man following her. The young man nodded as Sophie thanked him.

Continuing down the tunnel towards the station platform, she looked back to see the violinist causally wander into the man's way and continuously try to coax money out of him for his performance. Sophie's stalker brushed him aside as the violinist continued to walk backwards, refusing to give up.

Sophie waited until her stalker's gaze was averted, forced to tell the violin player to leave him alone before she hurried in a sprint towards the station platform. She could hear her stalker's footsteps follow suit. She reached the platform and hurried onto a train about to depart. She sat down in one of the empty seats, out of view from the window. The train car doors closed as she spotted her stalker standing along the platform expressing a look of defeat, searching the platform for her.

Sophie pulled her headphones out of her pocket and slipped them in her ears, expressing a smug grin of satisfaction. However, the question still remained: who had been following her?

Hyde Park Adventures

Four

This honor, *which has been gifted to me by our Führer, has become my legacy. Someone once told me, "Art is more than just the colors we see on a canvas, or the shapes we carve into stone. It is the telling of a story. Stories within each work embedded with life." And I am the harbinger of those lives. I am a conqueror of stories. An ambassador to those lives which have long since been buried beneath consecrated ground. Our Führer must have witnessed this ability within me, for he never makes mistakes.*

Before I was the Party's curator to a new era, I served our Fatherland by leading him through nightmares at the age of twenty-nine. As my men stood crouched at my side, each of us steeped in his own stench and covered in crimson-wet mud, we fought for our country. We charged an open battlefield littered with the bodies of our friends fighting for them and ourselves. We fought for our families. We fought for Germany. But our leaders fought only for themselves.

Hyde Park Adventures

We gave our mind, bodies, and souls in service to our Fatherland, and returned only to find he had been stripped of his pride and dignity. We were betrayed. And as we, the brave and loyal soldiers to our father, slipped back into the shadows but we never forgot, nor did we forgive.

I withered my spirit over the heated iron of a forge on an empty stomach amidst my hometown of Schondorf. I stood helpless watching my father sink into illness and decay, then watched my mother lose her faith.

My only solace during that time was painting. I rode my bike to the banks of the Ammersee, capturing Bavaria's beauty in oil every evening. It was there, along those banks, that I saw the glassy blues of the water, heavenly pinks from above, and purest of whites in the lilies turn to flesh.

"Pardon me," said a gentle voice from over my shoulder.

I continued to paint the shifting reeds along the water bank ahead of me, keeping my teal-colored eyes fixed on finishing off the last brush stroke of my white paint to capture the sun's rays before they passed. I dipped my brush in the clouded jar of paint thinner resting at my feet, then turned back to see who it was that had disrupted my concentration.

Before me stood a woman in a blue and white dress, wearing a wheat-colored straw hat with a red bow tied around it. Her eyes were a warm chestnut with blossom-powdered cheeks. She held an empty mason jar in her hands.

"I forgot my paint thinner at home. Could I bother you for just a splash?" she asked me.

I stood idle with the brush in my hand still dripping, my dirty brown bangs blowing in the breeze. I swallowed nervously, feeling my throat turn dry as though I had drunk the very paint thinner she had asked for. I glanced over her shoulder to see she had set up her own easel and stool along the bank a few yards away. I stared at her for what felt like the longest moment of my life.

I finally cleared my throat and turned back to my wood paintbox at my feet. I began sorting through the box while my hands trembled uncontrollably. I pulled my clean jar of paint thinner out and stood. I took a single step towards her, holding the jar out. I felt something grab hold of my shoelace as I stumbled to his knees, hearing the sound of my paint box tumble through the grass behind me. I looked back to see my painting supplies now scattered along the bank, with several of my own tubes of paint floating in the water.

The woman chuckled to herself and extended a helping hand out to me. "I suppose I owe you the use of my own paints now in exchange."

I took hold of her hand and rose to my feet, still holding the unbroken jar of paint thinner in my hand. I chuckled at the woman's remark, handing her the jar.

I turned back to see the oil from my paint streaking across the tops of the water. "I guess that's one way to paint the water," I said to her.

The woman laughed at me again. "An improvement upon nature altogether."

I turned back to her and extended a hand. "Peter."

"Andrea," the woman replied, shaking my hand with a warm smile. She was the most beautiful painting I had ever seen.

Andrea.

Andrea Marta Waschke.

She shared my fondness for color. My desire for unbeatable perfection. My love of light and shadow. We met many times along the banks of the Ammersee, sharing our passion as we painted the same lake from all sides. As we rode our bikes under a shaded green leaf canopy back towards our hometown together, we often stopped by our spot along the road which would later be claimed by our cottage. A field glittering with wildflowers, led by a trail made of lilies of the valley. We dreamt of a cottage so grand that it would rival the surrounding castles in decorum and charm. A castle of our own.

With the death of Herbert Shiess, the curator for the art museum in Munich, the Alte Pinakothek, came a need for new leadership. I had lost my job at the steel mill, alongside many others, and applied for the position against all odds. I won the heart of the owner, Heir Bedhurst, thanks to Andrea. Her tutelage in the masters combined with my passion and charisma became a marvel to Heir Bedhurst. I was sworn into the position with expediency, as the museum had fallen into dire times. It was there I first met Karl Fischer, a thin and rather weak man, but intelligent, whom I would later appoint as my secretary upon first joining the Party. I've come to trust Fischer with even my most prized possessions, knowing he will treat them with the same gentle love and care.

As I tended to the many needs of the art museum, I sought to expand its collection. I negotiated terms with the same command as when I was in the trenches: stern, determined, and unrelenting. During my first year as curator, I had turned a once-forgotten mausoleum into the new pride of Munich. Behind each new piece there was Andrea, mentoring me. She was the mind while I was the voice. She met me often for mid-day lunch, shared in one of the museum's many halls closed off to the public's eyes. The two of us would view each newly added painting with the same attention to detail as a master clockmaker.

"Do you still have your eyes closed?" I asked, my voice resonating through the halls of our museum. I guided Andrea to the newest renovated hall with my hands on her shoulders, walking backwards with her facing me.

She continued to keep her eyes closed, maintaining full trust in me. "Yes. Why would I want to spoil the surprise? It's my favorite part," she replied.

I moved her into position and stepped out of the way. "Open them."

Andrea opened her eyes. She remained silent for a second, taking in the black and white ink portrait of Samson fighting with the lion.

She shook her head in shock. "You did it?" she said, in a stunned tone.

"Look around you," I replied, overjoyed by her reaction.

Andrea scanned the room, seeing the collection of Albrecht Dürer pieces. Eighteen newly hung and acquired works from one of Germany's finest artists from the late 15th century.

Her jaw hung in awe. "You bought them."

"Wasn't cheap. The city was willing to cover part of the cost along with a few generous contributions from the Workers Party. They graciously paid for half, with great enthusiasm. Once I found them, I refused to take no for an answer. The proposition of having a grand exhibit of Dürer was enough for some."

Andrea began hurrying around the room, glancing at each piece in a state of bliss. She smiled at me from across the room as I strode around the room with pride. I snickered at her reaction, feeling my heart lifted with her own spirits.

"Joachim and the Angel. You bought Joachim and the Angel?" she asked, standing before the ink print of the father of Mary on his knees before an angel of the Lord. I simply smiled and continued to pace. Andrea turned back to the masterpiece and marveled at it before continuing her grand tour.

"I love the way your spirit soars over ink on paper," I said to her.

She turned to me with shock. "These are more than just works of art, Peter. They are his life! They're everyone's lives!" She began scurrying around the room, gesturing to each of the pieces. "This whole museum is a collection of people's lives! Souls transcribed in ink and paint! Stories carved into marble and granite! Each one filled with tragedy, and love, and hate, and happiness..."

Andrea stopped before me, her smile leaving me forever lost in bliss. "You saved them, Peter, saved them from being forgotten. Art is more than just the colors we see on a canvas or the shapes we carve in stone. They're people's lives."

I took hold of her hands. "And our lives? How will they be remembered?"

Andrea stepped into my arms, leaving us gazing back at one another. "The same way: through all of these works you've collected. This is our kingdom, Peter. Let it be shared with the world."

Andrea was the first to show me the true value of art. For me, art was a means to pass the time and create something beautiful. For her, art was life frozen in time. Windows for which we could glimpse into the soul. I would be a fool to say that what she taught me didn't have an impact on me. Her vision was one I strived to share.

Heil Hitler.

Colonel Peter Wagner

Sophie turned the page. She took a sip of her tea, holding Wagner's journal in the other hand. She glanced over at the clock on her computer as she sat before her desk in her flat. It was 11PM, or 2300 hours as she read it.

She stood up from her chair and stretched her arms out over her head.

The sight of a car parked out along the street below her flat caught her eye. She looked out the window over her desk and turned her desk lamp off; two gentlemen in dark coats stood beside the car, smoking as they talked.

Sophie sat back down in her chair and turned the lamp on again, keeping a wary eye on the men outside. She pulled her Glock from her backpack, hesitant to load a round in the chamber until there was a clear reason to. She placed her gun on the desk at her side and directed her attention back to the journal before her, continuing to read while drinking her tea.

The memory of *standing in awe before the Party's power and might is one I remember in every vivid detail. I attended a rally in Munich, feeling that ever-present betrayal that was festering within me that the Fatherland seemed to share. I cheered with the crowd, spurred with a renewed pride in Germany and its future. Our Führer stood at the podium, shouting words which played like a patriotic trumpet within me. He spoke of his own shared sense of betrayal we, who fought in the Great War, all felt. The world had taken so much from us and he spoke of a future for Germany when most of us saw none. A future set on reclaiming what was lost, demonstrating to the world what we were capable of. That we were a nation to be feared.*

I hesitated to join the Party in the beginning, keeping to the halls of my museum, continuing to drive out to Lake Ammersee to paint with Andrea. However, it wasn't long before our newly appointed Führer took his rightful place as leader of this great nation of ours and sought me out on his own. To say I was surprised would be an understatement.

    I sat in the waiting area amidst the cleanly-polished halls of Königsplatz. Ahead of me was a grand wooden double door, guarded by two Party members dressed in their sand-colored uniforms and red armbands. I held my hat in my hands, crumpling it with anticipation. I heard the sound of high heels knocking against the stone floor from the hall to my left. A woman with blonde hair in a black uniform, a Party pin fastened to her lapel, stepped out from the hallway holding a stack of folders. She stopped before me.

    "Heir Wagner, please follow me," said the woman. She turned her back to me and began making her way towards the double doors.

    I quickly rose to my feet and followed, feeling my heart beating in rhythm with the woman's steps. She opened one of the doors and stepped to the side, allowing me to enter first.

    I stepped past the two members standing guard as neither one made eye contact with me. I entered the room to see a man wearing a grey suit and tie sitting at a desk at the far end of the room, backed by a towering window overlooking the square outside.

    The woman approached the desk and placed the stack of folders down on top at the man's side. "Heir Wagner is here to see you, sir," she said to him.

Henrich Himmler, the Reichsführer and Hitler's right hand, looked up at me through his small, rounded glasses over his narrow mustache. He squinted with a seemingly disgusted expression in my direction.

He lowered his head again and continued to write, waving the woman away. "Leave us," he said.

The woman's heels echoed throughout the lavishly-decorated office as she walked past me and backed out of the door. She closed the door gently, leaving me standing idly with my hat clenched in both hands at my chest.

"Sit," said Himmler, his stern voice filling the empty space in the room.

I walked across the room anxiously and sat down in one of two black leather chairs before his desk.

A moment of silence passed, with only the clock in the room filling the void, before Himmler spoke again, still keeping his head down as though he was talking to the page. "You were once a Sergeant Major for the German Army during the war."

I cleared my throat, attempting to speak clearly. "Yes, sir."

"That was not a question, Heir Wagner. You are also the curator of the Alte Pinakothek."

I hesitated to speak, still unsure whether he was asking me a question or just stating the facts.

"Are you currently a member of the Party, Heir Wagner?"

I felt nervous, trying to give the Party leader a polite answer. I was certain he already knew the answer, though I could sense he was testing me. "No, but I've felt the call to join on several occasions."

"Yet you haven't. Curious. What's stopped you?" asked Himmler, finally looking up at me.

I released my grip on my hat. "I saw no way of benefitting the Party with my skills."

Himmler scoffed. He stood up from his seat behind the desk and walked over to the fireplace to my right. Above it hung a Ziegler painting of a woman cradling a baby lamb in soft shades of red, orange, and green. He stared up at the painting as he spoke.

"Art is a powerful tool, Heir Wagner. It speaks to the people in ways words cannot." He turned back and began pacing around the room. "Modern, degenerate art, such as the works of Otto Dix, has no place in this world. But the classics are something to be aspired towards. It divides people selfishly, when what we need are heroes."

Himmler stopped before a painting of the Führer. "Heroes like our Führer. Men who strive to unite us under one banner. A flag set on not only representing the might of Germany and its people, but one to be recognized, respected, and feared by the world." Himmler paced back around to his desk. He stood at the window. "Do you love your country, Heir Wagner?"

"Absolutely, sir. I gave my life for this country before, and I'd do so again," I replied without hesitation.

"Your patriotism is commendable."

Himmler turned back around to face me. He pushed his glasses up to the bridge of his nose and began sorting through the pages on his desk. "The Party wishes to appoint you as our new head curator. The Führer and I have been charmed by your sense of leadership, and ability to insure the preservation of Germany's greatest works. He and I share a fondness for the arts and wish to create the world's greatest collection, safeguarded under Germany's watchful eyes. Works which deliver a message: one of right; our right."

I sat stunned. My voice returned as Himmler slid a paper across the desk towards me. On it was the Party's symbol, accompanied with the various terms and rights that would be bestowed to me. "I- I'm honored, sir, but such a task would need more than just my command and negotiation to accomplish. Sir, you're referring to arranging agreements with museums, collectors, and even churches all over Germany, as well as Europe. The price for which these works may be far beyond our nation's—"

"We have no intention of paying for these works, Heir Wagner."

I fell silent, uncertain as to what he meant.

Himmler sat down in his chair once more. "With time,

these works will be yours to oversee as well as acquire. When this Party sets its eye on a goal, we see it through to the end, Heir Wagner."

Himmler picked up a pen from his desk and placed it on the document. He then set a Party pin alongside the page. "Are you with us and your fellow countrymen, Heir Wagner?"

I sat in disbelief with the document in my hands. It was the same meeting where I learned of the Party's long-term goal. A plan which demanded my expertise and knowledge. I couldn't refuse.

Heil Hitler.

Colonel Peter Wagner

Sophie jumped in surprise at the sight of something landing on her desk. Her cat, Marco, or Marco Polo, had leapt up in front of her, trying to get her attention. She set the open journal down on the desk and lifted Marco onto her lap, relieved it was only him.

"You're gonna get yourself shot one of these days, cat. Are you trying to startle me to get your dinner?" she said to him, petting Marco's tri-colored fur. Sophie stood from her desk and opened the journal, glancing out the window to see the two men who were standing outside were now sitting in their car out of the drizzling rain. She continued to read as she moved about her flat, filling Marco's food dish on the counter.

With my new *position came privilege. I had Andrea and my cottage built on our spot, and we lived there while I attended to my duty as Party Curator. My first order was to have all of Germany's prized works moved to the museum at König-splatz. A process which took both time and manpower. Many of the dimwits the Party sent under my command had no previous knowledge of art. To compensate, I appointed Fischer as the right hand of my kingdom. Like King Arthur, he became my Lancelot, seeking out that which I prized. He oversaw the movement of each work personally, putting together an efficient network via trains to have the works moved across Germany to the museum in Munich. Himmler soon ordered me to take my collection a step further. I issued my first order, which will forever live with me, that very winter.*

I stood along the streets of my hometown, wrapped in my heavy wool overcoat, fighting back the cold. I continued to smoke my cigarette in the snow, hearing my men searching the white-and-red brick house behind me as its owner yelled at them inside. The constant shouting had begun to irritate me. One of my men exited the home carrying a priceless Albrecht Dürer. I watched the owner follow him and continue shouting in a mix of German and Hebrew.

He was a stout man, well-groomed with a black mustache who loved to express his fury with his hands, seemingly used to bossing other people around. I threw my cigarette down in the snow and stepped in his path, choosing to try and remain calm before using force.

"These paintings have been in my family for nine generations!" he shouted at me, pointing at the truck being loaded with his collection.

"The Führer thanks you for your contribution and will take good care of your collection. I promise no harm will come to them," I replied, calmly.

"You are criminals, snatching what is not yours in broad daylight! Thieves! Bandits! You have no right! No respect!"

His words plucked at my lowest cord. I put my hand against his chest and shoved him back a step. I pointed firmly at his nose. "Criminals are those who stand only for themselves, keeping art where no one can see it. We stand for the nation, and its people."

The collector slid on the snow, nearly losing his balance as I pushed him again. I continued to walk towards him, pushing him back towards the door of his home, refusing to take his abuse. "Thieves steal what is not theirs. These works originally belonged to Germany. Bandits live by their own laws and not the laws of the land. We live by the laws of God and Germany."

I shoved him back in the doorway as he bounced against the wooden back wall of his home. I leaned in close, face-to-face with him, speaking with my lowest cord. "You are standing in our way, and you have stolen these works from Germany to keep for yourself." I glanced over at the fabric scroll hung on the wall to my right, embroidered with Hebrew scripture. "And you live by your own laws." I locked eyes with him once more. "You're the only criminal, thief, and bandit here. Now stand aside or I will have you and your family arrested like the villains you are."

The collector fell silent in shock, as I could see his upper lip quiver under his mustache. He backed away from me and walked into the living room of his home, sitting down on the couch beside his wife and daughter. A group of my men continued to search the living room around them, throwing aside anything which wasn't of value to us. The rest of my men continued to bring down the collection of Dürer paintings from the upstairs while I watched the collector from my place in the entryway. He pulled his silver and gold pocket watch with the star of David carved into the top from his vest and clutched it in his fist, as though in a moment of prayer.

The Party blamed the Jews for our burdens and troubles which led to us losing the Great War. I blamed the greed and weakness of our leaders and politicians more. However, I was under orders. And if they stood in my way, I was expected to deal with them. And I did, though I continue to weigh the cost.

Heil Hitler.

Colonel Peter Wagner

"Sounds like a real gentleman, doesn't he, Marco?" said Sophie with sarcasm towards Marco. Marco continued to sleep on her desk,

THE COLONEL'S LOST VAULT

unaware of her remark. Sophie glanced over at the clock again. It was 12 AM. She closed the journal around a café receipt from off her desk and picked Marco up. She leaned over her desk to look out the window, seeing the car from earlier with the two men inside had left.

Sophie grabbed her pistol and walked into her bedroom, placing Marco down on his bed near the window before hiding her gun within arm's reach, tucked between the bedframe and mattress.

"All that art, yet you hid it away and never shared it after the war. Why?" Sophie asked, thinking out loud. "Why the change of heart?"

Sophie stepped into the bathroom and stared at herself in the mirror, dwelling on Wagner's words. She opened the pill bottle resting on the sink and slipped one of her sleeping pills in her mouth, attempting to quell her dreams.

"Where'd you hide it, Colonel?" she asked herself in the mirror before swallowing the pills before turning in for the night.

Hyde Park Adventures

Five

Sophie felt her skin boiling under the desert heat as the sweat ran down her back. She tried to move her hands, feeling them chained behind her back to the chair. Her vision was obscured; blocked by the white-and-tan patterned cloth tied around her head. She breathed heavily, hearing only the distant sound of cars and motorcycles from within her shack prison, accompanied by the clatter of the chain holding the only door shut. She waited in her isolation, fearing for her life.

She heard two male voices speaking Arabic from outside the shack. Her breaths quickened at the sound of the chain being undone. The sound of footsteps approaching from across the sandy concrete made her gasp. She felt two hands grab her shoulders. The sharp edges of cutting pliers grazed the skin over her pinky finger.

She screamed.

Sophie's head rose from her pillow in fright, still screaming. She opened her eyes to see her darkened flat, finally falling silent. Marco stared at her from his bed, alerted by her usual nightmares. Her shirt and night shorts were soaked with sweat as she raised a hand up to her chest, trying to ease her heart.

A knock came at the front door, raising Sophie's anxiety. She took a deep breath and stood up from the bed. She grabbed her gun from its hiding spot and a towel from the bathroom, seeing her wet hair stuck to her face. She began wiping the sweat away from her face and neck as she crossed her flat. She peered through the peephole and sighed with relief seeing who it was. She opened it, hiding her pistol out of sight behind the door.

"Another troublesome night, my lady?" said Rupert, her elderly next-door neighbor across the hall. Rupert stood in the hallway, dressed in his blue-and-white pajamas, topped with a red robe. He stared at her with a concerned expression over his white mustache and thinning white hair.

"Sorry, Rupert. Yeah… More nightmares," Sophie replied, feeling sorry for causing such a fuss.

Rupert nodded in his usual polite manner. "I'll put the kettle on for ya," he said, turning his back, ready to limp his way to the open flat door behind him.

"There's no need, Rupert. Sorry I woke you."

Rupert turned back to her. "Pish posh. Was already awake. Just watching a little of 'Last of the Summer Wine.' Put on a dry pair of clothes and come join me."

Sophie relented a nod, returning to her flat to change and trade her pistol for Wagner's journal.

◆ ◆ ◆

Sophie sat on Rupert's brown-and-grey couch among his vast collection of old trinkets and mementos. She watched the late 70's sitcom on the tube television with the delayed subtitles, still wiping the sweat away from her neck as Rupert poured her and himself a mug of tea in the kitchen. She set Wagner's journal down on the seat cushion next to her, prepared to read once Rupert had inevitably fallen asleep. Rupert hobbled into the room and handed her a mug.

"Thanks," Sophie muttered.

Rupert smiled under his mustache and sat down in his recliner in front of the television. He struggled to lift his weak right leg up onto the foot stool before pulling a steel flask out from the space between his seat cushions. He dumped a splash of whiskey into his tea mug then held the flask out to Sophie. Sophie snickered at him and held her mug out for him to top off; he poured a small shot's worth into her cup before she sniffed at her cup, taking in the strong, warm smell.

Rupert took a sip from his mug and smacked his lips together in satisfaction. "Ah... A splash of life can make a rainy day dry."

Sophie took a sip of her tea, feeling the sweet whiskey sooth her throat. She immediately felt her nerves begin to settle, always enjoying Rupert's company as a distraction from her nightmares as she was certain he felt the same way. She stared at the cup with a grin, once again marveling at the brew's power to ease her woes.

"'Lots of us old boys came back from the war, sweating on even the coldest nights as though we had taken a walk through the gardens of hell," Rupert recounted calmly. "Some nights, I'd be screaming out for those lads we had lost as though they were still there. For other men, they'd be shocked to the point that fear blinded them or left them deafened by the screams of their fellow man. Nothing to be ashamed of."

Sophie bowed her head; very few people knew of her nightmares with Rupert being one of them. Not even Oz knew.

Rupert took another heavy sip of his spiked tea, ready to ease her wounds with the story she had heard many times before. "Was only fifteen on D-Day. Wasn't until I came home that I had my first drink in a pub," he chuckled in amusement. "Lied on my enlistment forms so I could join my brothers on the frontlines after they made it back following the retreat across the channel. 'Was the only day of combat I ever saw. Yet, it was more than a man should ever have to see."

Rupert took a drink from his mug and cleared his throat. "Juno Beach," he pointed down at his knee, "One round to the knee and I collapsed in the sand. Rolled around in agony for an hour, watching wave after wave of our fighting boys stomp past me in a hail of .42 fire. One young man, whom I never learned the name of, carried me into a mortar hole. He rose up out of the hole, ready to defend us; shot went right through his left eye and out the back of his head. Tried to help him, still gritting my teeth from the pain in my leg, but it was too late. Lad saved my life, but I couldn't save him."

Rupert fell silent; the low volume from the television filled the flat.

He pointed down at his knee again. "'Was in the hospital for six months. When they tried to send me home, I offered to be a runner and they agreed. Can you believe that? A bum runner." Rupert looked over at Sophie and laughed. Sophie chuckled, taking a sip of her drink.

"Spent the rest of the war as a scribe, running letters and filing documents behind the frontline; 'had me writing up reports here and there, even after the war. Wasn't the fight I wanted, but I was just glad to still be doing my part. Made it all the way to Germany as a postal boy." Rupert grinned and shook his head. "The pain kept me up most nights. Once I came home, it came back on its own, along with the face of that young man I never got to meet."

Sophie sank into the couch cushions, thinking back to her lost friends and fellow soldiers—her friend Yorkie's cries of pain and pleas for help under a pile of rubble, among a great many other things. "I wish I could have done more... I think it's the reason I can't sit in one place for too long. I can't find comfort unless I'm walking through that garden of hell."

"A warrior's burden. Can't save 'em all, though we may try endlessly in our dreams."

"Did you have any trouble readjusting when you came back?"

Rupert took a drink as he nodded. "I did. A soldier's place isn't always at home. It's out there. Fighting the good fight that he or she's been training for all their life. Was glad to be back, but never felt at-home again without the Lieutenant's orders repeating in my head."

Sophie took another drink in an attempt to wash away the memories. Rupert leaned back in his chair and watched the television. He chuckled, watching the three of the old men on the screen cracking jokes around the bedside of their elderly friend in the hospital.

Hyde Park Adventures

Sophie picked up Wagner's journal and opened it to the page she was on.

"What's that ya got there?" asked Rupert.

"An old journal from your war, actually. New story I'm working on," Sophie replied.

"Ha! Well, ain't that a coincidence! Be sure to let me know if you have any questions. I might be able to answer a few, assuming they're postal boy related. This old book's still full of some knowledge; I could go on for nights with tales."

"I certainly will, Rupert," Sophie replied, turning her attention to the journal. She read among the dim lamp light of the room, occasionally hearing Rupert chuckle at the television, just glad to know she wasn't alone.

While I pursued *my crusade for art across Germany, the Führer was making plans of his own. Germany had been stripped of its armaments and our leader sought to restore them, stronger than before. Much of my time was spent at Himmler's SS estate, the castle Wewelsberg, listening to Party plans and putting forward my own. A cold and dreadful place steeped in vicious rumors of the occult, housing Himmler's own visions.*

In 1936, I was obligated to attend the unveiling of Hitler's Luftwaffe strike force at the Olympic games in Berlin; 2,500 planes built with the intention of showing the world that Germany had returned strong and unmatched. As those planes flew over the stadium, Himmler made a request that I felt compelled to see through.

I watched the stadium cheer with the Party banners flapping in the breeze overhead, feeling as though I should have been more captivated by the sight. Yet, I felt only an emptiness that had taken hold of me. I watched as the Führer smiled and nodded in approval six feet away, with Himmler standing at his side, emotionless as always. The cheering sounds of the crowd were drowned out by the sound of the planes flying in formation.

"I have a new project for you, Colonel," said Himmler.

I averted my gaze away from the sky to see him leaning back to speak over my shoulder to me.

"Yes, Reichsführer?" I replied.

"We want those masterpieces you've been collecting to be well-protected for the future. Such treasures hold the key to raising the people's spirits once we've accomplished our goal."

"What did you have in mind, sir?" I asked,

"How does one keep our marks safe, our jewels secure, and our secrets hidden?"

"By placing them in a safe or a vault," I replied.

"Get to work on it," he told me, skipping right to the point.

I thought for a moment, conflicted. As safe as a vault would be, art was meant to be observed and enjoyed. I spoke my mind. "Wouldn't that defy the purpose of the museum, sir?"

"The Führer has plans to build a new museum to house them all. Germany will have plenty of time to stand and observe our nation's purity through oil and color, once it is all over," he replied.

I stood idly for a moment; the faint sound of the bombers flying low towards the stadium in the distance. "Sir?"

"These games represent more than just a competition against the world's athletes. It represents what is to come. The unification of the world under a single banner," he replied. He watched the bombers fly over with a long grin on his face. An unsettling sight from a man known to show no emotion.

A vault. One built to protect the world's most valued visual wonders from the conflict which was looming in secrecy. A vault with only three keys: one for Himmler; one I gifted to Fischer; and the last in my care.

Heil Hitler.

Colonel Peter Wagner

Sophie turned the page and eagerly read on. Rupert continued to laugh at the television, now having had his second cup of tea mixed with the remainder of his flask.

THE COLONEL'S LOST VAULT

The location of *the vault was and continues to be kept secret. Not even the Führer knows. Everyone who constructed the vault was lined up and put before a firing squad, to ensure its safety. Fischer and only two of my most trusted men—Captain Kurt Weller and Captain Willi Kindler—know its location and are in charge of storing the art inside. Upon its completion, I oversaw the arrival of the first train carrying the artwork myself, to make certain that there would be no issues.*

As I waited impatiently at the station platform, Fischer paced eagerly behind my back under the lamp light.

I checked my watch, expressing my irritation to him. "They're fifteen minutes late."

"Perhaps they were stopped," *said Fischer.*

I turned back to him and let the nightly shadows emphasize my scowl. "Their orders were to proceed here with the highest authority. They were ordered not to stop, not even for the Führer."

Fischer suddenly pointed back over my shoulder. A distant billow of white smoke appeared from the tops of the tree line. I held my relief as Fischer joined me at my side, awaiting an inevitable excuse from Volst.

The train rolled into the station with the steam fogging up the platform. I checked my watch again, expressing my irritation to the soldiers onboard as they each passed while riding along the freight cars. The train came to a shuddering halt as the men aboard all jumped down and began unlocking the cars.

Sergeant Volst hopped down from the last car and approached me, the orange lamps over his head illuminating his smug grin.

"You're late, Sergeant," I said to him, walking towards him.

"The third freight car door was stuck closed, so we couldn't open it to load it," he replied.

"Were you stopped?" asked Fischer.

"No," Volst replied, stopping before me. "Some fellow officers insisted on riding along, but I informed them I was under orders from Colonel Wagner himself not to let anyone else onboard."

I continued to glare at Volst as the rest of the soldiers began opening the wooden sliding doors to the freight cars. Volst's laid back attitude and smugness had always irritated me; he was young and overly confident, seeing no faults in himself, making him prone to mistakes.

"Fischer," I said.

"Yes, sir," Fischer replied.

"Count them all."

Fischer ran to the first car and began counting the wood crates as the soldiers unloaded them onto the station platform; each one five feet on all sides and labeled with the Party logo under a fragile, red mark. The soldiers all heaved and grunted as they carried the crates out of the cars, while I remained ever vigilant with Volst by my side.

"Major Holbist wanted me to inform you that curator Gurlitt will be shipping more works to you tomorrow from Vienna," said

Volst.

"Tell them to ship them to the museum," I replied.

"Yes, sir. Though, might I ask why these pieces aren't being shipped to the museum as well?"

"Asking questions isn't your objective, Sergeant. Now I suggest that you relay my order to the Major, and let the matter rest."

"Yes, sir," Volst replied.

"Where's Captain Weller?" I asked, not seeing the man I appointed accompanying the train.

Fischer stopped at the last car, having finished his count of the crates. "There's only eleven crates here, sir."

I turned to Volst, feeling my nails digging into my palms as I clenched my fists. "You lost one?!"

Volst stepped back away from me. "We couldn't get the door open—"

I lashed out and threw a fist at Volst, knocking his hat from his head as he fell on one knee before crawling away from me, blood dripping from his nose and mouth. I kicked him in the chest as the soldiers all stopped to watch with looks of terror.

"One of my crates is sitting on the platform in Stuttgart?!" I shouted.

"No! No—" I drove my foot into his side again as he coughed and rolled over. He began gasping for air as I waited for another pathetic excuse. "Weller loaded it onto a truck!"

"Where?!" I shouted down at him and kicked him once again.

"I don't know," Volst replied, now wheezing as he gasped for air. "It should be here by now."

I drew my pistol from my holster and pointed it down towards his head. Volst extended a hand to me, continuing to apologize and plead for his life.

"Colonel!" shouted Fischer, stopping me from pulling the trigger.

I turned my attention towards Fischer as he pointed towards the front of the station, through the waiting area windows. The headlights of a covered truck pulled up to the station, carrying with it my missing crate.

I stared down at Volst again, watching him continue to grovel in a pathetic manner. I put my pistol away and scolded him in silence. I had made it clear to him, as well as the rest of Germany's army, that these works were more valuable to me than any of their lives.

"Major!" I shouted back to Fischer. "Load them up!"

Fischer began shouting orders at everyone. The soldiers returned to unloading the crates, carrying them each onto the four trucks parked out front of the station where Kindler waited to oversee the loading. I turned my back to Volst, hearing him spit his own blood on the platform.

I picked up his hat and threw it to him as he rose to one knee. "Failure will not be tolerated, Sergeant."

I made my point clear. Word spread fast among the German ranks that I was not a man to be crossed and didn't tolerate mishaps or failure. Volst never lost a crate after that. When a fellow officer insisted on leaving four crates behind due to their weight, Volst relayed my disapproval in a similar fashion. He had them loaded onto another truck before driving them across the country himself, presumably fearing for his own life. Those first crates were the beginning of something grand. An achievement I thought I could be proud of, yet I still felt the emptiness.

Heil Hitler.

Colonel Peter Wagner

Sophie sat pondering Wagner's final sentence. She no longer saw any sign of the man who painted in tranquility through his writing, leaving her to question what had changed.

She heard the sound of a snort come from Rupert. She looked over to see his head resting back in his chair with his mouth hanging open.

Sophie stood up from the couch and picked up the blue-and-green wool blanket resting on the arm. She draped it over Rupert gently and sat back down, turning the page of the journal to continue reading.

As we began *searching every nook and cranny, the Führer set into motion a minor act which we knew would result in an even larger explosion. In no short time at all, we gathered a vast* collection of works across both Germany and Austria. Meanwhile, Poland fell easily to Germany's might as our tanks rolled into Warsaw September of '39, and our Führer's grand vision finally became clearer to me.

Within ten months, we took Belgium, Holland, Norway, Finland, Denmark, and France. Our forces could not be matched, just as foretold. Europe was ill-prepared, crumbling beneath our advances as we exposed their fragility to the rest of the world; nations made of glass which could easily be shattered with a single German stone. As we progressed in all directions, I was relocated to Norway, where I took possession of the works of the Nordic masters: Munch, Zorn, and Steinberg. I was then flown to France in no short time at all to oversee the transportation of the world's greatest works, all housed in the famous Louvre Palace.

My car rolled to a stop in front of the Louvre courtyard while our nation's flag waved from the rooftop at the far end and a banner blanketed the museum's exterior. A German soldier opened the car door for me as I stepped out onto the curb, smelling the faint scent of smog and burnt wood in the air. I turned and gazed over the top of the car in admiration of Paris. Our new nation had finally claimed in a few short months what we could not years prior, in my youth amidst the Great War.

I made my way towards the museum as Ziegler, Hitler's chosen private collector, crossed the courtyard to greet me. A tall and slender man, with a bulbous nose, dressed in a grey suit with the Party pin. My feelings towards Ziegler were—and still are—

mixed from when we first met back in Munich. He shared my vision of art, holding it in high regard over many of life's other virtues, but also lacked a sense of force and authority. A man easily pushed aside by the slightest wave of determination on my part, or anyone else for that matter

"Colonel Wagner," he shouted to me, saluting and shaking my hand as I approached. "Lieutenant Stein is waiting for us inside."

"Have they all been accounted for?" I asked.

"Most of them are missing. We found a ledger in the curator's office, so we know where some of them went, the majority to the countryside. We sent a few men out already to bring them back, though the Mona Lisa and the de Milo are still unaccounted for, including the piece in question. The museum curator continues to say they were loaned out to the London National Gallery since the start of last year."

"He's lying."

"Undoubtedly. I tried to pry it out of him before the Lieutenant arrived, but perhaps you can make more progress."

Ziegler and I entered the museum with two guards holding the doors open for us. Down the polished stone stairwell—decorated with ornate trimming and lavish walls, amidst the chilled air and the familiar smell of aged halls which greeted me—Lieutenant Phillip Stein awaited my arrival. A viper with little respect for art, Stein offered me a smug smile under his pointed cheeks.

"Colonel," he said, shaking my hand with a tight grip. I squeezed his hand in return with my own dominating grip.

"I told Himmler we didn't need to bother you in Oslo, but he insisted you join us for the inspection before the Führer's arrival. My men are already on their way to bring back some of the art before the day is out."

I let go of his hand, feeling the sting he had left. "The Reichsführer has many prizes that were stored here, Lieutenant. He wishes for me to find and inventory all of them for the Führer's more personal collection."

"Ah... You mean your mysterious-yet-famous vault?" replied Stein, in a mocking fashion.

I remained silent, refusing to engage with him. "Where is the curator?"

"The main entrance, under guard," Ziegler replied.

I pushed past Stein and began making my way down the steps; the heels of my boots echoing through the empty halls as I walked with Stein and Ziegler behind me. Empty frames sat on the floor and walls of the long hallway as I approached the marble stairs at the back. Large wooden beams and ropes littered the steps, with a leftover wood ramp leading from the landing down to the bottom of the steps, used to haul the statue away. I approached the landing on the stairs to see a clean outline of where the Führer's ultimate prize once stood.

"They've hidden her," said Stein.

I approached the wood ramp and circled the empty space. "Seems our angel still has her wings after all."

"They must have moved it before we arrived," said Ziegler.

I kneeled down, inspecting the thin layer dust on the floor. "Long before," I replied, wiping my hand through the dust, seeing months had passed since the statue's removal.

I marched back down the stairs and followed the museum signs to the main entrance. I could hear the sound of boxes being broken open ahead. I entered the main hall to see a man sitting in a chair as a captain yelled at him. He was the museum curator. A short, plump man, presumably in his fifties based on his greying hair and wrinkles, unrestrained and viciously beaten.

An endless line of soldiers appeared from the three hallways around me, carrying small frames of art covered in cloth along with small boxes filled with the museum's less-cherished artworks. Two of Stein's men remained close by, breaking open each of the boxes and removing the canvas cloth coverings, taking inventory of the paintings that had been hidden away inside.

"Where is it?! Tell us now!" shouted the captain.

The head of the museum remained silent in his seat, refusing to make eye contact. I approached the museum curator. The captain fell silent, offering me a salute. "Colonel."

I immediately sank into a crouched position and removed my hat, meeting him at eye level, trying to win the curator's trust. He continued to stare vacantly at the polished floor.

"Thank you for keeping them safe," I said to him in French, taking notice that neither Ziegler nor Stein spoke French based on their reactions.

The curator glanced up at me, expressing his hatred through his scowl. "They are not yours to steal. They belong to the world."

I took a deep breath and grabbed a vacant wooden chair resting along the wall behind me. I dragged it across the floor and sat down before him. "How many Caravaggio's did you have in your museum? Three?"

The curator continued to remain silent.

"You probably know as well as I do, Caravaggio was not just a painter, but a murderer as well. A painter, who killed a man in a brawl, forcing him to flee for his life from Rome. When I was younger, I never understood his struggle nor held any pity for him. Now I find myself here, walking in his shoes, and I carry with me all the same guilt and pity in the world."

"At least Caravaggio begged for forgiveness the rest of his life. One painting for every sin," the curator muttered. "You come here, having murdered thousands. You would need to paint a thousand paintings to make up for it. Even then, I pray that God would still cast you into hell."

"Then so be it. I'd gladly paint a painting for every one of your countrymen once this is all over. But before I can, I need to protect Caravaggio once more from his persecutors. I can't speak for the rest of my men, but I know I am willing to defend him with my *life, one man seeking forgiveness to another."*

"You already have him," the curator replied, gesturing over to Stein's men holding the ledger from his office.

"He's not the only victim here I've come to protect."

The Curator sat quietly for a moment. "She's in London, along with the rest. On loan since July," he muttered.

"You're lying," I replied. I stood up from my seat. "You know how I know? I was in London in July. I visited the National Gallery, taking inventory on the Führer's behalf."

I leaned in close and played my lowest chord for him. "I passed through here, too. I saw her on those steps, ever in her stride towards victory. I stood at her base and marveled at her faceless beauty on July twelfth."

The museum curator gave me a cold, worried stare.

"Same as Caravaggio, I can protect her better than you can. I cannot ensure her safety from others."

An uncomfortable void filled the room. I continued to pry the truth from his eyes as his pupils shrank. He was on the verge of telling me... when Stein interjected.

"Enough!" he shouted in German. Stein drew his Lugar and aimed it at the curator's forehead. "Tell us where the Victory is! Now!"

The curator retreated to his silence. Stein took a step back and fired one shot at the ceiling. The shot made all the soldiers stop as the curator sat with the the speckled dust from the ceiling raining down over him.

Stein stepped forward and placed the heated barrel against the curator's cut and bleeding forehead. "Where is it?!"

"Château de Valençay! Château de Valençay!" the curator shouted.

I placed my hat back on and turned to face Ziegler. Before I could speak, another shot rang out, causing me to jump. I looked back to see the curator now on the floor, blood streaking down from the freshly-made wound in his forehead. Stein returned his Lugar to its holster before combing his hair back with his palm in pride.

I shook my head, feeling both ashamed and disgusted. I turned to Ziegler. "Arrange a ride for me to Château de Valençay. You and Stein will remain here and give the Führer and the Reichsführer a tour of the museum. Show the few pieces left behind and inform them that I am seeing to the return of the Victory myself."

The Winged Victory of Samothrace. A marble woman found among the ruins of Rome, broken by time and robbed of her head and arms. Yet, even in her broken state, her beauty still shines. The Victory is the Party's ultimate prize. Once the Führer's museum is complete, it will be restored to its former glory with additions of the Party's influence set on symbolizing our own victory over the world. The winged goddess will be the figurehead at the bow of our ship deemed a new Roman Empire. I sought her out and had her shipped back to the vault in a heavy crate, along with several other significant works hidden at Château de Valençay. The rest were to remain in France for the time being, while other arrangements for safe locations were made throughout the Fatherland. Capacity in the vault was beginning to dwindle, forcing me to prioritize.

It became clear to me in France that I would not be spending much time in Germany anymore, so I left Fischer behind in my place, to oversee the care of the works. So far, he has proven himself loyal; I only pray he does not falter as this war carries on longer than anticipated.

As of late, I find myself in Athens on our great nation's behalf. Upon conquering the cradle of western civilization, I was brought here to do what I do best: secure the world's colorful treasures. However, the moment has come where I feel I must leave behind a path in case something happens to me. Our eastern advances have hit a stalemate, and I've spent far too much time in one place. My writings shall be the chronicle of my journey as I serve my country along its grand and glorious road to victory. Greece's treasures remain close at my side in secrecy, waiting to be transported back to the Fatherland. I hope to serve as their guard along the road, but for now, they remain hidden away along rolling banks. Along a coast of turquoise waters, where the gateway between Earth and Hell resides. A place where the River Styx runs dry, and the legion-headed serpent rests in eternity.

Heil Hitler.

Colonel Peter Wagner

"The gateway between Earth and Hell resides…" Sophie whispered to herself as the orange glow of the morning sun peeked into Rupert's flat. She slammed the journal closed and stood up from the couch with haste, then hurried over to Rupert and gently shook him awake.

"Rupert!" she said to him.

Rupert's eyes opened wide, as though trying to recognize where he was. "Yes, sir!" he grumbled to her, still groggy.

"Rupert," Sophie replied, crouched down on one knee.

Rupert looked around the room, finally able to get his bearings on the present. "Sorry, dear lady. Didn't mean to doze off on you."

"Can you watch Marco for me again?"

Rupert smacked his lips together as though he still tasted the whiskey on his breath. "It would be my honor. Where are you off to in such a hurry this time?"

"Greece," Sophie replied, hurrying back to her own flat to pack.

Six
Athens, Greece

WAIT... YOU'RE WHERE?" Oz asked through the phone speaker; the chatter of flight announcements over the intercom and travelers occupied the airport around Sophie. Sophie walked past the many gates among the terminal with her hair back in a bun, dressed in her favored choice of traveler's clothing: a shemagh around her neck, a tan buttoned-over shirt rolled to the elbows, straight-cut jeans and boots alongside her trusty backpack.

Sophie continued to talk to Oz through her headphones. "I'm in Athens. Wagner's journal said he was stationed in Athens. He worded it as though he was leaving a clue or trail for himself to follow, maybe one leading to the vault's location. So, here I am, getting my tan on."

"I thought you had agreed with Maple to stay local. No more trips?" asked Oz.

"Yes, which is why I may or may not need you to cover for me at the office. I paid for the flight myself, but if she asks, I'm in Liverpool following a lead."

Hyde Park Adventures

"No!" shouted Oz over the speaker, threatening his cover immediately. His voice fell quiet as though he realized he had just drawn unwanted attention to his sacred space among the cubicles. He whispered with a scolding tone, "Are you daft…!? I have bills to pay too, Broadway. I will not cover for you and get sacked the same as you."

"It's your story, Oz."

"Don't play coy, it's *your* story. I just do the digging because you don't wanna get your hands dirty."

Oz continued to scorn her as her shoulder collided with a man reading a magazine beyond the security gate.

"Sorry," she said to him, directing her attention back to the man.

"No worries," replied the man as Sophie caught only a glimpse of his face. Her heart seized for half a second, seeing his face; one with a familiar full brown beard. All that was missing was the red-and-black flannel.

Sophie directed her attention ahead of her again, continuing to make her way towards the exit, feeling uneasy. She glanced back out of the corner of her eye to see her stalker was once again following her from a distance.

Sophie continued to talk to Oz, pretending she hadn't noticed her old fan. "Tell you what: you cover for me with Maple, and I'll—"

"Don't say it…"

"—take you on a date to that Indian restaurant you asked me out to."

Oz sighed in her ear. "That's not a date, Broadway. That's a petty dinner in the friend zone. I asked you out two years ago, and once when we were in primary school together. Thought you didn't want to ruin our friendship?"

Sophie passed the carousels at baggage claim and stepped outside to be greeted by the potent smell of exhaust along the terminal curb. "Consider this your chance, then. Impress me with Maple, and who knows? Maybe a date among friends could turn into something more."

Oz scoffed. "Unlikely… Fine… Though I'm not doing this for a date. If I wanted one of those, I'd ask Maple out and risk losing my job when she discovers I'm not interested. Consider it a new addition to an ongoing debt that has yet to be paid in full."

Sophie snickered. "Love you, Wizard," she replied, jokingly.

"Ha!" Oz replied in an ill-humored, sarcastic tone.

Sophie tapped the end call button and removed the headphones from her ears before placing them in her bag. She took advantage of the moment, seeing that her stalker was still behind her. He was waiting inside the terminal doors, keeping an eye on her through the glass windows.

"'Meet me at the Athens International Airport, 15-hundred. You won't wanna miss this,'" said a male voice with a mid-western accent, approaching the curb behind her.

Sophie smiled, comforted by the friendly voice that was her back-up. She turned to see her old friend and fellow Raider, Corbin, walking towards her holding his phone up. His bright, white smile emphasized his dark complexion in the midday sun, along with his sunglasses shining back at her in a kaleidoscope of colors. He wore a white t-shirt over his sand-colored shorts, clean-shaven as always under his bald head.

"I see you still don't wait for a reply before running off. What if I wasn't here?" questioned Corbin.

"I knew you would be. Social media is a wonder. You keep posting about playing babysitter for all those celebrities here, so I figured I'd join you. Hanging at beach parties looked like too much fun to pass up," Sophie replied.

"You creepin' on me, Broadway?"

"It's what we were trained to do."

The two of them embraced in a hug. "How 'you been, Corbin?" asked Sophie.

"Could be better," Corbin replied, releasing her from their reunion. "You 'been staying out of trouble?"

"You already know the answer to that, so why waste time? What have you been doing with yourself?"

Corbin began walking back towards his car, parked along the curb. "Like you said: playing babysitter. Jumping between jobs, trying to keep my head above the surf. Ambassadors, musicians, movie stars, CEO's, you name 'em and I've probably opened the door for 'em. Anyone looking for US security around here."

"Gung-ho for life, huh?"

"Psh… Gung-ho for life *always*, girl. But this sure ain't the Gung-ho I was expecting in retirement," replied Corbin, shaking his head in disappointment.

The Colonel's Lost Vault

"Lizzy took more than just the house, huh?"

"She took the house, the motorcycle, *and* the States with her in the divorce."

Sophie snickered. "But now you get to live here in paradise, picking up supermodels."

Corbin began to unlock the driver side door to his Toyota Yaris as he scoffed. "Pff... You try eating flatbread for a year while driving this piece of shit; I'd rather have my truck back."

Sophie chuckled as she removed her backpack, glad to be in Corbin's company again. She opened the passenger side door and hopped in the car, placing her bag in the back seat. She closed the door, noticing her stalker hop into a yellow Mini Cooper parked two cars ahead of them.

Corbin started the car and began to drive away as they passed the Mini Cooper. Sophie watched the car through the side mirror to see it start following them.

"Care to tell me why I just picked you up at the airport versus leaving you on the curb?" said Corbin, adjusting the rear-view mirror.

Sophie rolled down her window and laid her head back, closing her eyes while taking in Athen's tropical atmosphere among a forest of pearl stone buildings. "Find us somewhere good to eat and I'll tell you."

"A'ight," Corbin replied. "First we have to lose your tail."

Sophie continued to speak with her eyes closed. "Was wondering if you noticed them,, too. Guy in the passenger seat chased after me in London. Ran into him when I was on the phone with Oz at the airport.

They were posted outside my flat, too; been following me for two days now, though I didn't expect them to follow me this far."

Sophie opened her eyes and glanced out the side mirror again as they merged onto the local highway. The two men in the Mini Cooper continued to keep their distance.

"Know who they are?" asked Corbin, removing his sunglasses and hanging them from his shirt collar.

"Nope. My guess is they're not friendly, either."

"What makes you say that?"

"The passenger's strapped. Felt it when I bumped into him; 'has a piece tucked under his shirt."

Corbin leaned forward and looked in the mirror again. "A'ight. Best hold on. This piece of shit's ain't quick, but it can maneuver."

Sophie set her seat upright and held onto the handle above her head as Corbin shifted down a gear. He began to speed up, merging between the busy lanes of traffic along the highway; with each car they passed, Sophie began to lose sight of her pursuers.

Corbin let free a sigh of relief as he checked the mirror.

Sophie kept her gaze fixed on the side mirror. "Don't relax just yet."

The sound of car honking and tires skidding came from behind; Sophie spotted a small-sized truck spinning out of control along the shoulder of the highway, forced off the road by the Mini Cooper.

"Might wanna punch it harder than that, Corb," Sophie said, masking her worry with an unconcerned tone.

Sophie heard Corbin's foot hit the floor as he accelerated. He swerved aggressively through the traffic as the other cars around them honked and attempted to get out of the way. Sophie held on tight to the handle, swaying side to side in her seat as she could hear the car tires screeching along the roadway.

Keeping an eye on the side mirror, she could still see the Mini Cooper behind them continuing the chase, showing no sign of giving up. A white Elantra jerked out of the way of the Mini Cooper, colliding with the guardrail along the shoulder before rolling over. The other cars behind them all screeched to a halt as the highway was now blocked, causing a pile-up.

"Christ, Broadway! Who the hell'd you piss off?!" said Corbin.

"I don't know! Who *haven't* I pissed off?! Just leg it, Corb!" Sophie shouted at him, continuing to watch her pursuers out the back window.

Corbin continued to race through the highway traffic, visibly eager to find an exit. He waited until the last moment, then steered the car onto an empty offramp, each holding their breath. The Mini Cooper skidded to slow down before following them, narrowly missing a concrete barricade as they drove towards the offramp. Corbin's car bounced and swerved as they drove through a busy intersection, narrowly missing an unsuspecting motorcyclist on the now-dense commercial streets.

Corbin turned onto a one-way street, only to find themselves speeding towards a series of small street cafés, bustling with patrons eating at folding tables along the road. Corbin began honking his horn, trying to alert everyone.

"When I said find us a place to eat, Corb, I didn't mean drive-thru!" said Sophie, bracing for them to hit the café tables.

Corbin remained focused on his driving with a serious expression. People began shouting and getting up from the tables in fright. The car crashed through the area, tossing the flimsy folding tables to the side as people continued to jump out of the way.

Sophie checked out the rear window again to see a man attempting to stop the Mini Cooper as he waved his hands in the air. They refused to stop, forcing the man to leap out of the way at the last minute, before continuing to plow through the remaining wreckage of the cafes.

Corbin turned onto another narrow one-way street, lined with parked cars and motorcycles. The Mini Cooper was still following them as they began to pick up speed with the white stone buildings around them whizzing by. Sophie turned to face the front window, seeing a crane truck pulling out into the road from a narrow alleyway; the crane arm jutting out into the roadway. The narrow gap between the crane and opposing buildings was shrinking, leaving Sophie rigid in her seat.

"Whoa, whoa, whoa! Corbin you can't make that!" Sophie said to him.

Corbin sped up as the gap continued to shrink. Sophie grabbed hold of the seat as she watched the crane racing towards them. She closed her eyes, awaiting the impact.

The car jolted, followed by the sound of screeching tires.

Sophie opened her eyes. They were still moving and now driving along the sidewalk beyond the truck. She looked back just in time to see the truck stop and the Mini Cooper crash into the crane arm, thinly scalping the roof of their car and catching the corner of the truck. The two men in the car stepped out and watched Sophie and Corbin drive away.

Corbin let out a sigh of relief as he turned onto a main roadway. Sophie sat back in her chair, thankful for Corbin's risky driving.

"A'ight, now I *really* want answers. What is it you've done to push someone that far over the edge?" asked Corbin.

Sophie reached back for her backpack and pulled the journal out. She held it up for Corbin to see. "Find us a place to eat."

"ARTWORK?" ASKED CORBIN, an ill-convinced expression on his face as he sat across from Sophie among the empty tables of the mom-and-pop Greek restaurant. "All that for artwork locked behind a metal door somewhere?"

Sophie continued to feast on her moussaka with a side of bread and olive oil in the warmly-lit atmosphere. The sound of a large family celebrating a reunion a few tables back from them in the nearly-vacant establishment helped muffle their conversation.

Sophie swallowed her mouth full of bread. "Maybe," she muttered, taking a drink of her ouzo.

"Who else knows you're chasing the story?" asked Corbin.

"Just Oz and my editor, Maple. And Rupert, but let's be honest: none of them have it out for me. Though something tells me the vault isn't what those guys were after."

"Meaning they only wanted one thing…" Corbin stared at Sophie with a concerned look.

"Yup! Me," Sophie replied with a less-than-worried tone, eating another bite of her moussaka.

"Christ, Broadway. You really don't know how to keep your head down, do you?" Corbin shook his head in disapproval. "Who do you think they're with, then? Naz—"

Sophie raised a hand to stop him as she swallowed, feeling her stomach ache at the sheer mention of the name. She cleaned her hands with her napkin, trying to brush off the feeling. "No. He's organized, but not *that* well-organized outside of Libya."

"Chow Zen?"

"Possibly, assuming he's outsourcing help now. Though, that'd mean he'd be after you too, and so far, it seems they're only after me." Sophie tapped her fork on her plate in thought, thinking back on her times with the Marine Corps Special Operations Command. "I don't think it's anyone we dealt with during our time with MARSOC."

Corbin perked up in the booth seat, expressing his own eagerness. "Then let's get what you came here for and evac. 'Cause I gotta be honest with ya, I'm skeptical. A whole vault full of lost artwork? Seriously, Broadway, think about it: is it really worth that much trouble?"

"A Van Gogh painting of poppy flowers worth $55 million was stolen from a museum in Egypt in 2010 and has yet to be found. If someone is willing to go through the trouble of stealing one painting of a flower bouquet, imagine how much a florist-sized shop filled with flower paintings by Van Gogh would be worth."

Corbin relinquished his skeptic look as Sophie continued. "You and I know very well that there are buyers out there in the underground—like Chow Zen—who could care less about the paintings, but the money they can get from it to fuel their causes. Which means that I now hold the treasure map to the motherload. If there's a trail to follow, I'm following it till the end. If it's all a fake, then at least that's a story worth learning the truth about. And it's not like I have a choice anymore: either I find it, or I lose my job."

"You find it, I'll come work for you as a personal bodyguard. With that much money, your career will become the least of your worries," Corbin replied, drinking his beer.

"If I find it, and there *is* anything left, I'll give you half just for helping me. So, what do you say, Corb? How about one more ride?" Sophie replied, snickering as she continued to eat.

"I'll watch your back for now, but that's it. You have a tendency of getting in over your head, and the last thing I want is grim news because I left you to fend for yourself. This is your show, Broadway; it's a shit show, but it's still your show. You've already made one day more interesting for me than the past several months. So… count me in."

Sophie smiled, feeling twice as prepared and at-home with Corbin now at her side.

"A'ight. Where do we start?" asked Corbin.

Sophie pulled the journal from her bag. She flipped the journal open with one hand and slid it across the table to him. "Read."

Corbin picked up the journal. His eyes scanned the page until he began reading the last part out loud. "Greece's treasures remain close at my side in secrecy, waiting to be transported back to the Fatherland. I hope to serve as their guard along the road, but for now, they remain hidden away along rolling banks. Along a coast of turquoise waters—' Shit, that could be anywhere around here. 'You ever been to a beach here? They're all that way."

"Keep reading," Sophie replied, chewing her food.

Corbin continued to read with a sigh. "'—Where the gateway between Earth and Hell resides. A place where the River Styx runs dry, and the legion-headed serpent rests in eternity.' Huh… The River Styx is a myth, though. Ancient Greeks believed it was the river you'd have to cross to get to the afterlife. When people died, they'd even burn their bodies with coins over their eyes just to pay Charon, the ferryman, to get them across. Some people around here still do that."

Sophie set her fork and knife down atop each other on her plate and threw her napkin over it. She wiped her hands together in satisfaction. "Ever heard of a place like that around here?"

Corbin continued to read over the page again. He set the journal down on the table and tapped on the surface, seemingly trying to thumb through the index of his mind. "A river of death? No."

"But you know a guy?" said Sophie, expecting a response from Corbin.

Corbin snickered. "As a matter of fact, I might."

Seven

CORBIN'S CAR ROLLED to a stop before a lavish two-story white limestone mansion, topped with blue painted roofing tiles and wooden window shutters.

Sophie stepped out of the car, marveling at the home's darkened silhouette as the sunset over the seaside view beyond it. "Super model friend of yours?"

Corbin opened the trunk of his car as he spoke. "His father owns several hotels in the area. His son's a graduate student of Ancient Greek studies from Stanford who works at the Acropolis. He's the only guy I know who might be able to help. His name is Niko Katsaros."

"You wanna go in hot or cold?" Sophie asked.

Corbin scoffed. "If I'm gonna keep traveling with you, I'm riding hot."

Sophie reached into the open passenger door and pulled her backpack out before making her way around to the back of the car. Corbin opened a carrying case in his trunk carrying an M16A4 assault rifle, alongside a tan M40 assault rifle and Sig Sauer handgun.

Sophie raised one eyebrow as she stared into the trunk, seeing even more carrying cases stacked in a row further in the trunk. "Traveling light these days?"

Corbin grabbed a knife from the truck and tucked it away in his hidden holster attached to his calf. He draped his pant leg back over the knife then pulled the Sig Sauer from the case and loaded a clip into the bottom of it. "Office supplies. I'd rather not travel with you any further without my pocket protector."

"What if you get pulled over? What are you gonna tell the local police?"

"The truth," he replied with a grin, pulling the slide back.

Sophie snickered and set her bag down in the trunk. She pulled the separated pieces of her Glock scattered among the pockets of her backpack and began reassembling her pistol.

"And what about that?" asked Corbin, arching a brow at her as he tucked his pistol away in the lining of his pants.

"What?" Sophie replied. "I buy the ammo when I get where I'm going. And airport security never seems to recognize it when it's in pieces."

"And what would you tell them if they did manage to find that in your bag?"

"The truth," she replied, grinning as she replaced the barrel and spring before locking the slide back into place over the frame.

Corbin shook his head and dug further into his trunk. He pulled a loaded clip of nine-millimeter ammunition from a box and handed it to her.

Sophie loaded it into her handgun and drew the slide back. "See? I knew you'd have my back. Now we're on the same page."

Sophie withdrew her leg holster from her backpack and fastened it to her thigh while Corbin closed the trunk. She holstered her weapon then pulled the journal from her backpack. "How do you know this guy?" asked Sophie, following Corbin towards the front door.

Corbin knocked on the door. "I led security detail for his engagement party last month, along with a few other events in the past that his fiancée doesn't know about."

The front door of the home opened to the sight of an elderly man with thinning grey hair and a mustache, plump around the waist, expressing a joyful smile at the sight of Corbin.

"Katsaros Senior! Good afternoon!" said Corbin, speaking in Greek.

"Mr. Corbin! An unexpected pleasure!" the man replied, offering Corbin a friendly hug. "What brings you to my home at this hour? I hope nothing serious."

Sophie watched the two men exchange words, only grasping part of what was being said with her broken knowledge of the language.

"Oh, no, no. We were just hoping to speak with Niko for a few minutes. I would have called, but—" Corbin replied.

"Say no more! Our home is always open to you. Who is your friend?" replied Katsaros Senior.

Corbin extended a handout, gesturing to Sophie, giving an introduction. "This is Miss Sophie Lions. A friend and colleague of mine during my years in the service."

Katsaros Senior stepped forward and shook hands with Sophie.

"Ya sas," replied Sophie, expressing her hello in Greek.

The man pointed a finger at her. "Ahh… It is pronounced *'Ya su'* when meeting one person," Katsaros Senior replied in English. *"'Ya sas'* is hello when meeting a group."

"Apologies," Sophie replied, feeling foolish while also relieved that he spoke fluent English.

"No, no. The pleasure is all mine. Savvas Katsaros. Please, come in, both of you. I'll go fetch Niko; we just finished dinner."

Sophie stepped inside, admiring the paintings and polished marble floors lining the grand foyer surrounding her. To her left was a quiet study, decorated with bookshelves around a dark, wooden desk, with a grand staircase leading to the upper floor directly ahead of her. Savvas ushered Sophie and Corbin further into the home, as she gazed out the wall of windows at the back of the home to see the full sunset out over the Aegean. At the center of the two-story mansion was a swimming pool, encircled by the home in a horseshoe shape, leaving only the rear open to the private majestic view.

Savvas led Sophie and Corbin around the left wing of the home, through a kitchen into a dining area where the home's other three occupants had gathered for dinner. Corbin and Sophie stopped in the kitchen, preferring to not disturb everyone.

"Have you had dinner yet? Care for something to eat?" asked

114

Savvas.

"No, thank you for the offer," Corbin replied. "We just wanted to ask Niko a few questions, then we'll be out of your way."

Savvas scoffed and waved a hand at him, presumably unbothered by their arrival. "Halara! Nonsense. We love guests." Savvas entered the dining room and walked over to a young man with curly black hair and a fine-trimmed beard sitting at the table. The young man nodded and stood up from the table, not before kissing the woman sitting next to him on the cheek.

The young man entered the room, dressed in a pressed, burgundy-colored shirt and tie. "Evening, Corbin," said the young man, shaking Corbin's hand. "What brings you here?"

Corbin stepped aside and gestured to Sophie. "Sophie, meet Niko. Niko, this is my friend, Miss Sophie Lions. She's a journalist from England."

Niko shook Sophie's hand, clearly hesitant at the mention of her being a journalist. "You wouldn't happen to be with any vanity magazines?"

Sophie exclaimed, offended by his assumption. "I write for STORY Magazine. Ones based on facts, not overly-dramatic gossip and assumptions."

Niko expressed a look of approval. "Allow me to express a genuine pleasure of having you in my home, in that case. Though, I don't detect an English accent on you."

"I'm an American; I grew up in England and moved back later. I served with Corbin in the US military for a short while."

"Ah! Well a friend of Corbin's is a friend of mine. What can I do for you both?"

"We need your scholarly advice with something," said Corbin.

Niko sighed and checked his watch. "It's a little late, Corbin. Perhaps we could do this at my office tomorrow?"

"We won't take long, Niko. I hoped we could catch you when you were away from the museum."

Niko glanced back over his shoulder at his family, still sharing conversation at the dinner table, as though he worried what his fiancée might say.

"I can pay you for your time," offered Sophie, picking up on his hesitation.

Niko's eyes turned towards her, a look of intrigue as though she had bought his attention.

◆ ◆ ◆

SOPHIE PACED AROUND the mansion study as Niko studied the journal while sitting at the grand wood desk. She watched him closely, making sure he wouldn't turn the page to read through the beginning of the journal entry. Sophie admired the many books and old artifacts on the shelves; old broken fragments of pottery and statues from a civilization long gone. Relics from the past which clearly shared their own long and troubled history similar to that of the journal.

She heard the journal pages crackle. She glanced back to see Nikko examining the backside of the selected journal page. She cleared her throat loudly at him.

Niko turned the page back, casting an untrustworthy expression at her as he read the page once more.

Corbin sat on the black leather couch before a coffee table opposite the desk, clasping his hands together with a tense stare as he waited for Niko to finish reading.

"'Along a coast of turquoise waters, where the gateway between Earth and Hell resides. A place where the River Styx runs dry, and the legion headed serpent rests in eternity,'" Niko read out loud, sounding invested. "Whoever this Nazi Colonel of yours is, he's definitely trying to leave a trail for either himself or whoever's reading this through cryptic messages."

"Know of the place he's describing?" asked Sophie, joining Niko at the desk as she looked down over his shoulder at the journal.

Niko sat for a moment in thought. "'The legion-headed serpent...' That line sounds like... A hydra... Hydra... Idra!"

"Idra?" asked Corbin, standing up from the couch.

Niko leaned back in the desk chair, directing his attention to Corbin. "Idra is the name of an island. It means Hydra in Greek. Your legion-headed serpent is a Hydra, which must be referring to the island. It's roughly three hours from here to the southwest by boat."

"Are there turquoise blue waters on this island?" asked Sophie.

"All around it. Pirates used to occupy the island during the 15th century, using it as smugglers' hideout. The Nazi's took control of it during their occupation of Greece. Even starved some of the locals there while doing so."

"Would there be a place on this island referred to as the River Styx, or a Gateway to Hell?" asked Corbin, standing up and approaching the desk.

Niko glanced back and forth between Sophie and Corbin. "Perhaps... Why? What's at the end of this trail?"

Sophie exchanged uncertain glances with Corbin.

"We think the Nazi's may have left something wherever this river is," said Corbin.

"Such as?" asked Niko.

"Artifacts," Sophie interjected.

Niko spun the chair around so he could face Sophie. "Miss Lions, if there are artifacts hidden in a cave somewhere, I and my colleagues have a right to know."

"So, it's a cave?" prodded Sophie.

Niko sat quietly for a moment, expressionless. "Perhaps... Though I refuse to tell you anything more until you tell me what kind of artifacts it is that you expect to find there. What does a journalist want from an old historical journal such as this? Media folk only care about the present. Never the past. It's always about who's divorcing who and what atrocities are plaguing this world that can be exploited to sell newspapers. Throwing wood on the pyres so the witch burning can be more to their liking."

"I'm not that kind of journalist. I'm an... adventurer of sorts.

While you boys from the chess club spend your time digging in the dirt," Sophie pointed towards the fragments of pottery, "I glue those broken pieces you all collect back together into stories worth reading about. I blow the dust off peoples' lives."

"You're a treasure hunter? Exploiting the misery of the past for your own financial gains?"

"Am not! I mean... I am. But, not for financial gain. My intentions are a little broader than that."

Corbin interjected. "Niko... Please. We'll pay you double—Make it *triple* the amount."

"I'm sorry, Corbin. But whatever your intention is, Miss Lions, I will continue to withhold my information until you tell me what it is you expect to find at the end of this trail. I have my own integrity to consider," Niko replied, turning his attention back to the journal, examining the page further with an eyepiece.

Sophie stepped away from the desk. She paced the room as Niko continued to examine the journal page. She continued to weigh whether to tell him the truth. Corbin stood at Niko's back, leaning up against the bookcase beside him, seemingly waiting for Sophie to make the call.

Niko closed the journal and held it up in one hand at head height. "You either tell me now, or I'll just keep this, and it'll tell me everything I need to know while I have you both arrested under false charges," he said with a sly voice.

Sophie glared at Niko's smug grin from across the room. She noticed an illuminated red dot appear on the cover of the journal in his hand, coming from one of the many windows lining the study.

"Red eye, Corbin," she said, pointing the laser out to him.

Corbin stood upright, now alert. "What?"

"Red eye! Get down!" Sophie shouted, diving down behind the couch.

Corbin leapt towards Niko, dragging him to the floor as the glass windows shattered. The journal fell to the floor at Niko and Corbin's side as a repeat of rifle shots outside continued to splinter the wooden desk.

Sophie drew her Glock as she lay prone on the floor with the padding fluttering down over her as the couch continued to be torn to shreds. The sound of someone entering the front door alerted her. She looked up through the glass study doors to see two assailants, both dressed in black face masks and night vision goggles, step into the foyer.

Sophie took aim and shot at one of the intruders through the doors, knocking him to the ground while the other sought cover behind the outer wall of the study.

"Corbin! Get Niko and his family out of here!" Sophie shouted over the continuous gun shots from outside.

Staring under the couch, she could see Corbin push Niko along towards the opposite doorway of the study leading to the family room. Corbin kept his head down with one hand braced over Niko's head as the two of them passed out of sight.

The shots outside finally stopped, allowing Sophie time to move around to the couch arm and seek better fortified cover. She looked back towards the now-shattered study doorway as the remaining assailant emerged from his hiding place and began firing his silenced assault rifle at her.

Sophie curled up next to the couch, seeing the shots pepper the wood floor near her feet. She waited for the shots to stop.

A brief moment of silence passed as the tension lingered. She reached up and grabbed the decorative marble piece on the study coffee table and threw it towards the corner. She then poked her head out from around the couch to see the assailant, now standing in the doorway, distracted. She fired two rounds at him, forcing him back against the bookshelf before he slumped to the floor.

She peered back to her left, seeing the journal still laying on the floor at the base of the desk. The sound of glass breaking in the living room drew her attention. She caught a glimpse of Corbin and Niko seeking shelter in the kitchen beyond the living room as another masked shooter rappelled through the living room skylight.

Sophie heard two of the windows behind her shatter. She glanced back over the couch arm to see two more intruders had swung in through the study windows, armed with assault rifles and wearing the same attire. She waited until both assailants had their heads turned away, searching the room, then dashed out into the foyer.

She drove her shoulder into the study doors, throwing both doors open as she took cover around the corner; the intruders firing at her wildly.

The sound of a woman's scream coming from the dining room beyond the kitchen. Sophie spotted another figure out the window near the swimming pool, tactically making their way along the exterior of the house towards where Niko's family was hiding. She now had four intruders to deal with: two at her back in the study; one around the corner in the living room; and another was on the verge of flanking Corbin and Niko from outside; and all were well-armed and well-trained.

She would have to choose; either make her move and reclaim the journal or defend Niko and his family.

Sophie took a deep breath in preparation. The journal could wait.

She sprinted towards the main staircase ahead of her, seeking the high ground among the second-floor balcony, which spanned the full length of the home like a catwalk. She felt the marble railing at her back being broken apart by gunshots, narrowly missing her shoulder. She passed out of sight from the study and hurried over to the far end of the balcony overlooking the living room.

She spotted Corbin and Niko in the kitchen through the doorway, hiding behind the counter. The masked figure in the living room below her was pressing forward in their direction.

"Corbin! Three o'clock!" Sophie shouted down at him.

The figure turned and fired up at her as she ducked down. Corbin used the moment to his advantage, standing up from his cover and firing three shots at the figure's back. He took hold of Niko by the arm and dragged him towards the dining room at the other end of the kitchen towards the rest of the family.

Sophie turned back around to see the assailants from the study now making ground on her as they moved slowly up the stairs. She hurried in the opposite direction, out through the upper patio doors ready to flank the intruder outside. She scurried along the upper walkway, checking her corners, seeing no further assailants. Six shooters total, which could only mean one thing: they were after her, and they knew what she was capable of.

Sophie reached the end of the upper walkway to see the masked assailant outside on the verge of breaching the dining room doorway below. She fired two shots down at him, missing both shots by a few inches at his feet. The figure ran out of sight behind the pool bar, while she claimed her own cover behind a nearby planter. She glanced back towards the patio doorway to see the two assailants following her trail appear in the window, still searching for her as they stepped outside; she was pinned down. Either she was about to be struck down by her target below, or she would have to risk moving and being fired upon from the two assailants advancing behind her.

Sophie raised her pistol, ready to make a final stand. She rose to a knee behind the planter and took aim at the figure behind the bar. Before her finger could squeeze the trigger, she heard the sound of two shots come from beyond the shadows below. The assailant behind the bar fell as she heard rustling from the bushes beyond the home.

Her brown-bearded stalker emerged from the bushes with his pistol drawn and aimed at the fallen assailant; with him was the bald-headed driver of the Mini Cooper, dressed in a white tank shirt and sunglasses hanging from his collar. The intruders along the walkway with her began firing down at her stalker and his accomplice, forcing them towards the bar for cover.

Sophie heard the glass door to her right slide open. She took aim at the door, ready to fire but stopped herself just in time. Corbin scurried out from the doorway and joined Sophie behind the planter.

"Only two left," she said to him.

Corbin peered around the planter through the bars in the railing towards Sophie's stalker below. "Seems your tail is on our side."

"Or they want to kill me themselves," Sophie replied.

"If they wanted to kill you, Broadway, they would have done it by now," Corbin replied, reloading his pistol.

Corbin whistled sharply towards the men below. Dirt and shattered tiles began to shower both Sophie and Corbin as the assailants switched targets and began firing towards them.

The bearded man peeked out from behind the bar towards Corbin. Corbin exchanged hand signals with him, coordinating for them to move at the same time as Sophie and him. The man nodded in agreement.

"Looks like your friends are military-trained. 'You ready?" asked Corbin.

Sophie nodded, ready to end this.

The gunfire over their heads stopped.

"A'ight. On my count," said Corbin, counting out their move on one hand to the stalker below. "One… Two… Three!"

Sophie and Corbin both rose up from behind the planter a half second after the stalker and his accomplice below. They took aim at where the assailants had been standing, only to find they had retreated back into the house. The two assailants hurried down the stairs, back towards the front door.

"Don't let them leave!" shouted Sophie, hurrying after them.

Another female scream came from inside the house. Sophie stopped. She turned back towards Corbin, seeing he, too, was alerted by the sound.

"You take the low road, I'll take the high road," said Sophie pointing to the stairway leading down from the balcony. Corbin nodded in agreement and ran towards the stairs. Sophie gazed over the balcony to see her now allied stalker advancing towards the foyer in pursuit of the fleeing intruders. She hurried through the sliding door behind her that Corbin had emerged from and into a guest room. She continued to hear the cries of a woman coming from the open door ahead of her. She approached the doorway cautiously to see a spiral staircase leading down to the lower floor at the other end of the hall.

Sophie crept down the stairs, continuing to hear the shouts of a heavy male voice speaking Norwegian, along with the combined pleas of Niko's family in Greek. She suddenly heard Corbin's voice join in halfway down the steps.

Peering through the partially open doorway at the bottom of the steps, she could see another assailant holding a gun to Niko's fiancée's shoulder. She was wrong: there were seven shooters total. At the opposite end of the room was Corbin, still aiming at the assailant as he tried to negotiate with him in English, as well as keep the shooter distracted.

The assailant dragged Niko's fiancée around, turning his back to

Sophie, unaware. Sophie approached and took aim, allowing herself time to line up her shot. The shouts of Niko and his family escalated as the intruder pulled the hammer back on his pistol, his voice growing louder.

Sophie fired.

Niko's mother screamed before everyone fell silent. The assailant's shoulder sank as he fell to his knees, then down to the floor, releasing Niko's fiancée. Niko's fiancéee ran back over to him as Savvas stepped forward, ready to defend his family in case the assailant got back up.

Corbin lowered his aim and let out a sigh of relief, seeing Sophie emerge from the doorway. "Could've gotten here a little quicker, Broadway," he said to her.

Sophie's eyes grew wide, realizing she still had one objective to account for. She sprinted past Corbin back through the kitchen to the living room, and into the study. She scanned the glass-covered floor near the desk as the sound of tires burning rubber along the road outside could be heard through the broken windows.

The journal was gone.

"Shit…!" Sophie said to herself as Corbin ran into the room. "They took it."

◆ ◆ ◆

NIKO STEPPED INTO the study holding two wet cloths. He handed one of the cloths to Corbin and the other to Sophie as they sat on the remains of the shredded sofa with worn-out expressions. The bald man in the white tank hung out in the foyer, talking on the phone, while Sophie's stalker stood watch nearby out the windows of the study. They refused to speak to her or Corbin, sharing only a brief conversation with Savvas.

"How's your fiancée?" Sophie asked Niko. She began wiping away the blood from the cuts on her forearms.

"Startled," Niko replied, sounding shaken, "but I think she's okay. Thank you, for saving her, both of you. I never knew my father had enemies. I'm glad you happened to be here at the right time."

Sophie sat confused for a moment, now unsure whether the assailants were after her or Niko's family now.

"I'm just glad we came prepared," Corbin replied, wiping the blood away from his neck.

The bald man reentered the study and stood before Sophie and Corbin with his phone in-hand.

"Mind finally telling us what's going on here?" ordered Sophie.

The man held the phone out to her. "Someone wants to talk to you," he said in a midwestern American accent.

Sophie stood up from the couch, exchanging wary glances with Corbin before taking the phone. She made her way into the foyer and held the phone up to her ear. "Hello?"

"I thought journalism was supposed to be a much safer line of work?" said a female voice, one that carried fond memories with it. It was her sister, Isabella or Izzie as she preferred to be called. "Those were your *exact* words."

"Hi, Sis… I should've known these two were your CIA watchdogs," Sophie replied, with a sheepish grin looking at the bald man. The man rolled his eyes at her and turned away.

"Why are you in Athens?" asked Izzie.

"Long story, one not worth writing about yet. Care to explain why you're having me tailed by Langley's finest?"

"I presume you know a 'Mr. Bjorn Skøriksen?'"

Sophie checked back over her shoulder to make sure no one else was listening in on her conversation. She saw Corbin getting a briefing from the bearded CIA agent along with Niko. She now understood the lie being told by her sister through her men, one meant to draw the heat away from her and the CIA, designed to keep the fragile ties of international relations in check.

"You know you're just as good at lying as your big sister," said Sophie in compliment, "If not better. I'd like to take full credit for my tutelage."

"Cut the shit Antigone Sophia Lions, I don't have time to bullshit right now. I need you to come clean with me for once in your reckless life. How do you know Bjorn?"

"We were neighbors at one time."

"Fine... Play dumb. I'll have you know though that your *neighbor* from Norway just so happens to be a major player in the international mercenary business. He recently placed a bounty on your hide worth more than all that old junk you chase after. When he found out you were still alive following your encounter at Newark—"

"You know about that, huh?" Sophie boasted.

Izzie scoffed. "It's my job to know! And you're quickly becoming a heavy file on my desk! Every time I hear of an incident in a foreign country involving a woman who fled the scene, I pray it isn't you. And eight out of ten times it is! I talked to the curator of the museum, and he described your appearance exactly. My stomach sank."

"Glad I'll at least be remembered for something, even if it is a living disaster."

"Bjorn heard you escaped and sent word out. Now he has men gunning for you."

"So, you sent me a CIA gift basket? Aw! Thanks, Sis! I always wanted my own security detail."

"This isn't funny, Soph." Izzie fell silent for a moment, presumably collecting her temper. "This life of yours you call an adventure is a disaster on my desk. You're miles up shit creek now, and I can't help you anymore. The only way you're gonna get this bounty off is you either have to kill Bjorn yourself or reason with him. My guys are now compromised, so they have to scrub up the mess you made before the local officials get wind and split. So, from here on out, you're on your own."

Sophie checked back to see Corbin still getting his briefing from the bearded CIA agent. "Izzie, I appreciate you still babysitting me, but I think Corbin and I can handle it from here."

"If you wanted to get back in the mud, you could have stayed here in Langley. The CIA has plenty of work. You can still come back if you want."

Sophie winced at the thought of returning to being a CIA contractor. "Two years was more than enough, Izzie. You know I prefer center stage rather than standing backstage like you. If I'm going to get in trouble, I'd rather the world know about it. I'm on a one-woman grand tour."

"Does that grand tour include the world's top mercenary's stage?"

"Ha… ha… I didn't do it on purpose. Bjorn seemed like a reasonable guy when I first met him. Wasn't until after we were in Marrakesh that I learned he was an asshole."

"Poor judgement of character on your part. Just… Don't get yourself killed. Would really put a dampener on next Christmas. I prefer not to be the only one entertaining dad, awkwardly eating dinner in silence as always."

"Speaking of which: have you talked to dad?"

"Once a month, same as always. Same old shit each time I call. Prioritizing his work over his children. I get thirty seconds in before he says he's got to go. I'd say call him, but maybe when you're… less busy."

"Speaking of which, I should probably get going so your guys can split. Seriously though, thank you for having my back all the way from Virginia."

"Don't thank me, thank Max and Wesley. They wanted to leave your ass high and dry after you ditched them twice, but I threatened their job security if they lost you again."

"They should have been more friendly. And learned how to drive."

"Yeah, you tell them that and see what they say. Just… Stay safe, Soph. Please."

"I will. Thanks, Izzie," Sophie replied, hanging up the phone.

Sophie stepped back into the study and threw the phone back over to the bald CIA agent, noticing Niko had left the room and was talking to his family. "Great driving, Wesley."

The agent scolded her. "I'm Max. He's Wesley," he grumbled, pointing to the bearded man.

"You espionage boys all look the same to me," Sophie replied.

"Would you mind telling me what's going on?" asked Corbin, still sitting on the couch.

"My sister sent us bodyguards," Sophie replied. "Seems we had our eyes on the wrong tail."

"Your sister thinks these two can do a better job than me?"

Sophie shrugged. "I know! That's what I told her. Said I had the best bodyguard around."

Corbin scoffed and shook his head. Sophie noticed the two agents rolling their eyes at her.

"So, who sent the killing squad, then?" asked Corbin.

"Looks like I picked a fight with the wrong mercenary. A guy named Bjorn. There's a bounty on me, which has yet to be claimed. Though, seeing as how they took the journal, I'm guessing he's now interested in more than just seeing me dead."

Corbin leaned forward, visibly ready to get on the move again. "So, what's our next move?"

Sophie could see Niko pacing around the living room. She waved him into the study again. Niko consoled his fiancée with a hand on her shoulder before heeding Sophie's call.

"Where's this cave you mentioned?" asked Sophie.

Niko stood with a conflicted expression. "I… prefer not to say."

Sophie relented. "Art. Stolen art. That's what we're after, Niko. And if we find it, I'll make certain it ends up where it rightfully belongs. Back in museums all over the world. But right now, that journal, the one those men stole, is the only key to finding it; and now it's in the hands of one of the world's most powerful mercenaries. It's only a matter of time before he learns about it and beats us to it. With it, he'll sell the art to the highest bidders among the underground, and those works will remain lost while the power-hungry gain more power. So, as one seeker of artifacts to another, I'm asking you: where is the cave?"

Niko seemingly took Sophie's words to heart. He walked over to the bookshelf in the study and pulled a book from the shelf bound in leather. He opened it and flipped through the pages as he returned to her side. He handed the open book to her; on it was a map of the island of Idra. He pointed to a spot along the northern coast, four kilometers west, near the main port city of Idra on the island. Sophie read the name on the map: Idra Foliá.

"The Hydra's Den," said Niko. "It's a seismically-active cave along the northern coast. The pirates used to refer to it as the 'Gateway to Hell' or 'The Mouth of the Styx.' It's been closed off to the public since the war because it was deemed too dangerous."

Sophie handed the book back to him and turned around to face Corbin. "You ready?"

Corbin set the wet cloth down on the broken coffee table ahead of him and stood up from the couch. "What about your journal?"

"Later. We're one step ahead right now. I prefer to keep it that way," Sophie replied.

Corbin snickered. "Gung-ho then, I guess."

Sophie patted him on the shoulder. She hugged Niko, expressing her sincerest gratitude before making her way towards the front door.

Corbin followed her as Sophie heard him offer one final word of advice to their CIA bodyguards. "Might wanna learn how to properly tail someone. Save yourself the trouble of future accidents."

Sophie glanced back to see Max grit his teeth as Corbin walked away. Corbin snickered along with Sophie, following her out the front door, leaving behind their mess for the agents to clean up.

Eight
IDRA FOLIÁ

FROM THEIR PLACE on the ferry, Sophie could see the windy shoals of the island of Idra matching Wagner's writings perfectly. The Aegean Sea bathed the island in turquoise, even in the morning sunlight; beyond the steep hills, the port city of Hydra floated over the ample blue waters. Upon reaching port, Sophie and Corbin wasted no time in following the lone road out of town which weaved between the white, rocky hills of the island in Corbin's Yaris.

An old wooden sign posted along the road caught Sophie's attention. She pointed to it as they approached. "'Idra Foliá Monopáti.' Does that mean what I think it means?"

Corbin stopped the car near the sign. "Hydra's Den Path," Corbin replied, affirming her translation.

Sophie stepped out of the car with her backpack into the wind as Corbin joined her. The sign pointed towards a steep, grassy hill leading down towards the shoreline below. Hearing the waves along the shore calling to her, Sophie began making her way down the forgotten path with Corbin following.

The jagged pathway ended at a large cave opening, blocked by a steel door tagged with graffiti and warning signs in Greek. Sophie approached the steel doorway blocking their entry to see a chain with a padlock wrapped around the handles.

"You got any bolt cutters in that armory you call a trunk?" asked Sophie.

"Why would I carry bolt cutters in my trunk?" replied Corbin, dusting off his pants.

"Figured I'd ask before I tried it my way." Sophie drew her pistol and fired down at the lock.

Corbin jumped. Her shot rang out over the distant waves, announcing their presence. Sophie holstered her Glock and removed the now-broken lock from the chain. She yanked the door open as the rusted hinges creaked, refusing to sway.

"Ya gonna help?" she asked.

Corbin sighed and began pulling on the door. The doors gradually opened just enough for the two of them to enter one at a time as a blast of warm, damp air blew out.

Sophie drew her flashlight from her backpack. She entered into the cave first, feeling the air blanket her as the faint smell of hard water and sulfur lingered in the air. The light from her flashlight remained smothered by the steam as it grew thicker further in. The faint sound of boiling water, hissing and bubbling, could be heard along the edges of the pathway ahead.

"You think it's alright to be here?" asked Corbin, coughing with a wrinkled nose. "The air's kinda... rancid."

"You can say it," Sophie replied. "Smells like shit. Probably best we don't stay here too long."

They wandered the clouded cavern, seeing the faint remnants of a creek bed now dried up at their feet, with small pockets of water along either side. Heated steam billowed from cracks in the floor and low points along the walls like chimneys as they followed the dried, winding pathway before them.

The path ended at a wide, steel dock, floating over a flooded cavern of sea water. Two small, motorized boats remained moored at the dock, both covered with rust and signs of decay.

Sophie looked to her left to see the flooded cavern led further into the darkness of the cave while the right led out to an unseen opening to the shoreline. She stepped onto the boat cautiously, checking to make sure it was seaworthy before committing the rest of her weight. The boat remained afloat.

"Come on," said Sophie to Corbin, turning her attention to the single prop engine.

Corbin stepped down into the boat. "Just like our trip along the Vichada in Columbia."

"I wasn't with you in Columbia. I was with Summers in Venezuela when we got the call you needed your asses bailed out after your boat sank.

Remember?"

"Right," Corbin replied. "Though if you're *here*, then who's gonna bail *our* asses out when this boat goes under? Now that your bodyguards are gone, who's our backup?"

Sophie pulled the cord for the engine a few times; the engine started with a sickly sputter. She untied the boat from the dock and pushed off from the dock.

"Nobody," she replied, sitting back down and taking command of the small vessel. "That's what makes it so much fun. No parents, no babysitters, just us and freedom."

"That's what I was afraid you'd say."

Sophie steered away from the dock and further into the cave, tossing her flashlight to Corbin for him to light the way.

"I didn't give you my two coins, boat lady," Corbin joked to her.

"Pay me later," Sophie replied, keeping a wary eye on the waters ahead as they began to weave deeper into the abyss.

"You know, it's discomforting, venturing further into a place called the 'Gates of Hell,'" muttered Corbin, scanning the waters with the flashlight.

"Are you having second thoughts?" asked Sophie.

"No, just… Didn't expect the company I'm with. I knew you'd be in this boat; but why am *I* here?"

Sophie chuckled. "If you have any more jokes, best get them out now."

"Can't think of anything right now, but I'm sure they'll come to me. Though, here's a serious question that's bugging me: why would a Nazi Colonel hid art away in a place this remote and unsettling? I mean, it's not the most ideal place for fragile paintings."

"Maybe that's exactly why he hid them here. You and I both share a military background, same as our friend, the Colonel. What would we do if we were trying to outwit our enemy?"

"Do the unexpected," Corbin replied, without missing a beat.

"Exactly," replied Sophie.

The corner of another small dock emerged from the dark and now-narrowing waterway. Sophie let the boat idle as it drifted towards the dock; Corbin stood up and readied himself. The boat bounced against the dock as Corbin jumped up onto the platform and tied the mooring line off to a cleat.

Sophie turned off the engine and joined Corbin as he offered her a helping hand. Ahead of them, along a rocky shelf, was another steel doorway with a lock on it. Sophie made her way over towards the door and drew her pistol.

"Hold up," said Corbin, putting a hand over her arm. "I prefer to keep what hearing I still have."

Sophie holstered her firearm as Corbin handed the flashlight to her. She watched as Corbin approached the door and drew his knife from its hiding spot. He rested the pointed end against the lock then slammed his palm against the handled end, breaking the rusted lock into pieces. He slid the door open, and then put his knife away.

"I suppose that's a better way," Sophie muttered to him.

Corbin smiled with appreciation; they turned to look inside at the darkened entryway ahead. Sophie pointed the flashlight into the room as Corbin entered first.

Sophie stepped inside after him, peering through the darkness for a moment in bewilderment. She pointed her flashlight to her right to see an old generator near the door. She walked over to it and gave the starter cord two hard tugs; the generator sputtered to life as the dark room began to brighten with a faint orange glow. It sputtered, struggling to maintain the light. Sophie kicked it, using brute force to jumpstart what little remained in it.

"I see your methods haven't improved," Corbin commented dryly.

Sophie chuckled, looking back to see the lights hanging from the ceiling had revealed a large cavern, filled with empty barrels and broken wood crates. The faint turquoise glow of a pool, forever being filled by a waterfall at the back of the room, refracted the light off the ceiling. The flat cave floor seemed to shimmer with that of white, glassy crystals, spotted with mold.

Sophie bent down and whipped her hand along the ground. She looked down at the white crystals, mixed with grains, now stuck to her wet palm. "Salt and rice," she said, snickering in delight. "There's your answer, Corb. Salt and rice to keep things dry."

Corbin bent down, inspecting the salt and rice covered ground for himself. Sophie walked further into the lit cavern to see the wooden crates and barrels were now empty. She spotted a pile of dark green cloth tucked away in the far corner. As she walked over to see it was a stack of wool blankets. She tilted her head to one side in curiosity.

She looked down at her feet to see a pair of glasses, broken and forever tarnished by the cave. She picked the glasses up to inspect them.

"Hey, Broadway," said Corbin.

Sophie looked up to see Corbin holding a small jewelry box that had been left behind over a stack of barrels, near the generator. "What'd you find?" she asked.

Corbin opened the box as Sophie approached. Inside was more salt and rice, used to preserve what had been left inside: a folded slip of paper. Corbin handed the old paper to her gingerly.

Sophie unfolded it as the grains of rice and salt fell to her feet; it was a torn page with familiar handwriting. She sat down on one of the empty crates and began to read it in silence.

If this page remains intact and has been found, then there is no sense in hiding my guiltiness any longer. My guilt will forever outweigh my transgressions. I'm either dead or imprisoned, for which either would be befitting punishments. If mercy somehow lives in Himmler's empty soul, he'll grant me a peaceful death by firing squad over the suffocating snap of a noose. Even the noose would be less agonizing than the punishment for which I expect God has planned for me. I suspect that Howls and Borgest have been given the task by Goring to investigate me. They sneak into my room during the day while I am away to read my journal, so I will continue to tailor its pages to their liking while maintaining a persona of clarity. Neither one of them possesses even half a mind. Even combining that which life has been so gracious enough to bless them with, they'd still lack any sign of intelligence. So, I shall continue to leave my clues with optimistic certainty that they'll never find them.

    I love my country, but she has been led astray. I will not sit here in this cave and pretend for even a moment that I am a victim. I made my own strokes upon the canvas of our nation's future and wish that I could wipe them away. I once believed in the Party's ideals; I wanted to believe we were rebuilding ourselves into something old made new and whole again. That we were being given the gift of determining our own future with the fall of the monarchy. Instead, I was led down the wrong path by charlatans and murderers. My only wish now is to see that there is something left of my country when this war is over. Something left of the world I stole. The lives I've stolen. The vault has become my sole purpose in this war now; within its thick walls, hidden away from the world, is my will and testament. Not a plea to God, but an attempt to right that which I have wronged.

    I commend the British for their courage. Our claim on Africa has passed, and our leader has betrayed those who were once called allies. The Party has no intention of sharing their power—they never have—and they will cut down all those who would stand in their way, so long as their minds still cling to their belief in a Third Reich.

    When I was still appointed the Party curator of the museum at Königsplatz, living with Andrea in our cottage, I came home one evening to find she wasn't there. She had missed our usual lunch at the gallery halls. She left no note at the cottage as to where she had gone, as she normally would. As it grew dark that night, I rode my bike to our place along the Ammersee to see if she had gone to paint. I found her box in the bushes, open with its contents spilled out. I rode further down the road to find her bike along the bank with no sign of her.

    I immediately returned to the cottage to find a car waiting for me outside with the headlights on. Two Gestapo officers in-uniform informed me that my presence was being requested. As I sat in the back of the car, taking in the unsettling silence, I knew something was wrong.

    The late-night streets of Munich faded away as we drove away from the city. After passing through a dense forest, the car came to a stop outside a castle, glowing in body and spirit as music played inside. The driver remained in his seat as the other officer stepped out and opened the door for me. He led me up the stone steps of the festive home as I passed under the Party flag hanging above the entry. I felt ready to get back in the car and drive away, preferring not to know why I had been summoned.

    The officer led me through a grand foyer, away from the festive music and sounds of party guests in the opposite direction. He opened an oak door ahead of me, revealing a dimly-lit study beyond, then stood at attention. I took a deep breath and stepped inside, feeling nervous.

Hyde Park Adventures

The room felt cold and dreary, with only the desk lamp and fireplace casting aside the darkness. Goring, the Party president, stood with a glass of jaeger by the fireplace to my right; an inflated man with a round waist and emotionless stare. Himmler stood with his back to me, looking out the only window.

I heard the door close behind me, sealing me inside with the two lions. I removed my jacket as I spoke. "Reichsmarschall... Heir Reichsführer... To what do I owe this pleasure?"

"A drink, Colonel?" asked Himmler, sounding ill-humored as always.

I threw my jacket over the arm of the couch and stepped further into the room, wishing not to express my growing fear. "I would enjoy one, but it is far too late for me. Might I ask what's the occasion?"

"My wife's birthday," Goring replied, in his usual, grumbled tone.

"Please offer her my dearest birthday wishes, sir. Though, I don't get the feeling this visit is meant to be an invitation."

Goring moved from the fireplace, waddling in his step as he took a drink of his jaeger, and then sighed. He gestured towards the couch, offering me a seat. I sat down beside my jacket.

Goring stood beyond the coffee table before me, his backside outlined by flames in the fireplace as though the devil had taken his place. "My job as Party Reichsmarschall is that of a mechanic, Colonel. I see to it that all the gears are oiled, turning, and that there are no leaks to be found. If one gear were to slip or be left dry, the whole machine stops working, which then leaves me with one of two options: I can either fix the problem, or simply replace it."

I spoke with hesitation. "I see... Well, as one of the gears of that machine, I hope my edges are still sharp?"

"You know that the Party recently announced the passing of the Nuremberg Laws?" asked Himmler, still standing by the window, looking away from me.

"Yes, sir," I replied.

Goring set his glass down on the table ahead of him. "You know that the laws specifically forbid the marriage of Jews, and most recently, Romanians and Blacks as well?"

"I heard the announcement about the addition to the laws, yes," I replied, ready to defend myself. "I still don't see how they relate to me. My family is from Bavaria. My father was Bavarian, my mother was Bavarian. I've even proven it."

"With the new laws in place," said Goring, as if I hadn't spoken, "those of us who sit on the highest chair are expected to be the prime examples of the Party's expectation for the people: people of pure race. And with that, it means burning frayed edges."

The double doors swung open with a heavyweight. I turned to look back over my shoulder. My soul was torn from my body.

Two Gestapo officers walked into the room dragging Andrea by the arms. Her eyelids were heavy. Her face was battered and bruised with a bloodied mark on her forehead. The two officers dragged her over to the center of the room and continued to hold her as she remained limp and on her knees.

I immediately stood up from my seat, restraining myself from expressing my outrage. Goring watched my reaction with a piercing stare.

Himmler turned around and finally faced me. "Do you know this woman?"

"Yes," I said, clenching one fist and quickly releasing it.

"How?" asked Goring. "What is your relation to this woman?"

I stared at Andrea with a smothered, heartbroken rage. She remained silent, clearly beaten to the point of unconsciousness; her arms and light blue dress were covered in dirt.

I took a breath and calmed myself, believing that whatever was happening was just a misunderstanding. "She's... a friend."

"Does she live in your home?" asked Goring.

"Yes," I replied.

Himmler walked over to the end of the dining table near the window, picking up a folder. He walked past Andrea and handed it to me; on the cover was the Party's symbol. I opened the file to find a series of records, all dating back to during the Great War.

"Your friend is a gypsy, Colonel. A runaway from Romania," said Himmler.

I flipped through the pages, unable to believe what I was reading.

"Did you know this?" asked Goring.

I glanced up from the pages at Andrea. She stared back at me with a broken, sorrowful expression, one of guilt and suffering.

"Colonel, were you aware of this fact?" asked Himmler, sounding impatient.

Andrea's eyes began to water under her swollen cheeks. I couldn't speak. During our many conversations, she always referred to her home as Germany. For the longest time I had begun to suspect she was from Austria, but never so far south as to Romania.

"Colonel," said Goring, walking over to me, whispering into my ear. "Now is the time for you to choose: are you a moving part, or a broken man in need of replacing?"

Andrea's bottom lip began to quiver as I felt a knot in my throat, dwelling on my answer.

"Did you know?!" Himmler shouted.

I held my breath. "No... No, I... I didn't know."

Andrea hung her head. I saw a teardrop fall from her eyes and hit the floor in the flickering darkness.

Himmler nodded to the two officers. They dragged Andrea back towards the door as I stood in place. I caught one last glimpse of her face; those heartbroken eyes forever burned into my memory.

Himmler took the file back from me. "An edge has been sharpened indeed."

Goring picked up his glass as he clapped me on the shoulder. I continued to stare blankly at the doors, watching Andrea's feet disappear.

"Dwell not on it, Colonel," said Goring. "We've all had rats living in our attics at one point. Come now. Join us for dinner. I have a cousin whom I believe would love to meet you."

I held no spite for Romanian's, or Jews, or Blacks. I witnessed the shouting and scorning at Jewish store owners across Munich, yet I turned a blind eye. Ignorance became my downfall. They had found her that morning along the lake, about to return home from painting. She got away on her bike, only to be driven down and beaten before being thrown into the back of a truck.

I said no, like a coward, clinging to the thought that I could maintain my status and seek a way to free her. The crime at that time for joining in marriage or relations with Germans as a non-racially pure individual was two years in prison. I'm almost certain Himmler and Goring knew Andrea was more than a friend, because they gave her the same sentence. I kept my distance over the next two years, sending Fischer on my behalf to plead my case while I continued to work on the vault. Once her two years were through, the Gestapo immediately sent her to Dachau; she was among the first.

THE COLONEL'S LOST VAULT

I never saw her again.

My once-rejuvenated spirit from meeting her faded once more. I drilled my men harder out of spite, did as I was ordered, and became lethal to those who crossed my path. Himmler saw it as an improvement towards my patriotic heroism, while Goring—even to this day—seemingly remains unconvinced. And he's right to keep watch over me; I changed that night, but not in their favor. I have my own plans set in motion, undermining their own.

The air raids by British forces over Athens have made me worry about preserving the safety and condition of the pieces. These works I've collected in Greece will be flown to the vault tomorrow night, while I am being relocated to Florence to aid the Italians in preserving their heritage. However, Himmler has already expressed orders that I am to play the part of a con artist, stripping them of their belongings with one hand while I keep their eyes distracted with the other.

I have already arranged a location for the next gathering to my collection. Much like that of back home, a place well-protected under a shaded canopy. A prison of stone, guarded by the Medici's halls of bronze and marble soldiers, and protected by the knight, Saint Donta.

These works will be my legacy. A legacy of righting wrongs.

~~Col~~ Peter Wagner

Sophie held the page in her hand with a heavy heart, staring down at the salt-covered ground in silence.

"Broadway?" Corbin asked quietly.

Sophie remained silent, feeling guilty.

"Broadway, what's wrong?"

"*I* was wrong…" she replied.

"Wrong about what? There's no vault?" asked Corbin.

"No. Wagner was a traitor; that's why the vault was never found. He had no intention of turning the art over to the Nazi's. He was collecting it to protect it from them. I was wrong about *him*. He wasn't the man I thought he was."

Sophie handed the page to him.

Corbin read the page to himself. "What did he plan on doing with it, then? He never handed it over to the Allies when the war was over, either."

"I dunno," Sophie replied. "Maybe he didn't trust them with it. After a life like his, I don't think *I'd* trust anyone, either. Though, something tells me we'll find out more in Florence. 'The Medici's halls of bronze and marble soldiers…' The Bargello; it's an art museum in Italy. It's where the Medici used to send prisoners during the renaissance. That's where he hid the artwork next, and I bet that's where he left another clue."

"Thank you for the information, Miss Lions," said an echoing voice from the entrance to the cave. "You've saved me a lot of trouble."

Sophie flinched and looked over to see two figures—both wearing masks similar to the assailants that had attacked them in Athens—standing at the entrance to the cavern with assault rifles aimed at Sophie and Corbin.

Bjorn's hulking figure stepped out from the darkness beyond the doorway, dressed in a V-neck shirt and dark tan cargo pants with his own pistols holstered across his chest. "Hands up this time, Miss Lions. I failed to shoot you before, but I won't make the same mistake again."

"'Was waiting for you, Bjorn," Sophie said to him, masking her embarrassment of being caught as she raised her hands up over her head.

Corbin watched Sophie raise her hands up. He did the same, still holding the journal page in his hand. The cavern lights flickered in rhythm with the generator as Bjorn and his men approached them.

"I may just keep you alive with how useful you've become. You can serve me as my own personal treasure magnet," said Bjorn.

"Did you learn where we were with help, or on your own?" asked Sophie.

"I'm a resourceful man; I prefer not to waste time. Having failed to kill you in Athens, my men came back to my private plane where I awaited your head, bringing only excuses. However, they manage to get the item they saw you clinging to in London. This journal of yours."

Bjorn pulled the journal from one of his cargo pockets and held it up. "After reading it, I see you've found something much more valuable than the Heritage Knife. Your CIA friends were not as tight-lipped as I had expected. As one of them was left choking on his own blood, the other offered me his last confession with haste. Now, I not only will get to kill you myself, but have the bounty I placed on you paid, tenfold."

One of Bjorn's men approached Sophie with his rifle still aimed at her. He pulled her Glock from her holster and tossed it into the water pool fed by the waterfall nearby. He removed her backpack and disposed of it in the same fashion along with her flashlight.

The other mercenary approached Corbin and disposed of Corbin's handgun the same way, and then grabbed the page from his hand.

The two men returned to Bjorn and handed the journal page to him. Bjorn examined the page with a smug grin in the flickering lights. "The greatest treasure the modern world has to offer is now mine, and mine alone to claim."

"I really do need that journal back at some point so I can return it to the library," said Sophie, coy and tired of Bjorn's monologuing. "You wouldn't want me to start getting fined for it. Maybe we can make a deal?"

Bjorn folded the page up and tucked it away inside the journal. "Our business is done, Miss Lions. No more deals."

"What if you can't decipher the next location?" asked Corbin, sharing the same causal tone as Sophie.

Corbin slowly began to take a step back towards the generator as Sophie could sense he had a plan in mind. Sophie began to do the same as to not seem suspicious.

"As I said, I am resourceful. I'm sure I'll manage," Bjorn replied.

"Oh!" Sophie added. "I'm sorry. Corbin, allow me to introduce you to Bjorn. Bjorn, meet Corbin. Bjorn's made a professional living out of backstabbing me now."

"A pleasure…" replied Corbin. "Glad I get to go out knowing the name of my killer."

The Colonel's Lost Vault

Bjorn snickered, drawing his own engraved, silver pistol and aiming it at Sophie. "As I am a gentleman, I will at least allow you both the honor of offering up your last words."

"Please delete my browser history," said Corbin.

Bjorn and his men chuckled. "And you, Miss Lions?"

"As I said before, Bjorn," replied Sophie, depriving Bjorn of the satisfaction of witnessing her fear, "parting is such sweet sorrow... And you talk too much."

The lights fell dim with the rhythm of the generator, leaving everyone nearly in darkness. Sophie heard Corbin seize the moment to draw his knife and cut the timing belt on the generator.

The cavern sank into pitch-black darkness. Sophie reached out and grabbed hold of Corbin's forearm, pulling him towards the pool, now glowing, thanks to her flashlight. The flashes of Bjorn and his men firing at where they had been standing illuminated the cavern.

Sophie and Corbin leapt into the pool and began swimming towards the bottom where her flashlight continued to shine. The patter of Bjorn and his men firing down at them over the sound of the cascading waterfall. Their shots lost all their strength as Sophie and Corbin swam deeper and deeper towards the bottom. Sophie grabbed her backpack and Glock off the bottom as Corbin retrieved his gun and her flashlight.

Corbin looked to Sophie for direction, still holding his breath as the gunfire above finally stopped. Behind him was a small opening, faintly glowing with a distant light source. Sophie pointed towards the opening, urging him to swim towards it. Swimming further into the sunken cave, Sophie could feel her need for a breath beginning to build; she could hold her breath for exactly three minutes and fourteen seconds—though she only hoped the tunnel was shorter than that. The tunnel continued to twist and turn with the turquoise light of the outside world growing brighter ahead.

The two of them emerged from an opening along the ocean floor, somewhere along the island coast. They swam for the surface until their heads finally broke the surface. Sophie and Corbin both inhaled and exhaled deeply in relief.

"You all right?" asked Sophie.

Corbin coughed and continued to take in deep breaths. He raised his hand up out of the water, giving an okay sign with two fingers. "Fine. And here I was thinking I'd never have to hold my breath for that long ever again."

Sophie hushed him, peering out over the water towards the beach. She could spot the entrance to the cave several yards away, where two more of Bjorn's men stood watch outside.

Sophie swam towards the beach, with Corbin paddling his way along behind her. They slogged their way up the sandy shoreline to a set of dried bushes and crouched down out of sight. Sophie continued to watch the cave entrance, shivering as the wind blew through her wet clothes.

Bjorn finally emerged from the cave entrance in a state of fury as he stomped his way back up the path. He turned back for a moment ordering the two men who had stood watch to continue watching the coast and the cave.

The two men nodded, starting their search of the area with their assault rifles. Sophie stood up a few extra feet to watch Bjorn climb the hill and jump into one of two SUV's parked next to Corbin's car. One of Bjorn's men threw a thermite grenade through the window of the Yaris before joining Bjorn in the vehicle.

Sophie slunk back down behind the brush as Corbin's car flared into an inferno with Bjorn making his escape with both the journal and page. The two mercenaries left behind continued to scour the beach.

"He's gone," said Sophie. "Though there's still two of them searching for us."

"What are we waiting for then?" asked Corbin, drawing his knife. "You take one, I'll take the other."

"I don't have a knife on me," Sophie replied.

Corbin stared at her, as though unamused. "You got hands, don't you? And last time I checked, you knew how to use them. Or do your skills now just end with using the heel of your boot since retirement?"

Sophie snickered in amusement. She started her way up the hill towards the SUV, staying low and out of sight as she slunk between the rocks and bushes. She took her position behind the back of the SUV, waiting for Corbin to find his own hiding spot among the rocks before the old wooden sign nearby.

They waited patiently while the two mercenaries gave up their search and returned to the SUV, sharing a casual conversation in Greek. One of them unslung his rifle and opened the driver side door as the other continued to talk while making his way towards the rear of the car.

Hyde Park Adventures

Corbin swiftly emerged from his hiding place behind the driver and thrusted his knife into his chest. The man fell to the road as the other stood up, alerted by the sound. The man spotted Corbin through the car windows and scrambled to raise his weapon. Sophie rushed out from her hiding place just in time to wrest control of his rifle and direct his aim away from Corbin towards the sky.

The mercenary struggled to aim his rifle at her as she maintained control over his weapon with one hand. Sophie threw a punch at his face only for him to be unfazed. Corbin finally intervened, quickly jabbing his knife into the man's neck before he fell at Corbin's feet.

"What took you so long?" asked Sophie.

"Should have broken his neck. Would have saved you the scuffle," Corbin replied, in a joking tone.

"Had I done that, you'd have had *three* ear holes instead of two."

Corbin replaced his knife and pulled the keys to the SUV from the driver's hand. He approached the back of the SUV and opened the trunk as Sophie joined him.

"Son of a bitch tried to steal my guns!" Corbin shouted, inspecting the thankfully-unburned boxes from his car.

"At least they did you a favor with the car. Now let's get out of here before the locals see the smoke," Sophie replied, throwing her backpack into the backseat of the SUV and jumping into the passenger seat.

Corbin hopped into the driver's seat and started the car, driving away as he looked back towards his burning Yaris in the rearview mirror.

He sighed with disappointment. "I was just starting to like that car."

◆ ◆ ◆

SOPHIE CONTINUED TO scan the surrounding coastline for any more of Bjorn's men, as well as looking for a good place to stop. After ten minutes, she spotted a vacant rest stop along the road and pointed for Corbin to pull over. Corbin pulled into the rest stop and parked the SUV facing the coast.

Corbin rested his head back against the seat as he turned off the car, expelling a sigh of relief.

Sophie sat in silence for a moment, feeling her frustration build. "That's the second time that man has stolen something from me."

"Just be glad he didn't steal your life," replied Corbin.

"I have to get that journal back, and the page."

"You? Don't you mean 'we'?"

Sophie looked over at Corbin, confused by his response.

Corbin scoffed at her reaction. "I'm not letting you go to Italy alone."

"I already owe you half that vault and then some, Corb. You don't have to go any further."

"I'm not in it for the money. I joined you on this trip because that's what soldiers do; brothers and sisters till the end. We're in this together now, Sophie. Now that I've seen what you're up against, I'm not letting you go in alone. Gung-ho for life, girl, whether you like it or not. And the way I see it, it's our mission now not to let that asshole use that vault to buy more mercs and more guns. I joined the Raiders looking to stop men like him, and just because I retired doesn't mean my mission is complete. So, I'm in this fight all the way."

Sophie smiled at him, feeling warmed and comforted by the reminder that she had a loyal friend.

"So, what's our next move?" asked Corbin.

"To Italy," she replied.

"Roger that," said Corbin, stepping out of the car. He smiled with a daydreamed look on his face. Sophie chuckled. "That, and a million dollars buys a lot of shoes and sunglasses. Oh! And you now owe me a new car, by the way. I like my trucks in silver with a red leather interior, just for the record." He closed the door and walked over to the bathrooms.

Sophie grinned, glad to have Corbin still around. She reached into the backseat and pulled a sealed bag of dry clothes from her backpack, then stepped out of the car and proceeded towards restrooms, ready to move on and get back what was stolen from her.

Nine
The Adriatic Sea

RESTING ON THE top deck railing of the ferry from Athens to Bari across the Adriatic Sea, Sophie marveled at craggy slopes of the Italian coastline steeped in twilight. The race for the vault had begun, and they were already one step behind; one length she preferred not to let get any wider. Bjorn was well-equipped, well-funded, and well-prepared, but what he lacked was what Sophie possessed: knowledge and cleverness. Without the two, she held every confidence Bjorn would always be second best.

Sophie's mind continued to dwell on Wagner's lost page; a story untold which now dwarfed the vault. The man, who once was painted in her mind as someone steeped in greys and dark shades, was now someone with a more vibrant pallet. A man no different than the paintings he had hidden away, someone who had hidden his own thoughts, passions, and beauty from the true enemies of humanity.

Sophie pulled her phone out of her backpack. She waited for

the screen to turn on, only to find it now broken and wet from her dive through the cave. In all her travels, she had learned to come prepared; she sorted through her bag and pulled out her backup in an airtight bag. Upon switching the number to her new phone, several notifications of six missed calls buzzed in-hand, four from Oz and two from Maple. Sophie immediately called Oz, dreading a report on Maple's mood.

Oz's voice answered. "Call Maple, right now," he said to her, without hesitation.

"What? No, 'Oh my God. I'm so glad you're alive,'" Sophie replied.

"Maple tried to call you this morning, but you wouldn't answer. She asked me where you were, and I said you went to Leeds to follow up on another interview."

"What else did you tell her?"

"Nothing. I said you were keeping me just as much in the dark as her, which you are. So, care to let me in on why you've chosen to ignore my calls?"

"Well… Yes and no. Just when I found the next step of the trail, the Vikings came ashore."

Oz chuckled at the other end. "Bjorn?"

"Yup! The devil himself dressed in his best Sunday clothes. Apparently, he's one of the world's top-watched international mercenaries, as told to me by a reliable source. He placed a bounty on me and stole a lost page from Wagner's journal… And the journal itself."

Oz applauded into the speaker. "Bravo… You now have a trained killer gunning for you and nothing to show for it? You sure you're really cut out for this whole adventure thing?"

"I still have my life, Wizard, that's something. Bjorn picked a fight with the wrong woman. Now I plan to nab that vault out from under him so all he's left with are a bunch of empty frames."

Oz sighed through the phone, speaking without his usual smug tone. "I'd tell you to be careful, but I know you won't listen. Yet, I'll say it anyway: be careful."

Sophie felt a crack of worry break through her toughened exterior by Oz's sentiment. "I'll try to be Oz. Corbin and I are on our way to—"

"Nope!" Oz interrupted, returning to his typical smug tone. "Save it. I don't want to know. The less I know the easier it is for me to play dumb when Maple finds out. Best call her—and have your best excuses ready."

"I'll call you later. I promise."

"Please do," said Oz, as Sophie hung up the phone.

Sophie immediately dialed Maple's number and waited eagerly for the sound of her answering.

"Hello?" said Maple's voice on the other end, sounding ill-humored.

Sophie opened her mouth to say hello just as Corbin called out to her from behind, accompanied by the cheers of several ferry passengers all celebrating their voyage at the bar.

"That Oz you're talking to?" Corbin shouted at her.

Sophie quickly covered the microphone on her phone and

shushed Corbin.

"Sounds like you're working plenty hard in Leeds?" said Maple's voice flatly over the phone.

Sophie laughed nervously. "Ha! Yeah, it's me. Sorry, Wonder Woman. I meant to call you. I just met up with a friend here in town."

"I better not be seeing any train slips. How'd you get there?"

"I… drove."

"I thought you didn't own a car?"

"The… same friend I'm with is driving me, as a favor," Sophie replied, looking towards Corbin.

Corbin held two drinks from the bar in his hands, expressing a confused look towards her. "You mean until my car was burned."

Sophie shushed at Corbin silently again.

"I thought you said you just met him there?" asked Maple.

Sophie's throat turned dry. She quickly reached over and took one of the drinks from Corbin. She drank it, feeling the stinging taste of lemon cello wash down her throat. She coughed and cleared her throat. "Yeah! No, that was another friend. I have a lot of friends. All over, you know?"

The phone fell silent for a long pause. Sophie drank the rest of the cello, staring at Corbin with growing anticipation.

"You know what, Sophie," Maple said at last, "So long as I don't see another one of these receipts, I don't give a flying fig how you get around."

Sophie let out a sigh of relief.

"How's the story coming? You found what you're looking for?"

"Not yet," Sophie replied, "I'm close, though. Like… super close. Like so close that if it were in the London Art Museum, the guards would be on my ass telling me to step back."

Corbin cocked his head back at her analogy. Sophie mouthed the word 'What?' to him.

"Good. 'Cause I am shortening your deadline by a week."

Sophie chucked the empty glass in her hand off the ship in shock. "You're what?!"

Corbin stood, stunned and disappointed by her reaction. "I had to return that…"

Maple continued. "I pleaded your case to the suits, and it didn't stick as well as you'd hoped. They want you out, but I told them you were already away and working on one last story for me. So, they allowed time for you to get back here, first. I may have stretched the timeline for how long you'd be gone, but it was my best effort to give you time. You can still convince me *and* them if you bring back the story, though. So, it best be something good, if not flooring."

Sophie began beating her head on the railing as Corbin watched her. She raised her head up and spoke with a false sense of optimism. "Yeah, no! I can have the story back to you by then. I'm super close."

"Good," Maple replied, "Then I'll let you get back to it then. Sounds like you're hard at work up there in Leeds."

"I'll get back to it right now." Sophie paused for a moment, clearing away her sarcasm and speaking with honesty in her voice. "And thanks for sticking up for me, Wonder Woman. However this thing pans out, just know I really do think you're a superhero."

"You've already buttered me up enough, Broadway, so don't oversell it. Save the thanks for when you get back. And I expect a damn good story."

"You got it," Sophie replied, hanging up the phone.

Sophie dropped to her knees in defeat and prayer before the railing. "I'm so screwed!" she shouted.

"That was my drink you took, by the way," said Corbin, still standing behind her.

"I now have two weeks to find this vault, or not only will Bjorn be sitting on a pile of stolen wealth up to his forehead, but I'll be eating biscuits from the corner store while I sit across the street from my flat in Hyde Park with nowhere to go."

"Don't forget the bounty on your head," Corbin added.

Sophie grunted in anguish, extending her hands towards the sky, begging for divine intervention. She returned to her misery with her head hung.

Corbin approached her and handed her the other drink in his hand Sophie took it from him as she sat cross legged on the deck of the ferry.

Corbin sat down beside her. "You can always come work for me."

"Thanks for the offer, Corbin, but babysitting movie stars and ambassadors really isn't my jam," Sophie replied, as she drank the cello.

Corbin and Sophie sat on the deck of the ferry together, listening to the sound of the passengers continuing to celebrate their own more fruitful journey. The glow of the ferry lights began to take over as the sunset cast its final glimmer of light.

Corbin finally spoke up, watching Sophie drink the last of her medication. "Why *did* you leave, Broadway?"

"By leave, do you mean the States?" she replied.

"The Raiders."

Sophie leaned her head back against the railing and set the empty glass down at her side. She looked down at her left hand seeing the shortened ends of her pinky and ring finger. "'Was time."

"I can smell bullshit, Broadway, I was born on a ranch. You had more brass below the belt than Summers, Quarter Mile, or me. You n' Yorkie used to put us guys to shame. First, I heard you guys were in Africa; then I heard you were in Germany; and *then* I was told you weren't coming back at all. Few weeks later I was being told Yorkie had died of an untreated heart condition, and Quarter Mile took a spill while rock climbing in the Alps.

"I immediately knew they were lying to me because Yorkie was the fittest woman I knew, and Quarter Mile hated climbing. So, now I'm asking you: what happened? This isn't about national security. This is about knowing the truth about what happened to my friends."

Sophie sat, replaying the story in her head. She remained silent. She finally stood up and gazed back out over the sea before them. She spotted Bari ahead of them as a glistening line along the darkened horizon which separated water from sky as Corbin joined her, still waiting for a response.

"Let's find a place to stay in Bari. We'll leave at first light for Florence," Sophie replied.

Corbin stood up from his place on the deck. He scoffed and shook his head at her, clearly frustrated that he once more was being left in the dark.

"Right…" he replied, making his way back to the SUV.

TEN

THE MIDDAY SUN baked the Libyan desert surrounding Sophie as she watched the main gate of the residential compound, guarded by armed men. She kept her face covered with her shemagh, blending in with the bustling crowd of people amidst Misrata as best she could. Her commander, Summers, stood at her side, pretending to be her husband as they sold dates and peppers from their facade as street sellers.

"Quarter Mile, have you got eyes on the target yet?" asked Summers into the mic hidden away beneath his collar.

"Negative. Nazer's bodyguards are shaking hands out front. Looks like they're having themselves a barbecue," said Quarter Mile, his low and raspy voice speaking into Sophie's earpiece.

"If he doesn't show, this whole thing is shot to shit," Sophie muttered, keeping an eye on the compound.

Quarter Mile coughed over his radio, sounding disgusted.

"Ya all right there, 'Mile?" asked Summers.

Hyde Park Adventures

Quarter Mile cleared his throat. "Yeah… Just drank out of my spit bottle rather than my water bottle."

Sophie snickered with a grin, hearing Summers chuckle along with Yorkie's laugh over the radio.

"'Should probably keep those two further apart," muttered Sophie, into her radio.

"I get in the zone up here, refusing to take my eyes off the scope," Quarter Mile replied.

A rusted and aged school bus pulled up to the front gate of the compound.

Sophie watched as the passengers on the bus got off, each one stretching as though having made a long trip. "He with them?" she asked, awaiting confirmation with eagerness.

"Yorkie? What's the word from your end? You got eyes on Nazer?" asked Summers.

"Still no sign of him. That bus is filled with a lot of boxes, though," Yorkie replied over the radio.

"Can you see what's in them?" asked Sophie. She watched the group of men, all armed and strapped with body armor speak to one another out in the open before the compound gate.

"No. I can't get a good look. The heat coming off the street is blurring everything. Definitely not food or clothing for the homeless though," Yorkie replied.

A black luxury car drove up to the front of the compound. A

man stepped out from the backseat with two bodyguards; he wore desert camo pants under an olive-green linen shirt, topped with a black bandanna wrapped around his head to hold back his black curly hair. His beard was finely trimmed, complimenting his dominating and authoritative presence as he scanned the street around him.

"That's him…" Sophie muttered in spite.

"Got eyes on Nazer," Yorkie confirmed.

Nazer turned and faced his men who had arrived on the bus. They began shaking hands, engaging in conversation while pointing at the bus with interest. A man wearing a red keffiyeh under a full beard stepped into view from behind the bus and hugged Nazer. At the same moment, a masked man wearing a blue-and-white scarf wrapped around his face stepped out from the passenger seat of the luxury car. The man's eyes scanned the surrounding street with suspicion before being introduced by Nazer to the man wearing a keffiyeh.

"Looks like Nazer's got himself a new best friend," muttered Quarter Mile, referring to the man with the blue-and-white scarf.

"Anyone know who he is?" asked Yorkie.

"Highboy, this is Crusader-1. We have the target in sight. The target is being escorted by a new bodyguard. Awaiting facial verification," said Summers into his radio.

A brief moment of static passed before command replied. "Roger, Crusader-1."

"Why do we need to see his face?" questioned Sophie, her gaze fixed on Nazer and his associates. "He's a friend of Nazer and that's all we need to know. If he stands in our way, we take him out with him. Let's take him now."

"Our orders are just to observe the meet. We don't move until we have a justifiable cause," said Summers. "So, unless Nazer gives us something worth moving on, sit tight until we've seen something. I don't wanna have to radio back to the CIA guys telling 'em we got trigger happy."

"We *are* trigger happy," Quarter Mile replied.

"You mean killing a church full of people wasn't justifiable enough for Langley?" Sophie argued. "Or what about the two US and three English reporters he kidnapped and killed? Or the explosion at the Brandenburg Gate he masterminded? This guy is like the heavyweight champ compared to Baghdadi. He's been evading us for months! I say we snag him now so we can ask him ourselves what else he's got planned. Off the books."

"We still can't confirm he was the one who planned those," Summers replied.

Sophie scoffed and shook her head in response.

The man wearing the red keffiyeh pointed towards the bus. He ushered Nazer inside the cab as Sophie and her fellow team members continued to observe from their various positions both high and low among the surrounding streets. The man opened one of the crates resting on the seat and began showing Nazer what was inside, pointing down into the crate.

"Yorkie, get me eyes on what's in that crate," Summers ordered.

An open-fence truck loaded with sheep drove past the compound, only to stop next to the compound, blocking Sophie and Summers' view.

"Shit! My view's blocked by this stupid truck," Yorkie replied.

"Quarter Mile?" asked Summers.

"Can't see into the back. Sun's reflecting off the window," Quarter Mile replied.

Sophie hurried towards the street corner, eager to keep tabs on Nazer. She heard Summers hiss at her. "Broadway! Stay in position!"

Sophie climbed up on the concrete wall near her, encircling a private garden across the street from the compound. She hugged the building atop the wall, gazing out over the truck and street traffic towards the bus.

"Way to expose yourself, Broadway," grumbled Quarter Mile over the radio.

"Just doing your job for you," Sophie replied, peering into bus windows from her vantage point, seeing what was inside the crate.

A green and white, metal, cylinder shaped object was inside the bus. The man with the red keffiyeh rolled the object over gently, showing Nazer the Russian text on the backside facing Sophie's view.

"Broadway, what do you see?" asked Summers.

Sophie spotted a former Soviet Union hammer and sickle emblem on the object, along with the letters M119-17. Sophie stood with a sickening feeling in her stomach. "That's a Lupis Missile payload…"

"A what?" asked Yorkie.

"A warhead. A Soviet warhead," Sophie replied.

"Did I just hear you say the word 'warhead'?" said Quarter Mile.

"Are you sure?" asked Summers.

Sophie continued to watch as the man wearing a red keffiyeh opened another crate. Inside was another Soviet warhead from a decommissioned short range Lupis missile. "He's got multiple. That bus is full of them."

"Jesus Christ…!" replied Yorkie.

"That enough justifiable cause for ya, Summers?" asked Quarter Mile.

"If they get those warheads to Tirana, they can easily sneak them into every major city across Europe and level each one in a day," muttered Sophie, watching Nazer hug the man.

"How big a blast are we talking about here?" asked Yorkie.

"Each one of those tubes packs a 50-megaton blast, perfectly wrapped in a space the size of a five-gallon drum. So, say if London were the size of a dime, the blast radius would be the size of a grapefruit," said Sophie.

"Holy shit…!" said Quarter Mile.

"All right, we have enough evidence," said Summers. "It's time we bring this asshole to his knees; once they move into the main building, we make our move. Quarter Mile, I want you and Yorkie on the west entrance. Broadway and I will enter through the east."

"Copy that," replied Yorkie.

Sophie jumped down from off the wall and rejoined Summers at their position across the street. They watched Nazer and his new friend exit the bus and engage in conversation, all the while with Nazer's presumed bodyguard in the blue-and-white scarf overseeing their safety. Nazer ushered everyone through the gate of the compound with a grand wave of the hand. The bus pulled into the compound just before the gate closed, while Nazer and his band of terrorists passed out of sight.

"Gear up," ordered Summers.

Sophie turned around and threw back the tarp over the food stall, unveiling the assault rifles they had stashed away underneath the table. She handed Summer's his rifle and a magazine before loading her own rifle.

Summers hid his rifle under his jacket then covered his face with his head scarf. He nodded to Sophie, leading the vanguard ahead of her as they crossed the street through traffic. "Radio in when you're in position."

"Roger," Quarter Mile replied.

Sophie and Summers entered the front gate of the compound, seeing the lone two-story building at the center enclosed by the surrounding stone wall. She scanned the corners of the compound; it was undefended. What once was a courtyard filled with men was now vacant.

"I don't like this. Who holds a high value weapons exchange without guards posted out front?" muttered Sophie.

"Yorkie, Quarter Mile, you see anyone?" asked Summers.

"Negative. It's quiet over here, too," Yorkie replied.

Sophie approached the bus, seeing the passenger door now closed. "Summers, give me a boost."

Summers joined her side, keeping an eye out. He slung his rifle, then gave Sophie a leg up. Sophie peered in through the window, seeing the bus was now empty as well. Summers lowered her back down.

"Now I'm really not liking this. It's empty," Sophie whispered.

"What?" Summers replied, expressing a perplexed look. "How'd they move all of it so fast?"

"Maybe they were ready to move it. Should we fall back?" asked Sophie.

Summers visually contemplated the suggestion.

"No. If we don't take him now, we'll lose track of the cache." Summers started making his way across the compound.

Sophie continued to check the main rooftop of the building, gathering an eerie feeling in her stomach. She heard no voices from within the building. The compound was a ghost town.

Summers stopped before the east doorway into the main building. Sophie joined his side as she spotted Yorkie and Quarter Mile moving into position on the opposite side near the western door.

"Call it," muttered Quarter Mile.

Summers stood with his aim at the ready. He took a quick breath in preparation. Sophie felt an urge to call a retreat, yet her hate for Nazer pressed her onward.

"Move in," said Summers.

Sophie kicked open the wooden door before them. Summers entered the building as the door flew open, scanning the hallway ahead of them.

THE COLONEL'S LOST VAULT

Sophie followed. The building was decorated with colorful rugs and home furnishings surrounding a grand traditional Muslim meal. It was as though someone had just been there, yet the meal had not been set for them.

Sophie suddenly heard the sound of shouts coming from beyond the closed doorway ahead of her.

"Back up, Quarter Mile!" shouted Yorkie's voice.

Summers approached the doorway. Sophie turned in preparation to enter the room ahead.

"Back up!" shouted Yorkie again.

A blast erupted from the doorway, throwing Sophie against the back wall behind her. Her vision blurred, accompanied by a sharp wailing sound in her ears. She felt an intense, stinging pain in her side as her ribs shifted freely under her skin. Her vision finally cleared as the sound of Yorkie's pain-fueled screams of agony filled her ears.

Sophie rose up from the stone rubble and debris over top of her, clutching her side. She hurried through the now-nonexistent doorway, calling out to her friend, "Yorkie!"

Yorkie's arm reached out to her from under a burning pile of stone and boards.

The sound of distant gunfire could be heard approaching the compound through the now open void in the destroyed building. Summers limped towards Sophie from beyond a cloud of debris smoke, a quarter-inch steel rod protruding from his leg as a trail of blood wetted the dust on his forehead. He grunted in pain, still keeping his aim raised and ready to fight as he joined Sophie's side.

Sophie began digging at the heated rubble, trying to get to Yorkie. She grabbed hold of her hand for a moment, trying to comfort her. "Hold on, York! I'm coming!"

The crackle of gunfire outside continued to approach. A hand grabbed hold of her shoulder.

"Broadway!" shouted Summers' voice.

Yorkie's screams continued as Sophie's ears began to ring with an endless high pitch.

"Broadway!" shouted Summers once more, muffled.

Sophie stared down at her feet to see what little remained of Quarter Mile: a severed arm and pieces of his right foot. Yorkie's screaming continued.

"Broadway!"

The seared image of Yorkie's scorched hand reaching out to her from beneath the burning rubble was cauterized into her mind.

Sophie screamed.

Her eyes opened to see Corbin grabbing her shoulders as he loomed over her amidst their lamp-lit hotel room in Bari, Italy. She let out one final scream, realizing it wasn't Yorkie screams she was hearing but her own.

Sophie laid in her hotel bed feeling the chill of her own sweat in the breeze from the window. Her eyes were wide and filled with horror as she panted out of breath.

Corbin let go of her shoulders and stood up at her bedside, a terrified look on his face. He stood silent for a moment, allowing her to reclaim her grasp on reality.

"'Guessing that's why you retired, huh?" he said to her.

Sophie sat up in her bed and buried her face in her hands, feeling the cold sweat chilling her both inside and out. She continued to quiver as she held out one hand flat before her, seeing her fingers tremble.

"You didn't choose to retire. They *forced* you. Didn't they?" said Corbin.

Sophie stood up from the bed and walked past Corbin into the bathroom of the hotel room. She gathered her breath.

"...It was 'recommended.'" She grabbed a glass from off the counter and filled it with water from the sink.

Corbin continued to stand in the bathroom doorway as she drank the water; her hands still shaking. "What happened, Broadway?"

Sophie dumped the remainder of her water glass into the sink, still feeling short of breath. Her chest grew tight, shaking with each breath. Each one of the damaged nerves in her legs surged with the haunting memories.

"We set up camp in Libya, in Misrata with two CIA agents. Summers led the operation, which MARSOC named Capsize. We snuck into the country by boat, then we were picked up by one of our insiders and driven into the city. Our target was a high value ISIS leader that had been evading us for months, but finally settled down. An arms dealer shipping guns to Syria and Iran."

"Nazer…" Corbin muttered.

Sophie nodded. "He controlled the supplies, which meant he controlled everyone. MARSOC had us posted to make sure he wasn't shipping anything larger than small arms in secret. Six months we hid in a flat building down the street from his compound. Day after day, night after night, waiting and watching. Everything was going smoothly. We just had to be patient.

"Our insider found out that Nazer was arranging to move something big via a ship to Albania, with a meeting to discuss the plan taking place at another compound on the other side of town. Command updated our mission to taking Nazer out if the intelligence proved to be true and we found justifiable cause. We found ourselves scouting out the location, waiting for the meeting to take place. Command gave us the confirmation to finally act. We saw all we needed to, so we moved in.

"As we breached the building, we found out our informant had been compromised; Nazer had gotten to him and was holding his grandson hostage. They used the meeting as a trap for us, and we fell for it. Our informant was dead inside, his body waiting for us, strapped with enough explosives set to bring the two-story building down over our heads. Quarter Mile and Yorkie found him first… Summers and I brought up the rear."

Sophie's bottom lip began to quiver as she continued. "Quarter Mile hesitated… He was killed instantly… Yorkie was buried alive under a stack of burning rubble. I was thrown from the doorway, peppered with shrapnel, and left with four broken ribs. Summers broke his left arm and had a piece of rebar sticking out of his leg. I tried to help Yorkie, but couldn't get her out… I tried and tried, but the rubble was too much…

Summers and I fought as best we could, but Nazer's men dragged us away as Yorkie continued to scream out to me. Her body was hung from our apartment balcony for everyone to see as a warning…

"Summers and I spent the next six days being interrogated by Nazer and his men. They wanted to know what we knew and who we were with. We didn't tell them anything. The first day, they beat me until my eyes swelled shut. The second, they drowned and shocked me till I passed out. They took my pinky and ring finger off with cutting pliers on the third day. Then my earlobe with a knife on the fourth, then drilled holes in my leg. The fifth day… they sterilized me with a hot poker…"

Sophie sat down on the edge of the bathtub beside her. She stared into the late-night darkness ahead of her as she continued to speak. "The sixth morning, I heard gunfire outside the shack I was held in. The blindfold was pulled away from my face, and I broke down into tears… A group of unofficial CIA operatives, led by a retired Navy Seal, came with three Delta Force members and two Army Rangers to rescue us. Nazer escaped the night before, never to be heard from again. Summers and I were evacuated out of the city by truck, then boat to the USS Virginia moored off the coast. From there, we were flown by helicopter to the US base in Stuttgart. Summers lost his leg to infection, along with part of his left hand. I spent three months in recovery undergoing surgery to repair the damage to my leg. Once I was back on my feet, they handed me my medals and my discharge papers.

"I stayed with my sister, Izzie, for the next few months. The only way I could sleep was by blacking out with a bottle of scotch. Once Izzie found me passed out in the garden one night, she arranged for me to meet with a doctor. Few weeks of therapy and pills, and the nightmares became less frequent. They've only recently come back…"

Sophie sat for a moment, taking in the silence; yet, even in the silence, she could hear Yorkie's faint screams. She started to sob, struggling to speak over her tears. "Every night is different. Sometimes, I'm on my knees trying to dig Yorkie out of the burning rubble… Others, I'm back in the shack, waiting to die. My lips turn dry… My shoulders start to ache from the restraints… My skin sweats from the heat… My vision darkens back to the sight of that white and tan cloth tied over my eyes… My ears replay the sound of the steel door creaking in the breeze as the chain holding it closed chimes over and over… I sat in that chair all those nights, and I… I cried. I cried… Fearing for my life… And I—" Sophie sniffed with a stuffy nose and took a deep breath, her eyes watering. Her breaths quickened with panic. "I didn't—I don't…"

Sophie's buried her face in her hands. She sank from her edge of the tub to the bathroom floor, overpowered by the memories. Corbin hurried over to her. He dropped to one knee and wrapped her in his arms. Sophie continued to sob. She clutched Corbin's arm for comfort as he rocked her gently.

"I don't wanna be alone… I don't wanna be alone…" she muttered, succumbing to her tears. "I'm sorry…"

Corbin held on to her tightly. "Shh… Ain't nothin to be sorry for, Broadway. I'm here. 'Till the bitter end of this, girl… 'Till the bitter end… Gung-ho for life…"

Eleven
BARI, ITALY

THE MORNING BUSTLE and honks of Bari outside her window woke Sophie from her sleep. She looked down at her bedside to find Corbin sleeping on the floor nearby.

His aid had led to the first decent night's sleep in several weeks as, for the first time, she didn't feel alone in her struggle. She tiptoed around him and allowed Corbin to continue to sleep while she sat outside on the hotel balcony as the sun rose, taking in the scent of the new day.

Before long, Corbin awoke and prepared himself to get back on the road. He spoke nothing of what she had told him as they got ready, offering her only a reassuring smile, which was all the comfort she needed. The two of them drove along the narrow cobblestone streets of Beri and began the long drive towards Florence, still set on beating Bjorn.

Sophie allowed her mind to drift along the drive, admiring the ancient castles and tantalizing vineyards which populated the Italian countryside. Briefly stopping in Rome, Sophie and Corbin continued to leave the night's events unspoken as they paused at a city street café, sharing a meal.

"Saint Donta…" muttered Sophie to herself, sitting across from Corbin at the table, dwelling on Wagner's words from the journal page.

"What?" asked Corbin, sipping his coffee.

"That line from Wagner's page. Saint Donta. Guarded by the knight, Saint Donta. It doesn't make any sense. There isn't a Saint Donta."

"Maybe he meant Dante? Maybe he was referring to the poet, Dante Alighieri. He was from Florence, I'm pretty sure. And he wrote that poem, Dante's Inferno. Perhaps Wagner's relating one clue back to the other with the whole journey through the gates of hell."

"Maybe," Sophie replied, feeling uncertain, "but Wagner was an art fanatic. I don't see him as one for writing. Especially with the Nazi's always looking over his shoulder. They opposed writings that went against their own ideologies."

"You said back at the cave you had him all wrong. Maybe that's the same case now."

"I guess it's possible. Though, I'm starting to wonder if he had other reasons for keeping the vault secret. Like he had something else locked away in there that he didn't want anyone else to find or know about."

"What makes you say that?" asked Corbin as he paid the bill.

"He wrote on that page like he was guilty of something. Some act of treason, worse than withholding that art from Himmler. Himmler oversaw the vault from the beginning. If Wagner had no intention of giving the art over to him, why did he give him a key? One peek into the vault and he'd have been found out."

"Probably had to. Probably relied on the hope Himmler was busy with the war and hoped he'd never get wise," suggested Corbin.

"Which begs the question: what was it that he wanted to keep so secret? What did he lock away with all that art that was so secret that he deprived the world of all those classical works?"

"Guess we'll find out once we get to Bargello," Corbin replied, finishing his coffee.

Sophie fiddled with the napkin on the table in thought. "Maybe whatever he hid away from the world was meant to remain hidden."

Corbin spoke with a surprised tone. "Are you thinking of backing out?"

"No. Whatever he hid, it's better we make sure Bjorn doesn't get a hold of it, is all. If there's more than just art in that vault, it's still our job to protect it. That and I still have a story to write."

Corbin stood from the table and grabbed his jacket off the back of the chair. "Then why waste any more time? There's only one way to find out. Keep moving onward."

Sophie smiled and finished her tea, feeling a hunger to pursue her newest questions.

◆ ◆ ◆

SOPHIE AND CORBIN crossed the open plaza of Florence under the clouded evening sky, wading through the busy crowd of tourists and street performers towards Bargello; a soaring, five-story red brick prison that loomed over the plaza, with its own watchtower keeping an eye on the busy streets below.

Sophie approached the prison with Corbin to see banners hanging over the entrance, advertising the repurposed prison's newest art collection of marble sculptures. They stopped outside the main entrance to see guests being let out through a locked gate, all the while observing new arrivals being denied entry as the museum closed for the day.

"Looks like they're closed," said Corbin. "Should we come back tomorrow?"

"And let Bjorn catch up? No way. Nothing's closed with the right attitude and presence," Sophie replied. She pulled up the museum's website on her phone and began reading through it, looking for contacts.

"Don't try any of your usual tricks, Broadway," grumbled Corbin.

"I'm not!" Sophie replied. "I'm just… compromising." She continued towards the museum entrance with a smug face, putting her phone away.

Sophie approached the gated entrance to see a balding man with black hair standing behind the bars.

He spotted Sophie approaching and presumed to know exactly what she was about to ask. "We are closed for the day. Please, come back tomorrow," the man said to her in Italian.

"No, no. We are here to see Signor Luca," Sophie replied in Italian. "My name is Vivian Solaso and this is my partner, Alexander." Sophie gestured to Corbin. "Luca said to come after the museum was closed."

The man stared back and forth at Sophie and Corbin for a moment. A group of museum guests approached the gate from within, seeking passage back out into the plaza. The man opened the gate for them, continuing to hold it open while presumably contemplating whether to allow Sophie and Corbin inside.

"Who do you work for?" he asked.

"We're with the McKenzy Artistic Heritage Committee, doing a study on Michelangelo," Sophie replied.

"And you say you are here to see Luca?"

"Yes," Sophie replied, offering him a polite smile.

The man looked back over his shoulder. He whistled to a grey-haired man wearing a polo shirt and glasses sitting in one of the museum rooms, converted into an office nearby. The elderly man approached with an authoritative stride.

Sophie could spot Corbin's smug grin over her shoulder, as though he expected her to falter at the unexpected change in the situation.

"Yes?" asked the man to his associate.

The man pointed to Sophie and Corbin. "These two are members of the…?"

"McKenzy Artistic Heritage Committee," Sophie interjected. "Luca, I presume?"

"Yes?" the elderly man replied.

"Miss Vivian Solaso. I spoke to you over the phone last week about dropping by to see the sculptures. You said to pop in after the museum was closed for the day."

Luca stood with a perplexed expression. As hard as he tried, he couldn't seem to remember, yet his manners and integrity seemingly wouldn't allow him to admit it. "I apologize, I can't recall. Though please, come in."

Luca waved Sophie and Corbin through the museum gate. The man standing guard allowed them to pass before closing the gate and locking it once more.

"You'll have to excuse me. My memory isn't as sharp as it once was. What is it you are here to see?" asked Luca, leading Sophie and Corbin towards the central courtyard of the museum.

"We're doing a heritage study, looking into the genealogical relationships between the many families of Europe during the Renaissance based upon the works commissioned by wealthy families. We were hoping to have a look at some of your busts and other sculptures for our study, analyzing their facial features depicted by Michelangelo to others we've seen in various regions around Europe. Hopefully, we can piece together a grand puzzle with it all," Sophie replied, laughing off the moment.

Corbin stared at her with a stunned expression. Sophie elbowed him. He turned his attention to Luca, assuming his role as Alexander.

Luca nodded, seemingly catching only half of what Sophie had said.

Sophie pulled a bundle of Euros from her backpack and held them out to him in an attempt to further sweeten her words. "Of course, we'd be willing to pay you for your time."

"I see. Well, uh…" Luca replied, taking the money, before gesturing to the museum around him. "Feel free to have a look around. Giovi or I will be here if you have any questions. If you could keep your visit as brief as possible, I'd greatly appreciate it. We will be leaving for the night in thirty minutes."

"Oh, thirty minutes is more than enough. Thank you," Sophie replied.

"Very well. There were some other gentlemen who showed up not long before we closed, looking to stay a little later, whom you might find wandering around. Hopefully, they won't be in your way."

Sophie glanced towards Corbin expressing her concern. "Did they say who they were?"

"Art collectors from Stockholm, I believe. Paid a handsome sum at the door as well just to inspect the works after hours," Luca replied.

"I'm sure they won't be a problem," Sophie replied, trying to hide her worry.

Luca returned to his office near the museum gates, leaving Sophie and Corbin alone in the old prison courtyard to explore the museum at will.

"What's our objective?" asked Corbin.

"Recon from afar and see if Bjorn's found anything first," Sophie replied.

Corbin nodded in agreement. The two of them stepped away from the courtyard into the western doorway of the museum, listening carefully for anyone ahead of them. Corbin circled around the gallery space in one direction while keeping Sophie in sight. The museum was eerily quiet.

Room after room was filled with marble and bronze sculptures pressed up against the walls and filling the dead spaces of the room.

Each room was vacant, with no sign of Bjorn or his hired help. Sophie checked her back to see Corbin was no longer in the room with her. She fell back, passing through the only other doorway leading into another converted gallery space to find Corbin standing near an old doorway, left ajar. Corbin waved her over to him as he continued to listen to the doorway. As Sophie approached, she could hear voices coming from within.

"Don't break it open. We have to make this place look the same way we left it. Anything in that one?" said one deep, Scandinavian voice.

"Another stubborn sod with head and shoulders. None of these people look very happy," replied another voice.

"Don't know *why* they'd be unhappy. If they were rich enough to have their faces carved in stone, they probably lived like kings. Drinking wine everyday while enjoying all the women they could lay their hands on," replied the deep voice. The other two voices laughed.

"Shut up and keep looking. We're not here for busts," grumbled Bjorn's voice.

Sophie crept through the door. Beyond it was an old staircase, leading down into the lowest foundation of the prison. A crypt of stone once used as a cellblock, now repurposed for the museum's added storage. Sophie spotted Bjorn sifting through straw stuffing among a row of crates and statues while his men did the same.

"Why don't we just kill the two guys upstairs? Then we'd have all the time in the world to check," suggested one of the men.

"If they get in the way, then we'll take care of them. For now, shut up and keep looking for the page," Bjorn replied.

"Maybe the curator knows something. You said there'd be books by a guy named Dante down here. All we've found is naked sculptures," said the man with a deep voice.

"I'm just guessing. He wrote a poem about hell and this is the lowest point in the prison," Bjorn replied.

"I think prison as a whole is hell," replied the deep voice. "Maybe we should have kept that Lions chick around."

"You wanna be another stone body down here? Shut up and keep searching," Bjorn replied.

Sophie took a step back up the stairs and joined Corbin at the doorway. She spoke with a whisper. "They're checking the storage."

"Obviously they haven't found anything?" said Corbin, whispering away from the doorway.

"Yeah, but who knows for how long. Bjorn's figured out the riddle about Dante, which means it's just a matter of time," Sophie replied.

"What do we do now?"

Sophie scanned the museum hall around her, checking to make sure the coast was still clear. Her gaze passed across the placard for a bronze sculpture depicting a man draped with a cloth in the middle of the room.

David - Donatello 1408-1409

"Guarded by the knight, Saint Donta..." Sophie muttered to herself.

Corbin watched her muddled expression while keeping an ear towards the door. "Broadway?"

Sophie turned towards Corbin in sudden realization. "It's not Dante!" she said to him, quietly but with eagerness. "It's Donatello!"

She hurried and began scanning the other placards in the room beside each one of the sculptures.

Corbin scurried after her. "What?" asked Corbin, following her around.

"It's not Dante. It's Donatello. 'Donta' is Donatello. And he wasn't a saint. He was a famous sculptor; a saint among artists. Look for a sculpture carved by Donatello. One that has something to do with a knight," Sophie replied.

Corbin stepped away from her in the opposite direction, checking each of the sculptures. Sophie continued to search, passing several sculptures among the collection carved by Donatello, but none of which shared a knightly pose or appearance.

"Sophie!" hissed Corbin's voice from beyond the open doorway next to her.

Sophie entered the hall to find Corbin standing before a marble sculpture, set into a relief along the wall. The carving was of a man dressed in a tunic, holding a kite shield with one hand while expressing a stern look of resilience.

Sophie read the placard on the wall next to the sculpture. "Saint

George, by Donetello." She began scanning around the edges of the sculptures, muttering to herself. "Guarded by the knight." She stepped up onto the old wooden carved altar at the base of the sculpture, scanning the relief more closely.

"What are you doing?" whispered Corbin.

"What does it look like I'm doing? I'm looking for anything left behind," Sophie replied, scanning the sculpture from head to toe.

She looked at the figure's closed right fist, seeing a space small enough to conceal a secret within. She poked her index finger in through the space, hearing something metal fall to the base of the sculpture. She looked down to see a steel tube resting at the statue's base. She picked it up and hopped down to the floor.

Corbin continued to keep watch as Sophie examined the tube. It was an old lipstick tube with the engraved letters AMW. She pulled the two halves of the lipstick tube apart. The tube had been repurposed, used to hide the secret within; inside were the same grains of salt and rice from the safe with another folded and rolled up piece of paper.

Sophie unfolded the page with the grains still falling at her feet, having only enough time to read the bottom line.

May this page *never see the sun and allow the works I've sworn to protect to live in peace.*

Peter Wagner

The sound of the door in the other hall closing echoed through the museum. Sophie and Corbin looked towards the doorway, hearing Bjorn's voice come from the other hall. "Search the museum. Check every dark space and corner."

"Let's exfil before they know we're here," Corbin whispered to her.

"No," Sophie replied, stubbornly. "I want my journal and page back."

"Forget it, Broadway. We've got what we came for, let's just get out of here."

"If Wagner's hiding something else in that vault, that journal may tell us. And… I promised I'd return it."

Corbin sighed in silence at Sophie's stern and stubborn look.

"Fine," Corbin replied, with a begrudging tone, "we'll get it back; but not here. Right now, we need to get out of here."

Sophie nodded in agreement. She peered around the statue beside her into the next hall, seeing one of Bjorn's men—tall with thick blonde sideburns—wandering through the museum, examining the many statues as he made his way in their direction.

Sophie folded up the page and tucked it into her bag. The steel lipstick tube fell from her hand as she fumbled. She reached out to snatch from the air, only for it to slip from her fingers and bounce against the floor. The sound echoed throughout the hall.

Sophie looked at Corbin with a fearful expression.

They both scurried towards the opposing doorway behind them, trying to remain quiet. Corbin peered around the corner from cover and stopped Sophie with his arm. Bjorn's other man—dark-skinned and beastly in size—was standing amidst the open courtyard. He was making his way towards them, seemingly also alerted by the sound.

Sophie and Corbin backed up against the wall behind a nearby column. Corbin kept an eye on the doorway as Sophie glanced back to see the sideburned mercenary enter the room with his pistol pointed at the statues.

Sophie dragged Corbin down by the shirt, forcing him to crouch behind the statue on a pedestal next to them. Sophie watched the sideburned mercenary approach the spot where they had been standing, in front of the statue of Saint George. He picked up the lipstick tube and examined it, feeling the grains of salt and rice on the floor with his fingers.

"Aron!" shouted Bjorn's voice from the courtyard.

Corbin suddenly grabbed Sophie by the backpack strap, dragging her towards the courtyard. She followed, spotting Bjorn standing with his back turned to them at the far edge of the courtyard, pointing to the museum map on the wall. The dark-skinned mercenary joined him from around the museum as Sophie and Corbin turned the corner and hurried towards the stairs leading to the second floor amidst the courtyard.

"It's Donatello. Not Dante, you dipshit. See the spelling difference? He changed the letters," said Bjorn's voice, echoing through the courtyard.

Sophie crouched low to the stone steps as she climbed, using the solid brick railing to conceal her movement. She peeked her head up over the railing as she reached the top to see Bjorn holding the journal in his hands as he pointed at the map.

"Boss!" shouted the sideburns man in his deep voice from the hall where Sophie and Corbin had been.

Bjorn turned his attention towards the doorway as the mercenary ran out across the courtyard, holding the tube of lipstick in his hand along with the grains of salt and rice. "What did you find, Tyge?"

Sophie waved for Corbin to follow her.

"I found this in front of a statue there," said Tyge, "along with that same shit from the cave in Greece. I think it's Donatello we're looking for, not Dante. There's a statue in there—"

"No shit," Bjorn replied, "We just figured that out."

"Someone was just in there," Tyge replied.

Bjorn began to scan the courtyard like a hawk searching for prey, holding the lipstick tube in his hand. Sophie ducked back down behind the railing among the balcony, continuing to listen.

"She's here…" said Bjorn in an angered voice. "Spread out and find her. She has it."

Sophie heard one of the mercenaries draw the slide back on his weapon, followed by the sound of the two hired guns hurrying away in opposite directions to begin their search. She hurried towards the open door at the other end of the balcony, leading into another gallery space with Corbin close at her side. Stepping into the gallery, she looked out the iron and stained-glass windows to her left, to see Bjorn making his way up the courtyard stairs, his weapon at the ready.

"Now where?" asked Corbin, pointing out the window at the stairs. "That's the only way out of here."

Sophie pointed towards the only other doorway in the room, leading to another converted gallery space. She hurried through the chain of upper gallery halls with Corbin behind her, scanning each room for another set of stairs leading out. She was forced to stop by a lone, old, closed doorway, finally reaching a dead-end. She turned the handle on the old door, only to find it was locked.

Sophie peered back out the stained-glass windows behind her to see Bjorn's distorted image stalking his way through the chain of halls behind them.

"Can you pick it?" asked Corbin.

"No time," Sophie replied. She kicked the doorway open, unleashing a loud crash which echoed throughout the museum. She looked back to see Bjorn's figure suddenly take off in a sprint towards the noise.

Ahead of her was another aged stone staircase, leading up into the prison's tower rather than downward. She grabbed Corbin by the arm and forced him into the doorway as she spotted Bjorn enter the hall.

"Lions!" shouted Bjorn.

Sophie hurried into the stairwell and slammed the old, heavy wooden door closed behind her. She grabbed the marble statue being stored in the stairwell and began dragging it across the floor to block the door. Corbin grunted as he helped, hearing the door buckle from Bjorn throwing his body against it.

The sound of gunfire beyond the door made Sophie jump as the handle near Corbin's waist exploded to pieces. Bjorn kicked at the door once more, only to have the statue block his path. "Lions!"

Sophie pushed Corbin towards the stairs, hearing Bjorn continuously try and force the door open. The spiraling stone staircase finally ended at the top of the watchtower, overlooking the whole of Florence. Corbin and Sophie looked out through the open cutout in the tower to see the eighty-foot drop to the plaza below.

"Shit! Now what?" asked Corbin.

"'Still know how to rappel?" Sophie replied, pulling out a length of climbing rope and a carabiner from her backpack.

Corbin expressed a brief look of concern, followed by acceptance. He drew his knife and cut two lengths of the rope for them to use as harnesses. Sophie handed him the carabiner as she could still hear Bjorn pounding against the stair door trying to break through.

Corbin fastened himself to the rope and threw the ends over the edge down to the street below. He climbed over the tower railing and positioned himself to begin his descent. "There's no such thing as a normal day for you, is there?"

Sophie smiled at him, keeping watch towards the door. Corbin began descending the tower as Sophie heard the sound of another body now smashing against the door. She pulled another carabiner from her bag and fastened it to the makeshift harness around her legs and waist. She clipped on to the rope as she heard the sound of the statue being toppled over resonate up through the stairwell.

Without hesitation, she climbed over the railing and looked down to see Corbin unfastening himself from the rope, safe among the streets below. She began repelling her way down the rope as she heard Bjorn and his men making their way up the stairs.

Halfway down the tower, she peered up to see Bjorn's face gazing down at her from over the railing, riddled with scorn. One of his men attempted to shoot down at her as Bjorn forced him back, gesturing to the surrounding plaza. He drew a knife from his belt and glared down at her once more.

Sophie started to descend even faster as her heart rate began to quicken with fear.

The rope fell slack in her hands. The top of the tower fell away from her as her stomach sank. She fell into the late evening shadow of the surrounding buildings of Florence, awaiting the inevitable impact of her back against solid cobblestone.

Her fears were set to rest as she felt Corbin's arms catch her as the two of them collided heads.

"You all right?" asked Corbin, setting Sophie down.

"Fine. You?" asked Sophie, rubbing at where the two of them had knocked heads.

"Perfect," Corbin replied, doing the same.

Gunshots sprang out from the tower above as the crowd surrounding them screamed and started to flee. Sophie and Corbin ran towards the plaza among the crowd as they could hear the bullets bouncing off the stone pavement behind them.

The shots finally stopped, as Sophie and Corbin passed out into the open plaza, making their way back to their stolen SUV parked along the outskirts.

"After all that, you still wanna get your book back?" asked Corbin, as they continued to run.

"After that, most definitely," Sophie replied.

Twelve

FLORENCE, ITALY

SMOLDERING WITH ANGER as he gripped the journal—the page from Athens tucked away inside—Bjorn sat in the passenger seat of his black Range Rover as his driver escorted him back to the private airfield. The car stopped out front of the private airport hangar; the airfield glowing under the Florence moonlight.

Bjorn opened his passenger door as he stepped out and slammed it shut in frustration. His two hired hands, Aron and Tyge, joined him as they arrived in their own SUV. The two of them walked around to the back of the car and opened the trunk, dragging the elderly curator from the Bargello out, beaten and bound with rope and duct tape. They hauled him across the tarmac towards the steps of Bjorn's private jet, waiting for them outside the hangar.

Bjorn stopped at the base of the stairs before the plane, waiting for Tyge and Aron loaded his hostage. He handed the journal off to Tyge.

"Put this somewhere safe." Tyge nodded and continued up the stairs.

Bjorn lit a cigarette as the co-pilot watched the curator being dragged past him through the aircraft with a nervous look before making his way down the steps, seemingly eager to speak with him.

"Are we ready to leave?" asked Bjorn, paying little attention to the co-pilot.

"Almost, sir," the co-pilot replied. "We're still waiting for the flight attendant. The captain wanted to relay a message regarding the sudden… *urgency* of the flight."

Bjorn turned his anger towards the co-pilot. "And what is it he wants?"

"Well, uh… He wants to renegotiate his rate."

Bjorn flipped his lighter closed and grabbed the co-pilot by the shirt. He spoke as the smoke billowed up from his lips and nose. "Tell the captain that if he wishes to negotiate, he should come speak with me himself rather than send his squire."

Bjorn let go of the co-pilot. The co-pilot scurried back up the steps of the plane, leaving Bjorn to continue enjoying his cigarette while he awaited the captain's negotiations.

The headlights of a black SUV pulled up to the plane. Bjorn turned around to see the silhouette of the missing flight attendant in the headlights step out of the passenger seat. Bjorn turned around as she walked past him, dressed in a blue skirt and top; her heels clicking against the tarmac.

"Sorry I'm late, sir," she muttered in an apologetic tone as she walked past him.

Bjorn watched the flight attendant make her way up the steps, admiring her backside before the SUV headlights drove away. The flight attendant loaded onto the plane as the captain appeared in the doorway. He walked down the steps with a kingly fashion, his co-pilot sticking close behind him as his feeble backup. The captain approached Bjorn with an unrelenting stare over his grey mustache.

"You wish to negotiate the terms of our agreement," Bjorn muttered.

"Three flights in less than twenty-four hours. Our agreement is for only two flights per day. No more," replied the captain.

"Are you telling me you refuse to fly my jet, captain," asked Bjorn, throwing his cigarette down on the ground.

"Yes. Especially when you bring hostages onboard my air—"

Bjorn drew his pistol and fired a round into the captain's forehead, silencing him before he could finish his sentence.

The co-pilot stood in shock with the captain dead at his feet. Bjorn holstered his gun and turned his attention towards the co-pilot. "Let that be a lesson to you, as you have just been promoted to captain of my aircraft. Congratulations. Now, please have the plane ready to depart when I have learned our next destination."

The promoted co-pilot continued to stand in shock, staring down at the dead pilot.

"Now!" Bjorn shouted at him.

The co-pilot turned around and made his way back up the steps of the plane in a panic.

"And I'd suggest you learn to calm your nerves before you do so," Bjorn added. "Otherwise, I don't foresee your promotion lasting very long."

Bjorn gestured to his private driver, ordering him to get out of the Range Rover. The driver stepped out of the car, ready to take his orders without hesitation following the sight of the pilot's demise.

Bjorn pointed at the dead pilot at his feet. "Throw him in the back and bury him in the vineyards with the other one." He started his way up the steps of the plane, readying himself to finally obtain the answers he came to Florence for in the first place.

"Hot towel, sir?" asked the flight attendant, standing in the shadows of the doorway. Bjorn raised a hand in rejection to her, turning his attention solely to the curator, left bound and sitting in one of the white leather chairs.

Bjorn removed his shoulder holster and set his guns down on the chair beside him. He sat down across from the curator, leaning forward with his elbows on his knees in preparation. He nodded to Aron.

Aron removed the tape from the curator's mouth and pulled back the strip covering his eyes. The curator winced in pain.

"Cosa vuoi!?" asked the curator in Italian, his face bruised and bloodied.

Bjorn shushed at him. "Shh… Lei parla inglese?" he replied, asking if he spoke English.

"Si," replied the man, quivering in fear.

"You are the curator at the Bargello Museum, yes?" asked Bjorn.

"Si—I mean, yes," the curator replied.

"What is your name?"

"Professor Luca Di Norcia."

"Luca," Bjorn replied, trying to play friendly, "I apologize for my rudeness at the museum. A friend, well… more like a rival now, managed to get away with something important to me."

"You shot my assistant!" Luca replied, seething in anger.

Bjorn snapped his fingers to the flight attendant. She brought the tray of hot towels over to him, ignoring Luca's pitiful plea. "Care for a hot towel, sir?"

"You're murderers!" Luca shouted at Bjorn.

Bjorn snickered, gesturing towards Luca. Aaron stepped forward and grabbed Luca by the jaw and top of his head. "I'm so sorry," Bjorn continued to speak. "My rudeness seems to be beyond my control today. Allow me."

Bjorn grabbed one of the heated towels from off the tray and began whipping the curators face with it. He then stuffed it into his mouth, then gestured back to Aron. Aaron replaced the strip of duct tape over the curator's mouth.

"Perhaps afterwards, we can share a bottle of Brunello. But for now, while I have your full attention without any further interruptions, allow me to ask you the same questions I asked your assistant. Hopefully, the car ride here gave you enough time to learn from his mistakes and reflect on your answer. Simply nod your head if the answer is yes, and shake if it is no."

Bjorn sat back in his chair. He took another towel from off the tray and gestured for the flight attendant to leave. He began wiping his hands clean with the towel, asking the curator his questions.

"First question: during the Second World War, a German Colonel named Peter Wagner claimed temporary control over the Bargello. As the museum curator, you must surely know this, as it is part of the museum's history. Yes?"

Luca continued to sit idle, scowling at Bjorn. Bjorn looked toward Tyge, knowing he didn't have to say anything. Tyge drove his fist across the curator's face, adding to the bruises. The curator sat wincing in pain for a moment before finally nodding his head yes.

"Already off to a much better start than your assistant. During this time, the Colonel kept several works of stolen artwork with him. You know of this artwork, yes?" asked Bjorn.

Luca turned his gaze towards Tyge. Tyge tightened his fist. Luca nodded yes once again.

"You're two for two, sir. Then you surely must know that the Colonel also left behind a page in your museum. A page which chronicled his journey, as well as the location of where he moved the stolen artwork after he parted from Italy. Yes?"

Luca shook his head with a no.

Bjorn took in a deep breath of anger. He looked towards Tyge again. Tyge once more threw his fist into the curator's cheek, dislodging the tape from over his mouth.

"Champagne, sir?" asked the flight attendant, returning with a tray of crystal glasses.

"No, thank you," Bjorn grumbled.

The curator took in a deep breath through the towel. Bjorn reached forward and removed the tape from his mouth, and then removed the towel.

"I don't know—I don't know where he took it," Luca replied weakly.

Bjorn extended an open hand towards Aron. Aron placed the empty steel lipstick tube in his hand. Bjorn held it out in front of the curator. "Have you seen this before?"

"No," the curator replied.

"It was hidden with Donatello's sculpture of Saint George. A sculpture in your museum."

Luca gathered his breath, trying to keep his eyes open. "The Saint George was moved to the museum in 1892. It hasn't moved since. It was there long before I took over."

Bjorn sat back in his seat in frustration.

"Champagne?" asked the flight attendant once more.

Bjorn huffed and turned to face the attendant. "I said *no*, woman. Are you—" He stopped, seeing the barrel of a Glock pointing at him from the flight attendant's waist. Bjorn turned his gaze upwards, seeing the flight attendant's face in full.

"I'd take it, Bjorn. Might be the last drink you'll ever have before enjoying your flight to the afterlife," said Sophie; her hair tied back as she wore a blue flight attendant uniform.

Bjorn's men began to reach for their guns. Sophie took a step back and pointed her gun at them. "Hold it. Hands away from your pants, boys."

"You're brave, Miss Lions," said Bjorn with a grin. "Though, I don't see your backup anywhere; where is your friend?"

"Look down at your shirt," Sophie replied.

Bjorn glanced down to see a red laser dot on his chest, coming from the port window of the plane.

"Got eyes on us, Corb?" asked Sophie, into her earpiece.

"Tell Bjorn if he makes any sudden moves, I'll leave a hole in his chest the size of a tennis ball," Corbin's voice replied over the radio.

"I'm sure he hears you, Corb," Sophie replied.

Bjorn snickered, seeing he had now been out-played. He had allowed himself to fall into a trap, brought about by his own blind obsession. "What is it you came for, Miss Lions? You already have the next page."

"My book and the page I found in Athens," Sophie ordered. "Along with the curator, now that you mention it. I don't like people stealing from me."

Bjorn nodded, understanding Sophie's aggravation. "Tyge."

Tyge turned his gaze away from Sophie and towards Bjorn. Bjorn pointed towards the overhead compartment. "Get the book."

Tyge stood up from his seat and reached for the overhead

compartment.

"Slowly," demanded Sophie.

Tyge slowly opened the overhead and pulled out the black duffle bag inside. He gently set it down on the seat and opened it. He pulled the journal out from inside and tossed it over to her.

Bjorn watched as Sophie didn't react, allowing the journal to fall to the floor. Instead, she continued to watch as Tyge attempted to reach out for his gun. She fired a shot at him, landing in the foam of the leather seat beside him. Tyge stopped and raised his hands again.

"I missed," Sophie said to him. She gestured to the curator. "Next one won't be so lucky. Now him." Sophie gestured towards the curator.

Bjorn pointed for Aron to let the curator go. Aron stood up and drew the knife from his belt slowly. He cut the ropes tied around the curator's hands, then put his knife away.

The curator stood up from the chair and hurried behind Sophie, using her as a shield as he slowly backed towards the door.

"You got all three of them, Corb?" asked Sophie.

"Roger," Corbin replied.

The red dot from the widow panned around between Bjorn and his men. Sophie slowly bent down and picked up the journal, keeping her eyes and aim on Bjorn. Bjorn watched her, waiting patiently.

"Might wanna reconsider your profession, Bjorn. Mercenary work just doesn't seem to be your thing," Sophie said to him.

Bjorn chuckled, watching her tuck the journal into her jacket.

"You would make an excellent addition to my team, Miss Lions. It's you who should reconsider your profession. Let me know if you ever have a change of heart; I could use someone of your talents working for me."

"I spent half my life stopping men like you. And I'm not one for being a hypocrite."

"Neither am I."

Bjorn reached for his guns on the seat next to him, willing to risk his life rather than let Sophie get away again. She shot once at him, missing by a few inches from his head. He grabbed his gun from the holster as Aron took cover behind the seats.

A shot burst through the plane window, shattering the glass and knocking Tyge to the floor with a loud thud. Bjorn began to fire back at Sophie from cover, rotating the plane seat to protect himself from the window.

Sophie fired back at Bjorn from around the corner near the exit to the plane; each one of her shots tearing into the upholstery before him.

Aron rose up from his hiding place, only to be struck in the vest by another shot by Sophie's companion outside. Bjorn looked back down at his feet to suddenly see a metal canister roll towards him from under the seat.

With a subtle pop, the canister began to smoke, filling the plane in a dense white smoke. He took another shot at the doorway, only to see it was now vacant as his vision became obscured by the smoke.

Bjorn hurried from his hiding place, hearing the sound of his driver outside being killed by the heavy sniper fire. He peered out through the smoke in the doorway with only enough time to see Sophie and the curator running across the airfield towards their stolen SUV. He was forced back inside by her friend from the hangar roof at the far end of the airfield as a shot pelted the frame of the door.

Bjorn remained in cover, waiting until he finally heard the sound of the SUV engine starting. He then stepped out from the plane onto the steps and began firing shots at the SUV from afar. He spotted Sophie's companion hurrying towards the car with his rifle in-hand before jumping in the backseat. The SUV tires screeched as they drove away from the airfield, leaving Bjorn standing among the corpses of his hired guns.

Bjorn reached into his pocket and pulled out his phone, calling up the most recent number. The phone rang for a moment before a male, middle eastern voice answered. "Did you find it?"

"Lions just made off with the journal," replied Bjorn.

"And you're calling me why…? Are you expecting me to help you?"

"No," Bjorn replied, expressing his aggravation. "I just wanted to let you know, the bounty's being called off, along with our deal. Once I find her again, I'm taking the treasure for myself. I want her alive so she can lead me to it. Then I'll choose whether to bury her in that vault or let her live should she choose to join me. I'm sure she wouldn't hesitate once I tell her the truth about you."

"You just signed your own death warrant."

"No. You just lost a partner."

Bjorn hung up the phone and continued to stare out across the airfield, seeing the value of Sophie Lions' expertise in full view now.

Hyde Park Adventures

♦ ♦ ♦

SOPHIE STOPPED THE car in front of the Florence police station, expressing her relief. Luca continued to sit in the passenger seat, wiping the blood away from his face using Sophie's shemagh. He finally handed it over to her with a sorrowful expression.

"I apologize for lying to you," said Sophie.

"I accept your apology," Luca replied. "Though, I should be the one thanking you. Had both of you not come, I would have ended up like my assistant. You are the only thing standing between those men and their goal."

"You really know nothing about the stolen artwork?" asked Corbin from the back seat.

Luca sat for a moment with a distant gaze, as though he was reflecting on a memory. "My predecessor, Giovanni di Mosca, was curator of the museum during the war. A polite man in every way. He taught me to see the beauty in art. As his young assistant, I heard him often speak of the Colonel. I was left confused for many years, questioning Giovanni's loyalty to our country. But when he finally told me of the stolen art before he retired, and how the Colonel used the museum as a fortress to hide it away from those who would do harm, I saw he was more than a patriot to my country; he was a patriot towards life itself.

"Colonel Wagner wasn't a bad man. I hope you both know that. He simply worked for bad men. He was an angel among demons." Luca opened the door to the car and stepped out. He spoke through the window. "If you find his vault, please keep it secret. The world still is not ready. Not while the hearts of humanity remain poisoned by flawed dreams. The same way I will keep your secret."

Luca stepped away from the car and began marching towards the police station with pride. Corbin crawled his way up into the front seat as he and Sophie both watched Luca enter the station, ready to file his police report regarding the death of his assistant and the robbery of his museum.

"You think he'll squeal?" asked Corbin.

"No," Sophie replied. "But let's get out of here before someone sees us."

"Roger that."

Sophie put the car in gear as Corbin looked over at her in the late moonlight.

"That's an unusual look for you," Corbin said to her, referring to the flight attendant outfit she bought from the real flight attendant, after intercepting her outside the airfield.

"Tell me about it. I haven't worn pantyhose since I was eighteen. And this bra chafes like a bitch," Sophie replied, tugging at her top uncomfortably.

Corbin began laughing at her as they drove back towards the heart of the city.

Hyde Park Adventures

Thirteen

SOPHIE SAT AT the desk of her hotel room along the banks of the Arno, allowing her hair to dry with the cool breeze blowing in from the open balcony door beside her. She read Wagner's journal, choosing to follow the tale of his life story from beginning to end before reading the page she found at the museum.

The time has *come for me to leave Greece. The British raids have begun to pose a major threat to my work. Our claim to this paradise is about to be challenged, and I intend to see that my last shipment back to the vault is unaffected before relocating to my next destination. Some of the shipments have been intercepted by renegade forces along the railway through Yugoslavia, leaving me with no other choice but to bring the remaining pieces along with me. The Rembrandts have me worried, however. At their age, they were never meant to endure such a long journey, and I have finally acquired the Girl Braiding Her Hair by Albert*

Anker. She's shy, but sweet in all her manners; though, she is not the only adolescent to be added to the collection.

The vault is nearly full, and yet I have been ordered by Himmler via coded message to take what is necessary from our allies to the south. Mussolini's place in the war has grown weak. While his forces continue to fight on, his country is being weakened by parties set on dethroning him. His people starve as their resources run scarce. Riots have begun to break out, so it's no wonder Himmler worries for the safety and security of their most prized works. My hope is that some of the pieces will still remain when I get there, assuming Mussolini's men and our own German forces haven't done away with them all carelessly.

I pray the Fatherland finds peace in these dark hours soon.

Heil Hitler.

Colonel Peter Wagner

Sophie dwelled on the journal entry for a moment. Now seeing the true man between the lines, she continued to try and unriddle the workings of his madness. She heard the sound of the bathroom door open.

"Where we headed next, commander?" said Corbin.

Sophie looked over to see Corbin wearing only a towel around his waist. She quickly turned her gaze away. "You know, some of the boys used to always walk out in the morning showing off their *rifles* trying to get a reaction out of me during training. At least you have the decency to put on a towel."

"Sorry," Corbin replied, sorting through his bag, looking for a clean set of clothes. "'You ever get any payback on 'em?"

"In several ways. I became a Raider while, the last I heard, none of them ever made it to Corporal. So I'd like to think so."

Corbin laughed.

Sophie opened up her bag and pulled out the folded page she found at the museum. "I was about to read up on our next destination."

"Care to read it aloud?" asked Corbin, putting on his clothes in the bathroom.

Sophie unfolded the page gently, seeing the text on both the front and back. She began reading out loud, doing her best to imagine Wagner's own voice in her mind.

When I arrived *at Château de Valençay, searching for the Winged Victory, I caught the French by surprise. French communications had been intercepted, leaving them with little defense and preparation. I was the first to arrive. Me and a single driver.*

My car passed over a mossy old stone bridge, and through a canopy of dense trees hanging over the road. I gazed out the window, thinking back on the road to my own home. To my cottage, stripped of its heart several years prior.

The crack of something hitting the metal hood of the car forced my driver to stop. The tires skidded through the dirt, followed by the sound of a gunshot and the glass windscreen breaking. My driv-

er attempted to duck down as another shot pierced his eye as he slumped over onto the seat. Through the webbed cracks of the glass, I could see a woman—dressed in a white-and-pink dress with dirty-blonde hair—firing a rifle at the car from the garden out front of the chateau. She was fearless.

I opened the car door and removed the white handkerchief from my pocket. She fired again, breaking the passenger window. I held my handkerchief up in the air and spoke in my best French trying to surrender. "Uh... No! Stop! Don't shoot!"

The shots stopped. I slowly stuck my head out to see she still had the rifle aimed at me. I raised my hands up over my head and exited the car slowly.

"Turn around, or I'll do the same to you as I did to him," the woman shouted to me, referring to my driver.

"I mean no harm!" I shouted back.

The woman laughed and shook her head. "Then go back the way you came, straight back to Germany."

I began to approach her cautiously, keeping my hands visible. I removed my hat and threw it on the hood of the car next to me. "I can't go back, nor does it seem that I can go forward. If I return without what I came for, they'll probably shoot me. So, if you're going to shoot, I ask only that you at least aim higher and better than before."

The woman expressed an appalled look. "Why are you here?"

"I've come looking to bring back something that was taken."

The woman squinted her eyes and raised the rifle. "What?"

"Art."

She fired once at me. I heard the shot pass over me, only a few inches from my head and get lost among the brush.

She cocked the rifle only to find she was out of shots. "Sorry! The next one will be much closer," she said sarcastically, trying to reload.

"Wait!" I begged with my hands still raised. "Wait! I'm not one of them! I came only to make sure they are safe!"

The woman stopped loading the rifle and retracted her head with a curious look. "You what?"

"I came to make sure they are safe. I know you've hidden works from the Louvre here. If you shoot me, they'll come and take them anyway by force. They'll burn the pieces they don't want and mistreat the ones they do. But if you allow me to at least see them first, I can help make sure none of them are harmed and stay out of their hands. Perhaps we can even make a deal."

The woman stood scowling at me for a moment. "Do you carry a gun?"

"I have a pistol on my right side."

She pointed the rifle at me again. "Leave it on the ground and take off your jacket."

I nodded in agreement and slowly removed my pistol. I placed it down on the ground, then removed my grey uniform coat and threw it on the hood of the car.

"Come closer," she said.

I crossed through the garden towards her with my hands raised. She finally lowered the rifle and gestured towards the Chateau. "Walk ahead of me. And you can put your hands down. You look ridiculous."

I lowered my hands. As I stepped towards her, I could see she wore an apron over her dress, covered in paint. Her hair appeared tangled and untamed pulled back into a bun, with heavy bags under her eyes.

"Do you have a name?" I asked.

"Arcadia. Yours?"

"Peter."

"Not so pleased to meet you, Peter."

I walked ahead of my new acquaintance cautiously towards the chateau, crossing the gravel path.

The three-story chateau towered over me as I approached. The exterior was elegantly decorated in white stone under a blue, steel rooftop in typical French fashion. The garden encompassed the whole estate, decorated with long lines of rose bushes and hedges, and accented with Roman style pots.

I approached the main entrance to see it through the doorway; the inside was similarly decorated to that of the Louvre, embedded with lavish French furnishings, polished floors, and stone columns.

"Turn left," Arcadia ordered.

THE COLONEL'S LOST VAULT

I turned and followed the series of doorways ahead of me until the path finally ended at a wide staircase leading down to the lower foundation. I made my way down the steps, hearing the sound of grinding and hammers chiseling away at rock. I reached the bottom step to find myself standing in a stone cellar, now converted into a makeshift artist's workshop filled with people.

Everyone inside halted working and looked at me with fearful gazes. I stepped further into the room, scanning each of them as I passed. Artworks of all various styles sat on easels, side by side next to unfinished works that were copies of the original beside them. I paced around the room, seeing each one of the dozens of artists around me covered in both stone dust and paint.

"You're making duplicates," I said to Arcadia.

"Of course," Arcadia replied.

I approached one of the painters. He looked tired and half-starved to death beneath his curly brown bangs. Before him was one of Monet's many garden pieces, speckled with vibrant splotches of green, blue and dotted pink lilies.

I stood before the painting, reflecting on the man who had painted it; one who had lived a life of hardship, yet was filled with awe-inspiring passion for color.

"Someone once told me, art is about more than the colors and patterns we scribble upon a canvas." I turned back to face Arcadia, expressing my sincerity. "They're stories." I continued to walk along the rows of art as I spoke: Di Vinci's, Carvagios, Rem-

brandts, even Jean Ingres's Grand Odalisque... They were all here. "They're people's lives. Lives stained on canvas. Lives printed in ink."

I stopped and turned to a tall statue in the center of the room, covered with a white cloth. I reached out and pulled the cloth back to see the Winged Victory hidden away underneath; beside it was a nearly finished replica. "Lives carved into stone..."

Arcadia approached me, carrying with her a cold glare.

I replaced the cloth. I turned back to face her, expressing my sincerest desire. "How long do you need to finish it?"

For a full year, an army of Paris's finest artists had joined together at Château de Valençay in an effort to create a collection of duplicates from the museum. They worked day and night, creating replicas that shared every inch of detail. When I arrived, they had only a quarter left to finish. I gave them a deadline of two weeks to finish, and only two days to finish the Winged Victory.

I returned to the museum with the duplicates they had finished, blaming the death of my driver on rebellious actions in the Paris streets along the way. Himmler never noticed the difference between the two statues. Two days later, I had the duplicate of the Winged Victory hauled to the museum for its unveiling before the Führer. As I watched the Party's self-proposed greatness drink and celebrate under a false idol and saw once more how easily they could be deceived. Their new empire was about to be built upon lies and deception. Half of the works they praised would be fake. And I couldn't help but smile for the first time in years.

The Colonel's Lost Vault

I hold hope that this war will soon end, as the Allies have begun to make an offensive in France, along with an offensive to the south pushing up to the north, here in Italy. Under orders, I have been called back to Germany. Fischer has already made arrangements for the artwork yet to be submitted to the vault to be hidden away in another location. The Girl Braiding Her Hair fears being locked up in a crate again. As a result, I've turned to keeping her at my side at all times during my journey home. For the time being, I've chosen to hide her in plain sight, using one of my own beloved paintings from my days with Andrea to conceal her from the world. Along a trail paved in white, where I first protected Dürer from the world, awaiting the day when I too shall share the fate of Saint John.

May this page never see the sun and allow the works I've sworn to protect live in peace.

Peter Wagner

"Are you kidding me?" grumbled Corbin. "The art's fake?"

Sophie rubbed at her forehead with mixed feelings after learning the most recent news. "*Half* of it is fake."

"So that cuts the reward for the finding down to what?"

"One point five million pounds?"

Corbin sat down on his bed. "Do you think the other half's still there?"

Sophie closed the journal. "Only one way to find out. Even so, the last thing we need is someone selling fake artwork on the black market. Money is money, and those fake works still have value to those who can be fooled."

"All right. So where to, then?"

Sophie opened her backpack and took one of her nightly pills from within. She made her way over to her bed and laid down. She draped the covers over herself. "To Munich. Back to Wagner's hometown," she said, turning off the lamp in the room.

Fourteen
GERMANY

Our lives have *been torn asunder. Germany is in even worse condition than when I left. The streets, which once were filled with people, rest in silence. The many houses which blossomed with window gardens under varnished wood shutters have been reduced to their foundations. Germany sought to build a glorious new empire, only to be left clinging to what little we have left. The vault continues to remain secure, yet I don't know for how long. Goring has given up on his investigation of me, now tending to more pressing issues, as the Allies have made it to the Rhine. The retreat from the south took a critical toll on us. Upon crossing the border home to Germany, Volst came to greet me at the station, bringing grim news with him.*

The train clattered to a stop out front of the station as I gazed out the window, remembering my first shipment which had once crossed the same platform nearly nine years prior. I took hold of my belongings and stepped out of the passenger car to see Volst standing with his usual smug grin. The young man was now grown, and with him the title of Lieutenant.

"Colonel Wagner," said Volst, approaching the passenger car.

"Lieutenant. It's good to see you again," I replied.

I extended a hand for him to shake. Volst stared down at my hand with a blank expression.

"I, uh, expected Major Fischer to be the one greeting me," I added.

"Might I share a word with you in privacy, Colonel?" asked Volst.

"Perhaps another time, Lieutenant. These newest works need to be—"

"It regards Major Fischer, sir..."

I could immediately tell by his tone and stance that something wasn't right. I nodded in agreement, handing my belongings off to the nearest private. "Have these put in my car."

The private nodded and hurried away as Volst turned around and shouted at a squad of young privates, no more than thirteen or fourteen years old, all unloading a crate from the train. "All of you! Take that box into the office! Now!"

The privates loaded the box onto a dolly cart and began rolling it towards the station office. I watched Volst's face, sensing my influence over him had been lost as he cast a scornful gaze.

"Lieutenant," I said to him, making my request, "would you mind telling me what's the matter with Major Fischer, or perhaps we can discuss this another time?"

Volst made an about-face. "No, Colonel... Now would be an excellent time."

I followed him into the station platform office. Volst waited by the door for the privates to bring the crate inside. The crate bounced against the concrete floor as I winced, fearing for its contents.

"Go," Volst ordered the privates.

The privates all exited the office as he closed the door behind them, leaving just the two of us alone to speak. Volst walked over to the windows and pulled the blinds down, obscuring the view from the other soldiers unloading crates outside.

"Why the secrecy, Lieutenant?" I asked.

"I've always admired you from afar, Colonel. I've tended to each of your shipments as they've crossed the German border, with Major Fischer always there overseeing everything. However, it seems I've been used."

"I beg your pardon?" I replied.

"Major Fischer had himself an 'accident,'" Volst replied, grabbing a crowbar from off the bench beside the window.

I fell silent, shocked and fearful for my oldest friend's safety. "An accident?"

"He shot himself."

"What?! Why?!"

Volst spoke with a sinister tone with his back to me. "I learned he was keeping secrets from me." He turned and faced me. "Your secret."

Volst stepped forward and wedged the crowbar between the gap between the lid of the crate. He pried the nails loose and threw the lid and crowbar down on the floor next to him. He reached down into the crate, dragging the Forli hidden away inside by the frame. I could hear the piece scream in fright.

I stood in horror, unable to move or think.

"This, Colonel!" he said, holding the artwork. "You are a traitor to your country!"

Volst drew a knife from his belt.

"You care for these works so much, Colonel, allow me to create my own masterpiece upon one of them!" he said to me, a crazed look in his eyes.

"Stop!"

He dragged the blade across the face of the painting, cutting it open.

The painting screamed.

I shouted at him and drew my pistol. "NO!"

I fired a single shot. The bullet pierced his throat. He let go of the piece and his knife, then stumbled back as he clutched his throat. The blood seeped through the space between his fingers as he stared at me with disdain. I raised my aim and fired another shot into his forehead.

Volst fell forward at my feet, the blood pooling around his head and chest. I stood idle for a moment before quickly turning back to the crate. I examined the Forli, seeing the cut wasn't deep. I hid it away again, back inside the crate, then replaced the lid in a hurry.

A knock came at the door as I began hammering the nails. "Colonel?! Lieutenant?! What's going on?!"

I finished hammering three of the nails before I opened the door to see a young sergeant, no older than fourteen, standing before me. "Sir, we heard gunfire!"

I stepped to the side, allowing the sergeant to see inside. "Lieutenant Volst attempted to charge me with his knife. A plot to assassinate me."

The sergeant stood wide-eyed, gazing at Volst's lifeless body.

"Have this crate loaded with the others and take care of it. Then contact Major Weles and inform him what has happened."

The sergeant continued to stare as though he had never seen a dead body before.

"Sergeant!" I shouted at him, dragging him out of his daze.

"Yes! Yes, sir! Right away," he replied.

I watched the sergeant hurry away before stepping back out onto the station platform. I cast a tense stare at the young privates all around me, reestablishing my place among my animal kingdom before heading to the car waiting for me, where I finally broke down seeing the blood on me.

Volst learned of my secret. Thankfully, he never found the vault, though Fischer paid the ultimate price for it. For that, I owe him my own life. He was a genuine friend, and the most loyal of soldiers. Both my captains suffered the same fate, having heard the news of Volst's discovery and ending their lives before he could interrogate them. The accident was never investigated, as there was no court available. Yet, Volst's death came with its advantages. The men fear me once more, allowing me to fill the gap left by Fischer tending to the vault. None of them are allowed to enter. Each one of the crates is placed outside the door, and I move them all inside myself once they leave.

Word has spread that the Russians are on the move to the east, and with the Allies to the west, I sense this war will be over soon. For now, the works that have yet to be moved to the vault continue to wait in hiding. My job remains the same: defend these works to my final days. Though now I've begun to question whether they should ever be seen again by the world. Even after the fires have been extinguished, and the armies have laid down their arms, does this world deserve to have back what it once sought to destroy?

Colonel Peter Wagner

Sophie closed the journal, staring out the window and the mountainous countryside of Bavaria. As they drove through the village of Flintsbach, along the south German border, she noticed the decorated wooden shutters and window gardens among the many homes, just as Wagner had described them, now returned to their former beauty. A quaint village surrounded by soaring hills of larch and spruce trees.

"Any news on the frontline?" asked Corbin, giving a nod to the journal.

"Some," Sophie replied. "It seems I was right: Wagner returned to Germany, only to have his secret uncovered by one of his officers. It confirms he had a secret, something else in the vault, but his journal doesn't say what."

"Any theories?" asked Corbin.

"Gold? I know the Nazi's stole gold as well. Maybe he was looking to embezzle it. Use the money to rebuild Germany after the war himself."

"If that's true, that would make up for half of the vault being fake artwork." A wide grin appeared on Corbin's face. "You just made my day, Broadway. A whole vault filled with art and gold; that's some treasure island shit right there!"

Sophie pulled her phone from her pocket and pulled up Oz's phone number.

The phone rang only once before Oz's voice spoke out from the other end. "Are you on a flight back to Heathrow? Please tell me you're sitting on a flight back to Heathrow. Say it to me: 'Oz, I'm on my way back.'"

"Nope! On our way to Munich. Just crossed the German border out of Liechtenstein," Sophie replied.

Oz huffed at her. "Why?! What's in Munich? No. Nope. Nevermind. I don't want to know. I already know too much and I don't need to know any more than that."

"Tell Maple I'm in Liverpool now."

"Liverpool, eh? You best get online and start buying up trinkets from each one of these places you supposedly went to as gifts for her. Might sell these half-baked lies I've been telling her."

"What did you tell her?"

"Said you were still in Leeds, set to head back this morning."

Sophie lurched forward in her seat. "You told her I was coming home!?"

"She's suspicious! She kept squinting at me like a detective out of Scotland Yard. Big sister sees all and knows all!"

Sophie sighed and pulled the phone away from her ear. She rubbed her forehead in aggravation before raising the phone back up to her ear. "Go into her office and tell her I just snagged another lead in Liverpool. An old geezer named, uh... Michael. Michael B-Bel-Borish."

"Better be the Archangel Michael, cause you're going to need him in your defense when she finds out the truth."

"Just do it, Wizard! I'll be back soon. I'm getting close." Sophie hung up the phone and let out another aggravated sigh.

"Trouble with the missus?" asked Corbin.

Sophie glared at him before continuing to look out the window, now feeling even more eager to get to Munich.

♦ ♦ ♦

THE ALTE PINAKOTHEK— a grand stone hall decorated with arched windows before a large campus of green grass—towered before Sophie and Corbin as they climbed the steps up to the front entrance. They entered the museum to see several groups of tourists wandering the lobby while awaiting guided tours through the museum. Hall after hall was decorated with works of art as Sophie and Corbin began to meander the halls themselves, admiring the many paintings.

"So, this was his museum?" muttered Corbin.

Sophie stopped before a painting by Carl Rotterman, depicting the Athen's coastline from the island of Aegina at sunset. She marveled at the colors, now knowing first-hand the beauty it was meant to capture. She turned back. "This was his kingdom. His and hers."

Corbin admired the same painting. "I see now why he fought so hard for it."

Sophie turned around, imagining Wagner and Andrea sitting among the grand halls of the museum, surrounded by the world's many lives painted in color; the two of them sharing a loving moment over lunch as Andrea taught the man Sophie had come to know so well. Raphael, Ruben, Manet, Di Vinci; they were all here. Pieces from the world's most beautiful minds, all protected by these halls of stone, collected by two lovers set on sharing their beauty with the world. This was their kingdom, their story.

"Broadway, you okay?" asked Corbin.

Sophie looked at him, now feeling her tears wet her eyes. "I'm fine. Just… caught up in the moment. Let's find what we're looking for and split."

Sophie walked over to the museum map on the wall. "Wagner's first collection added to the museum was by Albrecht Dürer. So, we find Dürer, we might find the painting holding the clue, same as the statue of Saint George. Best place to start."

Corbin began to scan the map with her. He pointed at it. "Found it. Listed under the 15th Century."

Sophie dashed away from the map and made her way across the hall towards the 15th century gallery. A sign hung beside the open doorway with a self-painted depiction of Dürer. She entered the gallery to see the vast collection of ink and oil paintings hung around the hall.

"Now what?" asked Corbin.

"Look for one of Saint John the Baptist. It was Andrea's favorite," Sophie replied.

Corbin began walking around the hall to the left, scanning each one of the works. Sophie started her way around the right wall. She found Samson Rending the Lion, along with Joachim and the Angel still hanging in their rightful places.

Sophie stopped before an ink print of a man being beheaded; his body slumped over the chopping block while his head was being passed off to a woman carrying a tray. She read the placard, written in German: The Beheading of Saint John the Baptist, Dürer, 1510. She scanned her left and right only to see a group of tourists nearby, all seeming to be focused on listening to their female tour guide as she pointed at the self portrait of Dürer in the far corner.

Sophie checked for an alarm, only to find that the painting seemed to hang freely, unguarded for the moment. She pulled the base of the painting away from the wall, feeling around the backside of it. On the back was a card tucked away in the frame. She pulled the card out and replaced the painting gently, checking to make sure no one saw; she was safe.

Sophie slipped the card into her pocket and continued on down the row, pretending to admire the other paintings. She eventually came to the end of the hall where she met up with Corbin.

"Find anything?" asked Corbin.

Sophie gestured towards the next hall subtly, seeking privacy. She pulled the card out and looked at it out of sight of anyone. Printed on it was a swastika symbol with the words *'West storage, 12 down, 25 left'* written underneath.

"Come on," Sophie said, leading Corbin towards the west end of the museum. She began scanning each one of the halls for a doorway or corridor leading further into the museum, one blocked off to visitors. She spotted a set of steel doors in the far corner of the museum with an "employees only" sign.

Sophie and Corbin approached the doors and scanned the surrounding hall around them. Seeing the coast was clear, Sophie subtly opened the doors with her backside and drifted inside. Corbin followed her, keeping his own eye out for security.

Entering the next room was an elevator shaft, surrounded by a steel staircase descending into the underbelly of the museum. The two of them hurried down the staircase, only to find two long rows of movable, steel artwork modular cases built into a brick warehouse beneath the museum.

"Down twelve," said Sophie, pointing towards the end of the cases. She counted them out, stopping at the row marked twelve near the end.

"Left twenty-five." She turned the handle on the outside of the case, moving all the other cases in the line, allowing her access. Inside were four rows of paintings, hung behind glass. She scanned each one of the works, counting them out. The row ended just as she reached twenty.

"There's only twenty here," said Sophie to Corbin. She looked down at the card again. "I don't understand."

Corbin took the card from her and looked at it. "Maybe these cases were put in after the card was written. Which means, either the previous shelves are gone, or this isn't what the card is referring to."

Sophie stepped back into the main corridor between the two rows. She counted out the cases again. There were only fifteen on either side. She looked at the brick wall at the far end, noticing the rows of bricks laid into the wall. "Wait a minute…"

Sophie ran to the end of the rows and stood before the brick wall. She started scanning the bricks.

"What?" asked Corbin.

"If you had to stage a bunch of art, stolen from your own country about to be stashed away in a vault, where would you stage it?" asked Sophie.

Corbin's eyes widened with understanding. "Hidden in a museum."

"Exactly," Sophie replied, proceeding to scan the wall. Sophie noticed a brick at the top of the wall ahead, engraved with a small swastika symbol. She pointed out the symbol to Corbin. "Found you. Twelve down."

Sophie and Corbin both counted the bricks down twelve spots from the marking. They both stopped at a brick in front of them.

"Left twenty-five," muttered Sophie. The two of them began counting the bricks towards the left side, finally ending at the same one.

Sophie placed her hand over the brick. She felt around it, noticing it wasn't cemented into the wall.

She pressed it.

She heard the sound of heavy steel moving on the other side of the wall. A doorway, part of the wall, swung open and away from her.

Sophie looked back at Corbin as they both shared the same look and feeling of intrigue and excitement. She pushed the door open the rest of the way. She stepped inside, only to find herself standing in darkness. She scanned the wall to her right, noticing an old light switch. She flipped it.

The old lights in the hidden space flickered on, revealing a long, stretched extension of the warehouse. Her excitement and intrigue quickly faded. The hall was empty, with only three open wooden crates. Sophie and Corbin stepped into the space, hearing their own footsteps echo.

Sophie approached one of the open wooden crates; inside were stacks of steel dinner plates, all aged and rusted. She looked back behind her to see Corbin reach into the crate before him. He lifted up an old, green, wool blanket, similar to the ones Sophie had found in Greece.

The two of them wandered over to the remaining crates. They were empty as well.

"You're not the first to find your way down here," said a female voice, speaking in German behind them.

Sophie and Corbin both looked back over their shoulders to see the female tour guide from the Dürer exhibit standing in the doorway; she stood wearing her black vest over her white button-up shirt, her hair pulled back with a black headband.

She approached the two of them with her heels clicking against the floor. "Several people have come looking for that card. One of them was old; a sergeant during the war who had known the Colonel, along with his secret stashed away behind the Dürer. Another was the grandson of the Colonel's best friend, Fischer. They all found the same thing as you, though: a dead end."

Sophie held the card in her hand. She handed it back to the tour guide, sensing she meant no ill will.

The tour guide held the card for a moment before speaking. "He never left whatever it is you're looking for down here. This place has remained the same for over seventy years. Wagner was arrested by the Allies before he could come back and place it."

"We came the long way," Sophie said to her.

"I'm very sorry, in that case," replied the tour guide, speaking with honest sympathy. "If you wouldn't mind, though, I do have a tour to get back to. I haven't alerted anyone you're down here yet, and I'd like to keep it that way if you both agree to leave now."

Sophie looked towards Corbin, feeling defeated. Corbin nodded in agreement. Sophie hesitated, now understanding why Wagner's vault was never found. She nodded in agreement and began following the tour guide out. She watched the tour guide turn off the lights and close the secret door by pressing on the same brick.

Sophie pointed to the card in her hand. "What will you do with that?"

"Put it back where it belongs," the tour guide replied calmly. "Leave it for the next person who finds it, only for them to be left with the same dead end, so I can tell them the same grim news."

Sophie watched the secret door lock with a heavy heart. She followed in Corbin's wake as they both made their way back up the stairs, back into the museum halls.

The tour guide rested a hand on Sophie's shoulder. "I'm sorry. But some treasures just aren't meant to be found." The tour guide walked back out into the middle of the hall and clapped her hands together, getting the attention of her tour group, who had been left to meander. "Sorry everyone. Shall we continue?"

"Now what…?" asked Corbin, sharing Sophie's heartbroken expression.

◆ ◆ ◆

I was at *Castle Wewelsberg when word came of the Allies' arrival. The tanks were on their way, and SS Captain Taubert immediately fled like the true coward I knew him to be. The fol-*

lowing day, Himmler sent men to destroy all documents related to the SS, as well as the castle itself. I collected what works he had hanging in the castle and hid them away with the Girl at my home in Paderborn.

The war came to an end a month later, with the Führer ending his own life. The US troops found me at my home and arrested me, learning from an unburned report in Munich about the vault. I was held captive in a holding cell for nine days before a British Captain by the name of Oswald who had arrived with a US Colonel named Maxwell. The two of them asked me about the vault while a Private—a young man with a limp, wounded during D Day—stood by, writing down every word. I told them of my journey and my disloyalty to the SS. They didn't believe me, so I offered them a cryptic message, one yet to be placed in its hiding place.

They agreed to let me go under house arrest, preferring not to punish me for my crimes until the lost works had been found. I refuse to tell them as I see no difference between the Allies and the Axis. Both sides sought to gain advantages over the other throughout this war, and I believe they will only mistreat and propagandize my collection for their own cause. These works belong in the hands of those who were wronged.

As of these late hours, I remain locked away in my home, with my secret being the only thing that's keeping me alive. The Girl Braiding Her Hair still remains under my care, as proof to myself of my struggle. I shall protect her the same as the others; though, I fear I may never be allowed to leave my home again. I *should feel pride and accomplishment, yet all I feel is grief.*

The war has taken a toll on me, as it has with all soldiers. The young man who once sat along the Ammersee painting the ripples in the water has now faded, his eyes no longer able to take in the colors he once worshiped, now blending into puddles. This may be my last entry in this journal. And if it were ever to be read by someone other than I, know that I did what I had to in order to protect the world's most valuable works. 'Cause someone once told me art is more than just paint on a canvas. They are people's lives.

Colonel Peter Wagner

"Tʜᴀᴛ's ɪᴛ," Sophie muttered, sitting on the steps before the museum, reading the journal out loud for Corbin. "That's the last entry."

"So, that's all? He never told anyone where it was?" Corbin muttered.

"The only record of any clue he gave now rests with the US and British governments, probably burned or destroyed after the war, or filed away in some paperwork lost in an archive somewhere."

Corbin sighed. He continued to pace before her along the steps while Sophie continued to feel a weight in her chest of sadness and heartbreak. She had come so far, yet her road would lead her no further.

"So *now* what?" asked Corbin.

"What do you mean 'now what?' That's it, Corb; end of the road.

There are no more clues to follow. No trail to take."

"You're just giving up?"

"The vault is safe from Bjorn. Mission accomplished. Without the clue, he won't get any further, same as us. We've done our job. That art is safe, and no one will ever find it."

"But what about your story?"

"I can write what I've got. Probably won't be enough to keep my job, but at least I can try."

Corbin scoffed. "No, there has to be more!"

Sophie stood up from the steps. "There is nothing more, Corbin!" she shouted, "Wagner, his assistant, and Himmler were the only ones who knew where it was! Himmler poisoned himself during interrogation, and Wagner's assistant was killed defending it! Wagner was the only one! And he took that secret to the grave with him! No one else knows where it is! They're all gone, Corb!"

Corbin stood at the steps, clearly taken back by Sophie's tone. Sophie sat back down on the steps and buried her head in her hands. "We made a good run at it... You can go home now, Corbin. You're dismissed."

Corbin continued to stand before her with a downhearted expression. "...Need a ride to the airport?"

"I'll find my own way back," Sophie replied, lifting her from her hands, looking out across the courtyard away from him.

Corbin stood before her, visually hesitant as though he didn't want to leave. He began to descend the steps of the museum. He stopped, offering Sophie his last words of advice. "Don't be afraid to call me if the nightmares come back. And thank you… Traveling with you reminded me of why I joined the Raiders." He took a deep breath laced with grief. "Gung-ho, Broadway."

Corbin descended the steps of the museum, leaving Sophie alone with her thoughts.

She continued to sit with the journal in her lap, watching him walk away. "Gung-ho…" she said to herself.

Hyde Park Adventures

Fifteen

LONDON, ENGLAND

The clattering of keyboards and telephones ringing among STORY Magazine's head office battered Sophie's ear drums. She sat before Oz's desk—her head propped up with one hand, her elbow resting on the desk—gazing blankly down at Wagner's journal. A cup of tea invaded her space before she sat back to see who was holding it.

Oz stood at the entrance to his cubicle, holding the cup in front of her with his own tea mug in the other hand. "Bright spark you are today."

Sophie took the tea from him. Oz sat down at his desk and spun his chair around to face her. He sat quietly, sipping his tea.

Sophie drank the warm tea quietly, still staring at the journal.

"You started writing the story, yet?" asked Oz.

"No," Sophie replied, expressing her depression, "can't seem to find the will."

"Best not tell Maple that."

"Not tell me what?" asked Maple, peeking over the wall of Oz's cubical.

Sophie looked at Maple before sipping at her tea while glancing towards Oz nervously.

"Uh, I'm still working on editing Deacon's article for next week," said Oz.

Maple expressed a displeased, yet suspicious stare his way. "So long as you get it to me by Thursday. Speaking of which, glad to see you're back, Broadway. I'll be expecting that story of yours on my desk later this week as well, shouldn't I?"

Sophie turned her chair towards Maple, casting aside her grief just long enough to offer her a half-hearted smile. "Working on it. Should have it for you by Friday."

"Good. I'm eager to read it," Maple replied before walking away.

Sophie released her cheek muscles being held captive against their will. She rested her head back down on her hand, staring back at Oz's pencil holder.

Oz continued to drink his tea, seemingly enjoying her misery in his own way. "Almost midnight, Cinderella," he muttered.

"Shut up, Oz," Sophie replied. She turned away from him and hung over the journal. She stared down at the leather cover, trying to conjure up the will to write a story which she knew had no ending.

"You've got the pages you found, plus the journal. That's more than enough," Oz muttered.

"No, that's not enough. Without finding the vault, the story will just fall into the bin like all the other myths about it."

"Well, at least go take the journal back and fulfill one of your promises. Hopefully, she won't press charges."

Sophie sighed and stood up from her chair. She picked the journal up off the desk and tucked it into her bag, slinging her backpack over her shoulders as she draped her scarf around her neck. "Was fun working with you while it lasted, Oz," she grumbled before walking away.

"What about our date?!" Oz hollered at her.

SOPHIE WILLED HERSELF up the front steps of Oliwia's home, feeling every urge to get away. She stood before the door, hesitant to knock. She spotted the mail woman from before making her way towards the residence. The mail woman turned from sorting the stack of letters in her hand to see Sophie on the steps.

"Oh! Hello again," she said to her. "'Suppose I'll pass these off to you again?"

The mail woman held the stack out to Sophie. Sophie took the stack from her with a plain smile. "Thanks."

"Enjoy your day," the mail woman said, continuing down the block.

Sophie held the letters in her hand, now feeling obligated to knock on the door. She pulled the journal out of her backpack, ready to use it as a peace offering. She finally knocked.

The subtle sound of the floorboards beyond the door creaking caught her attention once more. The door opened to the sight of Oliwia; her smile disappeared upon seeing Sophie standing on the steps.

Sophie took a heavy breath and held the journal out to her. "I believe this is yours."

Oliwia took the journal from her delicately, along with the stack of mail. She held the journal for a moment, checking its condition. "I called my insurance agency after I found this missing. They told me they didn't send anyone. It would be at least polite for you to tell me who you really are."

Sophie swallowed, feeling her guilt now outweighing her wish to retreat. She spoke, feeling compelled to tell the truth. "My name's Sophia Lions. I'm a journalist for STORY Magazine."

Oliwia raised her chin. "A tabloid writer?"

Sophie nodded with a grimace.

Oliwia scoffed. She opened the journal. Her breath escaped her. She pulled out one of Wagner's missing pages, tucked away inside.

"I was going to write a story about your father, but… not anymore," said Sophie.

Oliwia's hands trembled as she unfolded the page from Athens. She began reading it; her eyes slowly started watering. She unfolded the second page Sophie had found in Florence. "You found his missing pages?"

Sophie nodded politely. "They're yours to keep. And rightfully so."

Oliwia held the pages for a moment in shock. She waved Sophie inside. "Come in. Come in, I want to hear all about your journey."

Sophie's guilt turned to confusion. She followed Oliwia into her home as she closed the door behind her. The elderly woman made her way into the kitchen, clasping the pages as though they now meant more to her than the journal itself. Sophie spotted the Mezuzah on the door frame, now understanding it was Andrea, presumably Oliwia's mother, who had been of Jewish heritage as well as Romanian. She watched Oliwia sit down at the table to read the pages more closely, finding it strange that Wagner didn't seem to mention Oliwia in his writings before.

Sophie watched Oliwia struggle to compose herself, reading the story of her father and mother's final heartbreaking moment together. Oliwia stood up and grabbed the dry cloth draped over the sink; she held it over her nose and mouth as she continued to read the page and weep. Sophie stood in the kitchen doorway, remaining silent, allowing her to cherish the moment.

Oliwia finished reading the page. She dabbed her eyes dry. "Sorry," she said with a sniff. "I remember him writing these pages when I was a little girl. I always wondered what was on them. I suppose you've read them?"

Sophie nodded. "Yeah... He was a good man. A sweet man. I'll admit, I had my own assumptions about him at first, but I'm glad I learned the truth. I found the first one in a cave off the coast of Athens. The second was hidden with a statue at the Bargello Museum in Italy. I never found the one he planned to leave in Germany."

Oliwia chuckled. "He was arrested by the Allies before he could write it down. I could have told you that *before* you went traveling across the globe for them."

Sophie smiled and laughed. "Yeah… 'Guess I should have told you who I was from the beginning."

"No. Now I'm glad you didn't. Had you told me you were another tabloid writer, I would have shooed you out the door and these pages would have never found their way home."

Sophie offered her a warm smile. "They belong to you."

"No," Oliwia replied. She picked the journal up off the counter. She slipped the pages back inside and handed the journal back to Sophie. "They belong to you, now."

Sophie held the journal in her hands, feeling humbled. Oliwia offered her a teary smile before shuffling into her living room. Sophie turned around to see the painting by Wagner hanging on the wall in the kitchen, now seeing the caring man within, painting along the Ammersee. A man forced to live a martyr's life among demons.

Sophie leaned over to see Oliwia open the lid of an old wooden box near her sitting chair in the living room, similar to the one she had found in Athens.

"There were three keys originally. Himmler's was always fake. It would never open the vault. The other one was the one my father entrusted to his best friend, Fischer. He destroyed it following his death, leaving this as the only one left."

Oliwia pulled a brass key out of the box. She admired the key for a moment before handing it to Sophie.

Sophie held it in her hands, admiring the ornate design of it. The man of beauty had even crafted a fitting key for the secrets he held.

"It's yours," said Oliwia.

Sophie looked up at Oliwia in shock.

"Let it be proof," Oliwia added, "proof for you at least that it really does exist."

Sophie smiled with gratitude.

"And," Oliwia wandered into the kitchen. She pulled the painting off the wall and handed it to her, "take this."

Sophie took the framed painting from her with her free hand. She stared at Oliwia, confused as to why she was giving her everything which she seemed to hold so dearly.

"He would have loved to meet you. A soldier, one with heart. I'm just happy to know his most cherished belongings are now in the hands of someone who sees him for the man he truly was; not the one he painted for the world. A good man."

A knot formed in Sophie's throat. She rested the painting against the wall at her feet before embracing Oliwia in a hug. "Thank you."

Sixteen

WITHIN THE HALLS of history's troubled past, Sophie sat in London's Imperial War Museum, surrounded by relics of war as she typed Wagner's story out on her laptop. She could find no other place of comfort to write such a story. She continued to type her newest—and possibly her last—story with each keystroke focused on painting a vivid picture of the martyred man.

She glanced away from her laptop for a moment, seeing Himmler's fake vault key in the display case nearby. In her bag was the truth, and she was now compelled to reveal it to the world. Beyond myth was a vault built on deception, with the purpose of never sharing its treasure with tyrants and selfish ideologies.

Sophie flipped through Wagner's journal, refreshing her memory as she wrote. As she reached the final paragraph, she hesitated. She had built up a beginning, but now found herself faltering at the end. Once more, her mind dwelled on the ever-lingering question.

"Where did you hide it?" she muttered to herself.

"Holding up alright in here, Lions," asked the museum security guard, Charlie, over to Sophie.

Sophie was drawn from her thinking to see her older friend Charlie standing in the doorway to the exhibit hall, dressed in his uniform while messing with his favorite yo-yo.

"We're closing in fifteen," added Charlie. "I can keep the room open longer if you'd like? Just don't try nothin' funny again."

Sophie chuckled. "I'm good. Thanks for the offer though."

"You look puzzled in here? Something on your mind?"

"Just... Running out of road to follow at the moment."

"Well, you know where I would go then?"

Sophie shrugged at his question.

"Back the way I came," Charlie suggested. "Ya never know what you might have missed."

Charlie returned to his watch as he strolled away with a carless sway in his step, playing with his yo-yo.

Sophie chuckled at Charlie's carefree attitude. She closed her laptop, choosing to think about the ending more at home. She picked up Wagner's journal and flipped through the pages lazily, taking Charlie's suggestion She looked at the last page as her eyes crossed a series of words.

...a young man with a limp, wounded during D-Day,...

The Colonel's Lost Vault

Sophie closed the book and put it back into her backpack along with her laptop. She flung her backpack over her shoulder as she made her way towards the exit of the museum. She stepped out onto the busy sidewalk of London's southern city of Lambeth, then stopped.

"A private... A young man with a limp, wounded during D Day," said Sophie out loud to herself, "No... No! No way! There's no way!"

Sophie unslung her backpack and pulled the journal from her bag again, flipping back to the page. She read the line again.

I was held *captive in a holding cell for nine days before a British Captain by the name of Oswald who had arrived with a US Colonel named Maxwell. The two of them asked me about the vault while a Private—a young man with a limp, wounded during D-Day—stood by, writing down every word.*

Sophie stared into the void before her in realization.

"Rupert...!"

Sophie took off towards the underground station, her feet now following the rhythm of her heart rate.

♦ ♦ ♦

SOPHIE RAN UP the stairs of her flat building and down the hall. She quickly began pounding on Rupert's door, waiting eagerly while hearing movement on the other end.

253

Hyde Park Adventures

The door opened to the sight of Rupert holding a pot of table flowers. "Oh! My lady. Pleasure to see you when the sun is about for once. 'Was just given the flowers a drink."

"Rupert, you said you were a transcriptionist during the war while stationed in Germany, right?" asked Sophie, partially out of breath.

Rupert chuckled. "Is that what they called it? I just always called me'self an errand boy."

"Did you ever work for a British Captain named Oswald?"

"Oh, you mean Doc Oswald? 'Course! We always called him Doc though on the account he was a quack before the war. Stern man, sharp as a knife."

"Were you there when he interrogated a German Colonel by the name of Wagner? Something about missing art?"

Sophie held her breath.

Rupert squinted for a moment. He tapped on the flowerpot in his hand in thought. "Mmm... Can't say I've heard the name before."

Sophie let out a disappointed sigh.

"We did interview a Colonel about some missing art, though. Waschke, I think his name was," Rupert added.

Sophie's eyes grew wide. "Waschke... Andrea Moreen Waschke. He used her last name…!" she muttered.

"Yeah! That was the name of his wife. 'Said the poor thing died before the war. We interrogated him in Paderborn. I still have a copy of the transcripts in one of the boxes here in my flat."

254

Sophie stood in shock, her skin covered in goosebumps.

Rupert waved her into the flat. "Come on in. I'll see if I can find it for ya."

♦ ♦ ♦

`A year. A year to the date` as a matter of fact. A year had passed, and my knee was still on the mend. Was D-Day, June 6th of 1945, when I was called from my cozy office in Borchen—a few kilometers outside of Paderborn—with a request to scribe the week's interrogation of several soldiers and officers who had surrendered to the Allies, and were currently under house arrest. I can only guess that Doc Oswald wanted to keep an eye on me while I awaited my grant to return home.

And on that day of days, unlike D Day, I was late. Without the white noise of artillery and gunfire in the distance, lulling me to sleep every night, I had become restless. And today I was paying for it. I hobbled across the square to the town hall with my typewriter in my arms, my shoulder bag dragging me down with paper, and hurried into the lobby to find Doc and an American Colonel sharing a discussion before the lobby sofa.

"Sorry I'm late, sir," I said to Doc as I approached him.

"No harm done, Private," Doc replied, reading through the pages. "Go ahead and get yourself ready and we'll be with you in a moment."

I nearly dropped my typewriter as I tried to point to the council chamber doors. "In there, sirs?"

Doc looked away from the pages and smiled at me. "Yes, Private. Hop to it."

"Sir," I replied, hobbling away.

I heard the American Captain's grumbled voice speak to Doc as I stepped away. "Young buck, ain't he?"

"Old enough to have fought, Captain," Doc replied. "Private McBride has been with us since Normandy. He's as loyal as he is stubborn. There's no better man fit for the task."

I opened the door to the council chamber to see two tables setup before the council desks, witness to only the vacant audience chairs. At one table was a man, sitting patiently, dressed in a wrinkled grey cotton shirt, aged well into his forties or fifties, with his hair neatly combed.

I shuffled down to the open table beside him and began setting up my typewriter, trying not to make eye contact.

"Are you all right, Private?" the man asked politely in English, with a German accent.

I hesitated to responde, both nervous as well as caught off guard. "Fine. Just take a bit of time to get around, now. That's all."

I continued to set up my typewriter.

"How did it happen?" he asked.

"D Day, sir," I replied, in kindness.

The man expressed a look of heartbreak as he averted his gaze down to the table before him. "I'm sorry to hear that."

I pulled the blank sheets of paper from my bag, struggling to see any evidence or inkling of a man motivated by hate or selfish pride as I had expected to find in the Nazis. I sat down before my typewriter as I heard the doors to the chamber open. The man raised his chin up, almost as though he was ready to face whatever justice the Allies had in store for him.

Doc sat down at the table beside the American Colonel.

"Ready, Private?" Doc asked me.

I nodded. "Ready, sir."

I watched Doc's lips under his brown mustache closely, typing out his every word as he spoke. "I'm Captain Oswald of the 20th Infantry Brigade. This is Colonel Maxwell of the US 3rd Armored Division."

The American Colonel, now known to me as Maxwell, continued to sneer at the man sitting across from them.

"And your name?" asked Doc.

"Peter Waschke," the man replied.

"Don't you mean Colonel?"

Waschke didn't respond. He continued to share the same cold and stone look as the Colonel, almost as though he was adopting the face I imagined.

Doc expressed a frustrated look. He whispered something to Maxwell in his ear, who then stood up and proceeded out the council doors for a moment.

"Where's my daughter?" asked Waschke.

"Your neighbors agreed to look after her while we conducted our investigation," replied Doc. "Do you have any other family, Mr. Waschke?"

"I had a wife... Andrea..."

"And what happened to your wife?"

Waschke sat quietly for a moment. He hung his head as I got another glimpse of the man I had seen inside. A man who's troubles must have lasted longer than the war itself. He finally spoke in a grumble. "She died before the war."

"I'm sorry for your loss..." Doc replied.

"We've all lost many, Captain. Some more than others, and in ways that'll haunt even our grandchildren."

Then Maxwell reentered the room carrying a folder with him. He handed it to Doc. "We may not know your real name, Colonel, but we did find your address here in Paderborn. Seems you are one of a few Colonels that worked up at Wewelsburg Castle. One standing second row behind Himmler himself it seems, devoted to gathering art."

Maxwell examined the documents with a smug grin. "You boys weren't very tidy about your clean-up it looks like."

"I'm not your enemy, Colonel," Waschke replied.

"Not anymore," said Maxwell, throwing the paper down

on the desk before him. "Now you're our prisoner. And until we pardon you - if we pardon you — you will continue to be our prisoner."

Doc leaned forward in his chair, adopting a strict and serious tone of voice. "Where is the art, Colonel?"

Waschke sat quietly, visibly weighing his own options in his mind. "Hidden."

"Hidden where?" asked Maxwell, sounding ill-humored.

"Somewhere safe."

"Safe from who? There's no one to hide it from anymore. If you're not our enemy, then why keep it a secret any longer?"

Waschke sat back in his chair and offered the Colonel his testimony. "From one Colonel to another, you and I know there will always be men who will seek to poison the beauty of this world and use it for power. I have witnessed my country's own soul be torn from its body by such men and sewn back together with a dark needle and thread. So long as the folly of men continues to corrupt the innocent, I will not tell you where it is."

"Surely there's a paper trail you boys overlooked," said Doc.

"There is. The one I left for myself..." Waschke replied.

"Leading where?" asked Maxwell.

"A vault."

I stopped typing for a second. Waschke met my gaze

with a glance before continuing to speak. I continued to type.

"The one I built. I filled its halls, hoping to protect the world's works from men like those you stopped, as well as men like yourselves. Men who now break down my door, all doors of my home country, and take what they wish like marauders and bandits. Civilized men turned greedy. I left a trail behind that only I, or someone with all the pieces, would be able to follow. However, I never got the chance to leave my final bridge needed to cross the river of my mind. Which leaves me as the only one who knows where it is. Of course, what is a puzzle without its final piece?"

"What was this 'last bridge' you wanted to leave behind?" asked Doc.

Waschke sat quietly for a moment. He glanced towards me as I finished typing out Doc's last sentence.

"Beneath our Castle," he said.

Maxwell snickered, standing up from his seat. "Looks like we know where to look then."

"You'll never find it, Colonel." Waschke replied. "No one will. And for the better."

"We seek only to return those works to the people they belong to," said Doc.

"They belong to the world, Captain. Not to any one man, or woman for that matter. And until the world is ready to have them again, they will remain hidden. A day I fear may never come again."

Doc scoffed and stood up from his chair. "Start your search at Wewelsburg."

"I'll send my men up there this afternoon and have them start combing the place from the top down," replied Maxwell.

"Thank you for your honesty, Colonel," said Doc, nodding to him before turning around. "I'm sure we'll be in touch. That'll be all, Private McBride. Thank you."

Doc and Maxwell both marched towards the exit as I finished my last line.

"Captain!" Waschke shouted, still sitting in his seat.

Both officers turned back to face him as I pulled the sheet from the typewriter.

"My daughter?" he asked.

Doc looked towards Maxwell with a less than serious face. The two of them exchanged words out of hearing range.

"I'll see that she remains under your care," Doc replied from across the chamber. "You will remain under house arrest for the time being in case we have further questions. You should be thankful, Colonel. I've agreed to spare your life because of her."

The two officers walked away, leaving myself and Waschke alone in the chamber. I continued to pack up my sheets of paper as Waschke sat in his chair, staring off into the open air.

"Might make a copy of that for yourself, Private," he said to me, glancing at the transcript in my hand.

Sophie finished reading the last line of the transcript. She sat on the floor, surrounded by Rupert's copied transcripts with a grin forming across her face. "Wewelsburg."

"So, you have his journal? Always wondered what his real name was," grumbled Rupert, sitting in his chair, reading through the journal.

Sophie stood up from her place on the floor and grabbed her backpack, then ran over to Rupert. She took the journal from Rupert's hands and kissed him on the top of the head. "Thanks, Rupert!"

"Any time, my lady! I suppose you'll be needing me to watch Marco again?" Rupert shouted to her as she ran out the flat door.

Sophie hurried down the stairs of her flat building, dialing her phone. The phone rang for a brief moment as she stepped back out onto the street, facing towards Hyde Park.

"Hello…?" said Corbin's voice on the other end, sounding ill-humored.

"I found it, Corb!"

Corbin fell silent for a brief moment. "You what?"

"I found the vault! It's at Wewelsburg Castle in Germany."

"Wait… How?"

"Someone close to me held the answers. I'll tell you about it later. Can you meet me in Paderborn, Germany?"

"Sure. When?"

"As soon as you can," Sophie replied, making her way down the stairs to Hyde Park Corner station, already on her way to Heathrow Airport.

"A'ight," Corbin replied.

"And Corb... I'm sorry for what I—"

"Forget it, Broadway. As I said, you have nothing to be sorry for. Remember: gung-ho for life, girl."

Hyde Park Adventures

Seventeen

PADERBORN, GERMANY

Sophie stepped out onto the curb of Paderborn's Lippstadt Airport, under an early morning sun. Her phone rang as she pulled it from her pocket to see Oz was calling her, once again. She declined the call knowing she would explain everything to him once she got back. She waved down a local taxi, eager to get to Wewelsburg Castle.

A cream-colored taxi began to approach the cub. The driver was suddenly forced to swerve out of the way of a merging black Range Rover stopped a few feet down the curb from Sophie. Her fatigue from the late-night flight was replaced with fear. A pale-skinned man in his mid-thirties wearing a brown leather jacket stepped out of the passenger side. He began to approach her with one arm tucked into his jacket, his attention solely on her with a forceful stare.

Sophie took several steps backwards, sensing he wasn't one of her sister's friendly CIA escorts as his pace quickened with her own. She turned around and began running through the crowd of people standing along the curb as the man started to chase after her.

She hurried through the sliding glass doors of the terminal, colliding with someone standing in her way. She took a step back to see the stranger's face.

"Miss Lions. Funny running into you here in Germany," said Bjorn, in his usual thick, Scandinavian accent.

The man who had been chasing her stopped at Sophie's back and waited. The man kept his hand tucked into his jacket, seemingly waiting for Bjorn's word.

Sophie turned to Bjorn and sighed. "You plan on killing me in public, Bjorn?"

"No. If I wanted to kill you, I would have done so while you were back in London. While you were writing at the war museum or even on the plane ride here. During that time, I sensed that you discovered something. Otherwise, why would you come all the way back to Germany?"

"Maybe I needed a vacation away from you. I don't know how to say this Bjorn, but I think we should really look into seeing other people."

Bjorn snickered. "Load her in the car."

The man behind Sophie took hold of her by the bicep. He pulled her backpack from her with his free hand, then dragged her across the curb towards the Range Rover. Sophie hopped into the car willingly, seeing another man waiting for her in the backseat with an UMP submachine gun resting on his lap. Sophie sat in-between Bjorn's newest hired hands as her capturer hopped into the passenger seat.

Bjorn pointed towards the airport exit ramp. "Drive."

The car pulled away from the airport, leaving Sophie with nowhere to go.

Bjorn drew his pistol and pointed it at her. "I know you found it. So now I want you to tell me: where is the vault?"

"I don't know. Wagner never left his clue in Munich," Sophie replied calmly.

"Yet, you came all the way here. Why?"

"Just a hunch."

"You journalists have a knack for getting too far in over your heads; you seek to show the world the truth, only to end up as casualties yourselves. So, allow me to offer you my security services once more, Miss Lions. I'll protect you from those that may do harm to you and this time, all I ask in exchange is one thing: the vault."

"I felt safer at the airport, Bjorn."

"You lead me to the vault, Miss Lions, and the treasure inside, and I will consider our previous arrangement settled. I will go my way, a wealthier man, and you will have your story. If you cooperate, I might even allow you to keep one or two pieces for yourself as evidence. Refuse…?" Bjorn pulled the hammer back on his gun.

Sophie scanned the car, seeing the steely gazes of the two men beside her. She pointed towards her backpack at the feet of the man in the leather jacket. "Can I have that for a moment?"

The man looked towards Bjorn.

"Why?" asked Bjorn.

"My answer's in there," Sophie replied.

Bjorn nodded, keeping his gun pointed at her. The man handed her the backpack.

"Nothing funny, Miss Lions," Bjorn said to her.

"You really think I brought my gun to the airport?" Sophie replied.

The two mercenaries both shrugged in agreement.

Sophie pulled out the typed transcript page from Rupert. She handed it to Bjorn. "Wewelsburg. Wagner's last clue says it's 'beneath our castle.' The SS used Wewelsburg Castle as a headquarters, and Wagner was found living here—in Paderborn—at the end of the war. So, there you have it. The vault is beneath Wewelsburg Castle."

Bjorn began to read the transcript while the man with the automatic weapon took over guarding Sophie.

Sophie noticed the road sign for Wewelsburg Castle posted along the road out the window. "Might wanna turn left up ahead."

Bjorn looked away from the transcript. He glanced back at Sophie with a glare of contemplation.

"Do as she says," he said to the driver.

The driver made the left turn.

Bjorn handed Sophie back the transcript page. "An honor to be working with you again, Miss Lions."

Sophie smiled back at him, feeling less than flattered.

THE COLONEL'S LOST VAULT

◆ ◆ ◆

GAZING THROUGH THE windshield, Sophie could see Wewelsburg Castle ahead perched along the top of a hill overlooking fields of farmland. A single tower to the north guarded the lower plains while the rest of the castle watched its flanks.

The castle disappeared behind the surrounding township, then reappeared as they drove up to the visitors' parking lot. The castle and parking lot were vacant as though closed for the day. Bjorn and his men stepped out of the car as the man with the submachine gun waved Sophie out.

Sophie stepped out before the grand stone castle in the drizzling rain and turned back to grab her backpack from the car.

"Leave it," muttered Bjorn.

Sophie stopped. She let go of her backpack—now feeling disarmed—watching the car door close.

Bjorn directed her to take the lead with his gun. "You first, Miss Lions."

All four men kept their eyes on Sophie, seemingly waiting on her. She started up the sloping walkway leading towards the castle. Approaching the exterior, the stone halls began to loom overhead with a haunting feeling. She approached the main gate and inspected the old lock.

"Looks like it's closed. 'Guess we'll have to try again tomorrow," Sophie muttered, turning back to face Bjorn.

The man with the leather jacket kicked at the gate forcefully. The old lock gave way and clattered to the ground.

"Wow!" said Sophie, in a joking tone. "Look at that! 'Guess they're open! My mistake."

Bjorn waved her through the gate. Sophie took the lead again, stepping into the triangular shaped courtyard, lined with high walls dotted with windows.

"Where is it, Miss Lions?" asked Bjorn.

Sophie scanned the courtyard around her, noticing a visitor's map near the gate entrance. She began walking towards the map.

Bjorn and his men all pointed their guns at her with the clatter of hammers being drawn back, startled by her motion as though she was about to make a run for it.

Sophie raised her hands and expressed an appalling look at all of them. "Jesus Christ, can't a woman check a map? Not like I've been here before."

Bjorn and his men all exchanged glances of shame. They lowered their weapons.

Sophie shook her head and scoffed, annoyed by Bjorn's new trigger-happy companions. She checked the map as she spoke, "Just like men, not wanting to ask for directions."

Alongside the map was a brief summary of the castle and its history. Towards the bottom was the year 1933, accompanied by the notice of the SS expansion to the North Tower, the same year Wagner

The Colonel's Lost Vault

agreed to build the vault. Sophie pointed towards the tall tower across the courtyard to the north. "Base of the North Tower."

"After you, then," said Bjorn.

Sophie took point, making her way towards the doorway leading into the tower. She scanned the windows and rooftops above her, trying to formulate a plan of escape. She spotted movement in the tower window above, behind the reflection; someone else was here.

Sophie opened the old wood-and-iron door at the base of the tower before her. Ahead was a short hall with a stone spiral staircase leading down to her right and up to her left. She waited for Bjorn and his men before moving on.

Bjorn approached the doorway and looked down the steps. The lights were off, leaving the stairwell steeped in darkness. He nudged Sophie towards the steps leading downward.

"Pff!" Sophie snickered at him. "What's the matter, Bjorn? Expecting a dungeon filled with ghosts?"

"I don't like surprises," he replied.

Sophie took in a deep breath of the aged castle air and began to make her way down the steps. The darkness continued to get worse as she held onto the railing. She could hear the faint sound of water droplets trickling over the stonework ahead as she reached the bottom.

Sophie pressed forward, seeing only the black outline of the hallway ahead with a display case to one side. She ran her hand along the display case, hearing Bjorn and his men following her.

"Find a light switch," said Bjorn.

Bjorn's men moved ahead of Sophie and began feeling around the walls. Sophie's hand crossed over something metal resting on the glass top of the display case. She felt it with her fingertips, immediately knowing what it was by memory; a Glock seemingly left for her, and she knew by whom.

Sophie picked up the gun and tucked it into the waist of her pants and under her shirt, before hearing one of Bjorn's men flipping on an old light switch.

The old lights flickered on as she found herself standing before an open, arched doorway. Beyond it was a circular stone chamber with a sunken circular floor at the center, decorated with eerie paintings of thin, starved, mournful people. Sophie stepped into the chamber as a sign beyond the archway told the story of the room. It was called the Crypt.

Sophie made her way around to each one of the paintings, seeing they were depictions of victims of the holocaust; a grim reminder of those who had life's greatest gift stolen from them. The chamber which had once been used for cult gatherings was now a memorial to those robbed of life.

"Where is it, Miss Lions?" asked Bjorn, his voice echoing throughout the hall.

Sophie looked up towards the chamber ceiling; in the center was a round stone relief of a swastika. She looked down at the sunken pit in the center of the chamber, presumably used for either bonfires or as a gathering point. She inspected the floor. All around the central pit was a gap between the stone as though the floor itself was independent from the chamber.

"Here," Sophie replied, pointing at the floor.

Bjorn inspected it. Sophie began scanning the room even further.

Her eyes spotted a single stone column tucked away next to the wall as though it were the joining point between two halves. She approached the waist-high column. To one side was a small slit, just big enough to fit a key into.

"Looks like you'll go no further, Bjorn. Not without the key," Sophie said to him.

Bjorn turned his attention towards her. He stepped out of the pit and made his way over to the column. He felt the slit with his fingertips. "Wagner made three keys, Miss Lions: one for himself, one for his assistant…" Bjorn reached into his pocket. He pulled out a brass key. Sophie stared at it, realizing it was one she had seen before. "And one made for Himmler himself. One graciously 'gifted' to me by the Imperial War Museum."

Bjorn placed the key over the keyhole. Sophie grinned, knowing the key wouldn't work.

Bjorn slipped the key into the keyhole. The stone column began to turn as a whole, clockwise. Sophie expressed her confusion, watching the key spin and the column rotate.

The stone pit behind them quaked with the sound of grinding stone. Sophie and Bjorn turned around to see the stonework at the base of the pit now sliding away, revealing an open well into an abyss. The base of a stone platform rose up from the darkness below, spiraling clockwise as it ascended. The platform—engraved with the Nazi SS lightning bolts into the base—stopped at the top of the well. A single pull lever at the center of the platform controlled the platform's rise and descent.

"Into the mouth of Jörmungandr," said Bjorn, stepping onto the platform.

Sophie joined Bjorn on the platform, still uncertain as to how Himmler's false key had worked. Bjorn's men joined them, all sharing worried and fearful expressions.

"What's the matter, boys? Afraid of boobytraps?" said Sophie, trying to keep Bjorn's men on edge.

"Don't listen to her. She's trying to distract you," Bjorn replied.

Bjorn pulled on the lever. The platform slowly began to spiral counterclockwise, sinking down into the depths of the castle. Sophie looked up as they descended, watching as the chamber drifted away from her, along with her chances of escape. The stone counterweight for the platform, affixed by a series of ropes, rose past them towards the top of the well as they continued to sink deeper and deeper into the ground.

The platform came to a stop with a shuttering echo amidst the darkness. Sophie could feel a cool opening ahead of her as she took a few steps forward. The sound of her footsteps carried throughout a large room as she could hear Bjorn and his men right beside her.

"Anyone got a light?" asked Sophie.

She heard the flicker and saw the spark of a lighter behind

her. She looked back to see the man with the leather jacket holding the lighter, now aflame. Sophie gazed out through the dim, flickering darkness to see three rows of wood crates leading away from her. She spotted a lamp hanging on the wall to her right.

"Hey, you with the light," she said to the man.

"Isaac," the man replied with his name.

"Sure, Isaac. Whatever your name is. Bring the light over here."

Isaac walked over to her. Sophie took the lighter from him and held it up to the lamp to see it was an old gas lamp, tethered together to a chain of similar lamps; age had blown out the pilot light. She relit the pilot, then handed the lighter back to him.

"There's gotta be more. Light the rest," she said, pointing down the chain of lamps connected by piping along the wall.

Isaac continued further into the chamber, lighting the pilot for each lamp along the wall. Sophie looked back to see Bjorn and his other men lighting the remainder of the lamps along the far wall using their own pocket lighters.

Sophie followed the gas line to its source. She spotted a lone valve along the wall near the platform and slowly began turning it, hearing the gas once more flooding the line. The room began to brighten behind her as she turned around in awe.

A twenty-foot-high chamber made of solid stone, lined with three long rows of wooden crates, each labeled with black ink. At the far end was a winged angel—armless and headless—forever in stride up on a lone platform.

Bjorn flipped his lighter closed with an awestruck expression. Each of his men gazed around the chamber, seeing the hundreds of crates, each labeled with a system of inventory numbers.

Sophie began making her way down the far-right row towards the Winged Victory. Her eyes caught the sight of a power switch mounted on the wall. She traced the power line, noticing several holes drilled in the ceiling, scattered throughout the chamber, each packed with explosives; a trap presumably left behind by the Nazis to bury the vault, in case the Allies arrived, one that—thankfully—was never used.

Sophie continued on down the row, up the steps to the base of the Winged Victory. She stood before the statue, skeptical.

"You do not disappoint, Miss Lions," Bjorn said to her. "Dig in, boys!"

Bjorn's men scattered, each one looking for ways to open the wooden crates. Isaac found himself a crowbar and began cracking open the lid on a crate nearest the base of the steps to the Winged Victory.

Sophie circled the winged statue, noticing small chunks were missing from the wings. She glanced down at the floor, hearing something crunch at her feet. She pulled her foot back to see a cracked piece of the sculpture beneath her shoe. She knelt down to pick it up.

Isaac removed the lid from the crate, Bjorn joining him as he pulled the straw away. Isaac wrapped an arm around Bjorn in excitement, seeing the top frames of the artwork inside.

Sophie felt the piece of sculpture with her fingertips. It wasn't marble. She looked at the base of the statue, seeing the inside was made of a rocky, grey substance. She felt the rock, discovering it was concrete—concrete used to mimic the weight of a fake.

Sophie turned to see Isaac lift a painting out of the crate. It was a Monet. Only there was something wrong. The canvas was now riddled with spots of mold.

"Is it supposed to look like that?" asked one of the other men.

Bjorn took the painting from Isaac. He looked more closely at the surface, then checked the back. He threw the painting down on the ground, then withdrew another painting from the crate. A Rembrandt also covered in splotches with mold.

Bjorn tore each one of the paintings from the crate and continued to throw them across the room in anger. Sophie stood up beside the Winged Victory, unable to hold back her smug smile.

"They're fake!" bellowed Bjorn, throwing another painting against the wall.

Another of Bjorn's men opened a crate at the far end of the room nearest the platform. He reached into the crate and pulled out a stone the size of a watermelon. There were more stones inside—similar to those found along the Barvarian slopes—meant to give the impression of valuable weight.

"Looks like Wagner had us all fooled, Bjorn," Sophie said to him. "He never wanted Himmler to have the art. And neither will you."

Bjorn huffed in place for a moment. His anger-fueled breaths gradually began to transform into chuckles. He began to approach her, holding his pistol lowered at his side. Sophie continued to back away from him.

Bjorn stopped before the Winged Victory, breaking off a piece of the concrete from the wings as he spoke. "It was a disaster, what happened to you in Libya."

Sophie stopped in place, a cold sensation resonating within her, sown with fear. "How did you know about that?"

"I became partners with an old friend of yours when he learned he was being watched," Bjorn said, twiddling the concrete between his fingers. "He reached out to me, seeking my expertise, wanting my help in trying to find out what enemy was watching him and seemed poised to eliminate him. So, I formulated a trap."

Sophie watched Bjorn pace around the vault, inspecting the crates as he continued to speak.

"We arranged for one of his weapons exchanges to be made in public, where whoever was watching could see. And once it came time to talk business, we prearranged for the weapons to be moved with haste while I led him out through a tunnel we dug under the compound. We retreated to a more secluded location to talk business, all the while leaving a surprise for the ones who followed; a surprise… for you."

The pained cries and image of her friend Yorkie buried under rubble invaded Sophie's mind again. She felt a sweat start to brew on her skin as her heart rate quickened with her nightmares coming to life.

"Believe me, it pained me to do so," Bjorn said, tossing the concrete aside with his back to Sophie. "You all held potential in my eyes—skills which could be turned to a better line of work with no rules—which I could benefit from. I never told my client that I learned it was the CIA who had been watching him. And not only that, but Marine Raiders; a group of killers long forgotten, reborn. You can imagine the joy I was forced to suppress when I heard you had survived and got away. Captain Summers came back a broken man. But you… Sophie… Your name truly carries meaning with it! Antigone Sophia Lions! A woman born to be a warrior! A rogue lioness!"

Bjorn made his way around her with a crazed and obsessed look in his eyes. "I kept my eye on you from afar, seeing a possible prospect. Imagine my surprise when *you* contacted *me*, seeking my services. I was flattered. I thought to call my old client to tell him the good news but chose not to; I wanted to see how my hands had shaped you for myself. But after your failure to show me your worth to me in Marrakech, I decided to inform my client and perhaps claim some sort of reward on your life. *He* was the one who called for the bounty on you. Not me."

Sophie could feel her own fear starting to paralyze her.

"After learning of the possible fortune you had uncovered, I began to rethink my decision. I told my client of the treasure, and he agreed to allow me to keep half of the stolen works, as a finder's fee. Then you stole the journal back from me and showed me your true value: the value I always believed you had. So, I ended my partnership with my old client forever, all for you."

Bjorn approached her. He loomed over her as she stared into his maniacal gaze. A gorgon's stare which had already begun to turn her to stone.

"But I don't have to say his name. Because you're going to say it for me."

Sophie turned to stone as the name crossed her lips against her will.

"Nazer…"

Bjorn smiled, placing a hand on her shoulders. "You… You and I are of the same spirit, Sophie. A true crusader. One destined for glory. Seeing as there is no longer any treasure, I still prefer not to leave this vault empty-handed. So, I'll extend my offer to you, one final time."

Bjorn pulled the hammer back on his gun as he kept it down at his side.

"Join my ranks, and you'll have all the money and glory you could ever want, and you and I can kill Nazer together, along with anyone else who stands in our way. No more bureaucracy. No more taking orders. Just you and me, partners, bending the world's leaders to our will, using their secrets against them. You are the only treasure left here, now. And if I can't have you, then no one will."

Sophie remained petrified before Bjorn, unable to make a move or speak for the first time. Her nightmares held a conscious grip on her.

Bjorn raised his aim up to her stomach. "You are all alone down here, Sophie. No one will judge you. Make your choice."

Sophie tried to speak. As hard as she tried, she found her voice now held hostage as well.

The voice which suddenly spoke on her behalf was not her own, coming from the entrance to the vault. "She's not alone."

Sophie's paralysis weakened. She turned her gaze.

Corbin stood on the entry platform—a climbing harness around his waist and a climbing rope dangling at his back—holding an assault rifle aimed at Bjorn. "And she never will be. Gung-ho for life."

The sight of Corbin broke Sophie free from her nightmares. She seized control of Bjorn's pistol by the muzzle and forced it aside. Bjorn fired a shot past her as she drove her forearm into his throat, knocking him backwards.

Corbin opened fire. Each of Bjorn's men drew their weapons and began returning fire in Corbin's direction as the man standing beside Isaac fell to the floor, bouncing off one of the crates as he bled. Corbin dove down behind cover under the row of wooden crates nearest to him.

Bjorn recoiled from Sophie's strike, bashing her in the side of the head with the blunt end of his pistol. Sophie stumbled back and shook the stars from her vision in time to see him readying his aim again. She yelled in a headlong charge, driving her shoulder into his stomach in a tackle.

Bjorn slammed his back against the fake statue as the concrete crumbled around the two of them. He rolled to the floor as Sophie fell to her chest beside him, his gun sliding away from the two of them towards the far wall.

Sophie hurried to her feet, running back towards the row of crates where Corbin was hiding, hearing the whistle of Bjorn's men firing all around her. She dove behind the row of boxes, drawing the Glock hidden at her waist.

Corbin rose up from his hiding spot, firing off a series of rounds towards Isaac across the room. He ducked back down behind cover, locking eyes with Sophie at the opposite end of the row.

Sophie hurried towards him, crouched while keeping her head low. She shouted over the gunfire blasting throughout the vault. "'Could have jumped in a little sooner!"

Corbin shouted back at her as he reloaded. "'Saw you with Bjorn when you pulled up; 'figured I'd maintain the element of surprise!"

Sophie expressed her amusement and faith in her friend with a smile. She pulled the slide back on her pistol and rose out of cover to take two shots at Bjorn as he grabbed his gun from off the ground. Bjorn hurried down behind the opposing line of crates along with the rest of his men with Sophie's shots missing.

"I got a quick way out of here, but we need to deal with these guys first! I'm not stacked on ammo!" Corbin shouted over to her. He fired another volley of shots at Isaac before ducking back down again.

One of Bjorn's men suddenly stood up from behind the crate directly in front of them, forcing them to duck even lower to avoid being hit.

"Push!" Sophie shouted to Corbin.

Corbin and Sophie both propped their backs up against the crate. Together they forced the crate across the concrete floor, crushing and pinning Bjorn's man between it and the opposing row.

Sophie rose and fired two rounds into the man as he attempted to unwedge himself before ducking once more.

"We gotta get out of here," said Corbin.

Sophie looked over towards the wall behind her, seeing the switch for the trap laid into the ceiling only twenty feet away.

"Cover me, then get ready to run!" Sophie shouted to Corbin.

Corbin nodded. He rose up out of cover and began firing the remainder of his magazine towards Bjorn and Isaac. The two of them were forced to yield behind cover as Sophie hurried over to the switch.

She turned the switch, awaiting the sound of a timer.

Nothing happened.

A bullet buried itself in the stone wall to her right. She turned back to see Bjorn firing at her as she leapt back down behind the row of wooden crates again.

"Whatever that was, I don't think it worked! 'Got any other bright ideas?" shouted Corbin.

Sophie took a quick breath, trying to think of a new plan. She rose up from her hiding spot again and aimed towards the holes in the ceiling over Bjorn. "This is for Yorkie and Quarter Mile!"

She fired a single round. The hole above Bjorn exploded. A rainfall of rock and dirt showered over him as he disappeared behind the falling rocks. One by one, the explosion caused a chain reaction throughout the remaining charges one after the other. The vault quaked all around them with the ceiling caving in over them.

Sophie rose to her feet and ran towards Corbin, grabbing him by the arm before hurrying towards the elevator platform. She looked back over her shoulder just in time to watch Isaac be crushed by a large mass of rocks from the ceiling.

Corbin fell from Sophie's grip as a melon sized stone crossed his shoulder. He grabbed hold of his shoulder in pain as Sophie hurried back and helped him once more, leading him towards the climbing rope he had used to repel down.

Corbin fastened the rope to his harness. "Grab on!" he said to her.

Sophie wrapped her arms around Corbin's neck as he raised his arm, trying to fire up at the counterweight for the platform tied off to the end of the rope climbing rope above. He yelled out in pain, unable to make the shot.

"Lions!" shouted Bjorn's voice over the thunder from the chamber.

Sophie spotted Bjorn clawing his way towards her as the chamber continued to collapse all around him.

"Parting is such sweet sorrow, Bjorn!" Sophie took aim at the counterweight above her. She fired several rounds at it, dislodging the counterweight from the ropes which held it aloft. The weight plummeted, dragging Corbin by the belt up the elevator shaft as Sophie dropped her gun and held him by the belt with one hand.

Rushing towards the top of the elevator, Sophie felt her hand slip. She began to fall as Corbin suddenly reached an arm out and grabbed hold of her, hollering in pain from his shoulder as they continued to rise. The counterweight crashed against the base of the vault as Corbin and Sophie came to an abrupt stop.

Corbin hung from the rope near the top lip of the elevator shaft, unable to reach the ledge as he held onto Sophie with one hand. "Climb, Broadway," he grunted to her.

Sophie climbed her way up the front of Corbin, using his harness for support. She grabbed hold of the ledge and pulled herself up, then turned back and hoisted him up by the harness.

The two of them rolled over onto the ground among the crypt, both out of breath. A plume of dust billowed up from the opening to the vault as Sophie rose to her feet and removed the key hidden away behind the column.

The stone slab covering the vault entrance slid back into place as the column rotated back the other way. The crypt trembled with the sound of the well being closed as the collapsing vault fell silent below. Sophie sat down on the ground with her back against the wall, catching her breath.

"I'd be willing to settle down with one of those supermodel wives, now," said Corbin.

Sophie shared a laugh with him, thankful to know that—once more—she was never alone.

Hyde Park Adventures

Eighteen

BERLIN, GERMANY

THE BUSTLING CHATTER of travelers among Berlin's Tegel Airport encircled Corbin and Sophie as they stood in the terminal. The two of them stopped before Sophie's gate back to London, ready to share one final goodbye.

"You sure you don't want me to ride with you back to Athens?" asked Sophie, dressed in her usual flannel and scarf.

Corbin shook his head. "Nah. Thanks, but no thanks. I can only handle being around you in small doses. For all I know, we'd end up halfway around the world instead."

Sophie laughed. "I still owe you a car."

Corbin held up the keys to the SUV he had been driving. "Consider the debt paid," he replied. "I might hit your sister up about forging a new title for it though. Once I tell her who previously owned it, I'm sure she wouldn't mind."

"Whatever you tell her, just leave me out of it."

"You know, I was still in Germany when you called. Figured I'd take some time off. Maybe find a nice fraulein to have drinks with."

"Any luck?"

Corbin scoffed and shook his head. "I came to rescue your ass, didn't I?"

Sophie expressed a heartfelt smile. She wrapped both arms around him, feeling like the luckiest woman in the world to have such a great friend. "Thank you for being there."

"You know I always got your back, girl," Corbin replied, hugging her. "We Raiders stick together till the end. Don't ever be afraid to call me if you need anything."

Sophie stepped back from him and adjusted her backpack straps. "I will."

"And sorry you didn't find what you were looking for."

Sophie shrugged, accepting fate. "Guess the world's better off. It won't make the greatest ending of all time for my story, but having found a vault full of fakes is better than no ending."

"'Glad you got what you came for then," Corbin replied. "And thank you for dragging me out of retirement. You helped remind me of my purpose: defending this world from those who would do it harm. Sharing an adventure with you is something I'd be willing to do again one day."

"You could always come work with me in London?" Sophie offered.

Corbin chuckled with a nervous laugh. "Yeah… nah. I'll stick to the beach party security gigs for now. I won't tread on Oz's turf."

"Fair enough," Sophie replied.

Corbin expressed a long-lasting smile as she turned away. He started his way towards the terminal exit as Sophie watched him. He turned around and walked backwards as he offered her one final word of advice. "Keep your head down more, Broadway. But never stop moving."

"You too," Sophie replied.

Corbin turned back around and walked away as he made his way out of sight through the terminal security tunnel. Sophie took in a breath of relief, ready to return home, even without the ending she wanted.

Hyde Park Adventures

Nineteen

LONDON, ENGLAND

Hearing the busy phones of STORY Magazine's main office surround her, Sophie paced back and forth around Oz's cubicle, anxiously awaiting Maple's response to her story. Oz hovered over his desk, still studying Sophie's parchment page from Newark Castle. He continuously referred to a Latin guide open on his computer, then returned to reading the page with his magnifying glass.

"She hates it," Sophie said to him, expressing her anxiety. "If she liked it, she would be out by now."

"Would you just bloody stop?" Oz said to her, turning away from his work. "Just wait before jumping to conclusions. I'm trying to read eight-hundred-year-old Latin, meanwhile you're freaking out about the present at my back and it's very distracting."

Sophie sat down in the empty office chair next to his desk. "She doesn't usually take this long."

Oz placed the magnifying glass down on his desk with an aggravated grunt. "Would it help if I read this out loud for you? Maybe take your mind off your pending demise?"

"Yes, please," Sophie replied.

Oz picked up the magnifying glass again and pointed at the notepad and jar of pencils on his desk. "I'll read. You write."

Sophie grabbed the notepad and a pencil, awaiting Oz's word.

"Befallen thy divine King," read Oz, "hastened by armies of Louis and Alexander. Valiantly, he fought until his dying end, a loyal servant of God's good graces. As the Lord's angels carried him away with his final breath, the name for whom he entrusted God's crown he spoke. A ship bound for the inlet of the mud flats, guarded by knights in red cross: the son of Pembroke, keeper of England's name."

"That's it?" asked Sophie.

"Best translation I can give," Oz replied.

Sophie read the translation on the notepad.

"The 'knights in red cross' has to be the knight's templar, yes?" queried Oz.

"Most likely. 'The son of Pembroke?'" Sophie thought for a moment. "William Marshal I was the Earl of Pembroke during John's reign. When John retreated to Newark Castle, some of the barons who had cast him out rejoined his cause when they didn't agree with the French king, Louis VIII, becoming their new king. One of which was William Marshal's son, William Marshal II, who was the Earl of Pembroke."

"So, this William Marshal II took the crown jewels with him across the sea?"

"Based on this page, that'd be my best guess. Now to *where* is the big question."

Sophie jumped in fright as a set of papers hit Oz's desk beside her. She looked up to see Maple standing before the cubical, expressing an ill-humored look towards Sophie.

"You were in Leeds, huh?" said Maple, standing with her hands on her hips.

Sophie smiled, sheepishly. She raised a finger. "It was off the books. I didn't spend a single cent of your money."

Maple sighed, leaving Sophie to brew in her own suspense for a moment longer. "It's slow…"

Sophie felt a lump of worry start to form in her throat.

"But I like it, and you kept your word on not giving me any more receipts. So, I'm going to run it."

"Yes!" shouted Sophie, throughout the office, jumping up from her seat with joy. Sophie felt her feet come off the floor as everyone in the office stared at her.

"I'll pass it along," Maple added, trying to get her attention. "Though I want you to revise the ending again. End it on a higher note."

"Absolutely! I'll do it now!" Sophie replied, never having felt so relieved and excited in her life.

Hyde Park Adventures

Maple stood before Sophie with an embarrassed expression. She scoffed, watching Sophie drag Oz from his chair to hug him with joy. "All right! Have your victory lap and just get the revised version back to me by Wednesday," Maple said as she walked away from Oz's cubicle shaking her head.

"Wait! Wonder Woman! Does this mean I get to keep my job?!" Sophie shouted after her.

"What do you think?" Maple shouted back, stepping into the office elevator.

Sophie continued to smile with joy as she quickly grabbed her backpack from off the floor. "I gotta get home and make those changes."

Sophie dashed away from Oz's cubicle, then quickly stopped to hurry back and grab the translated page from the notepad. She kissed Oz on the cheek in a rush. "Thanks, Oz!" she said to him, before hurrying away towards the elevators.

Oz sat with a dazed look and smile, before he flinched and called after her, "Wait! So, does that mean we get to go on a date?"

Twenty

MARCO SAT PURRING in Sophie's lap as she read her article over again for the seventh time, petting him as she did so in thought. The blinking cursor on her screen waited impatiently for her response.

Sophie scoffed in defeat, setting Marco down on his bed before she began pacing around her desk.

"What was your secret, Peter?" Sophie mumbled to herself.

She noticed the painting Oliwia had gifted to her still resting on her kitchen counter. She sorted through her kitchen drawers, pulling out a hammer and box of nails. She turned to the wall beside her desk and pounded a nail into the wall, then hung the painting, surprised at the weight and thickness of the canvas.

Sophie adjusted the frame to be level, then took a step back. She admired the painting, taking in Wagner's colorful strokes of pure light along the Ammersee. She raised an eyebrow with an idea forming in her head.

◆ ◆ ◆

SOPHIE WAVED FAREWELL to her taxicab driver from the airport as she stood on the streets of Schondorf, a quiet village surrounded by farmland and nestled along the banks of the Ammersee. With one look, the beauty Wagner saw in every building was back to the way it once was: wooden-framed homes with flowers growing beneath every window—topped with red tile roofs—only now outfitted with satellite dishes and power lines. Yet, the peaceful inspiration remained all the same. The perfect place for her to finish his story.

A group of tourists rode past her on bikes before stopping at a local bike shop that was renting them out to visitors, as a way of enjoying the town's lakeside view. Sophie watched the shop owner reclaim the bikes from the tour group, knowing she had one view left to see.

◆ ◆ ◆

RIDING A BIKE along the dirt road hugging shoals of the Ammersee, Sophie's imagination began to wander into bliss. Thinking back on Wagner's story, she couldn't help but feel as though a chapter of her own had now come to rest. Her nightmares had subsided for the time being, yet the memories still weighed heavy on her heart.

Sophie brought her bike to a stop along the roadway and dismounted, walking towards the banks of the lake. She stood with the reeds blowing along the shore before her, watching the shifting waves dance in the sunlight. She looked to her right, imagining the sight of Andrea and Peter painting in each other's company, two lovers blissfully unaware of the future as they lived in the moment.

The sailboats floating with the breeze caught her attention before she heard the sound of something clatter a few yards away from her. A wildlife painter stood over a fallen easel, with the wind having dragged his work to the ground. He picked the easel back up and smiled at her.

"Guten tag," the man said to her.

Sophie smiled back in acknowledgement. She averted her gaze back out at the view, listening to the trees rustle behind her. A flicker of sapphire blue bounced off the water, reflecting off the skies above in the evening sunlight. She stared down at the water, seeing the ample blue ripple with the waves.

"'Hidden away along rolling banks. Along a coast of turquoise waters'…" she said out loud to herself.

Sophie scanned the road behind her, staring up at the rustling green trees covering the road with shade. She reached into her backpack and pulled Wagner's journal out. She unfolded the page she found at the cave in Athens.

"'A place well-protected under a shaded canopy'…"

Sophie placed the page and journal back into her bag and mounted her bike. She began riding back towards Schondorf, scanning along the left side of the road, opposite the bank.

She pulled the brake handle with her bike skidding to a stop along the road.

"'Along a trail paved in white'… " said Sophie, seeing a pathway of white stones leading up a hill through a meadow.

Sophie left her bike along the road and began following the pathway on foot. Ascending the hill, she looked back to see the lake in its entirety, sunken beneath the hills. At the end of the white stones was an old wood-and-stone cottage, long-since abandoned. The windows had all been broken and the planters were now filled with weeds.

Sophie entered the broken doorway of the home, seeing the inside was vacant. She passed through each of the rooms, sensing a lost liveliness to the home. She stopped before the fireplace and crouched down, seeing the depiction of a grand castle carved into the stonework at the back.

"'Beneath our castle.'"

Sophie sifted through the soot in the fireplace. Her fingertips crossed over a metal ring attached to the floor. She pulled on the ring to reveal the base wasn't attached to the fireplace. The stone slab slid back, revealing a wide, wooden staircase leading down into the hollowed-out foundation of the cottage.

Sophie pulled the flashlight from her backpack and turned it on, checking to make sure no one else was around; no one was in sight, except for the birds now living in the rafters. She began making her way down the old staircase cautiously, hearing it creak beneath her feet.

The stairs ended before a large room with dirt and stone walls. At the opposite end, a seven-foot-tall, seven-foot-wide, steel vault door laid before her.

"You sneaky son of a bitch…! You built two," said Sophie with a joyful grin.

She approached the door and examined it. A single keyhole was in the middle.

Sophie removed her backpack and pulled Wagner's key out. She paused, taking in the moment.

She slipped the key into the lock. A perfect fit. She turned it clockwise.

The lock behind the door clattered. The door swung open a few inches under its own weight. Sophie pulled the door open the rest of the way and pointed her flashlight inside.

Sophie stepped in, utterly at a loss for words.

Row after row of rusted bed frames lined the walls of a wide stone chamber, meant for the one remaining secret in Wagner's story.

Sophie stepped inside, cautiously. She pointed her flashlight up at the ceiling, seeing several small, steel tubes leading up to the surface above used to circulate the air. Amidst the bed frames at the back of the chamber sat several stacks of empty art frames. She looked down at her feet, noticing the floor was covered in the one thing the fake vault lacked: salt and rice.

She lifted up an empty wooden frame from the floor and read the placard at the bottom.

The Girl Braiding Her Hair - Albert Anker, 1887

Sophie snickered. "And you gave them away."

Sophie replaced the empty frame and continued to scan the now-empty hiding spot. In the far corner was a stack of wool blankets and steel dishes, similar to those she had found in the previous hiding places.

Her foot brushed against something metal on the floor, lost within the rice and salt. She bent down to pick it up. It was a broken pocket watch with a star of David carved into the silver and gold. She held the pocket watch for a moment, seeing the good man whom she had been so wrong about now in full light.

Sophie spotted something pink on the floor at her feet. She bent down and inspected it. It was a broken white and pink glass teacup. Beside it was a dark, glass cork bottle. Sophie picked up the empty bottle and read the label written in pen: *Butterscotch*.

Sophie sat down on the floor and held the bottle, feeling an ache in her heart. She held the bottle up to her chest, then uncorked it, smelling the sweet scent lingering inside. Looking down into the bottle, she noticed a rolled-up piece of paper within it.

She pulled the paper out and unfolded it. She read it to herself, the lights from the vents above illuminating the page for her like rays piercing through a clouded sky.

The works I have hidden here shall always remain hidden. Hidden in the hands of those who deserve them the most. Those who have had their lives taken away. Perhaps by giving a part of the world to them, it might be the first step towards filling the grand void left behind. Their journey has been just as harsh, side by side with humanity's prized possessions.

Let them remain hidden in plain sight. Passing unnoticed until their owners feel it rightfully so as to return them to the world. I've seen the errors of my ways, and I have come to regret them all my life. I can never repay the debt that now rests on my soul, no matter how many I have saved.

So, let them remain hidden. As someone once told me, art isn't about the colors we see on a canvas, nor the shapes that we carve in stone. They are people's lives: the world's greatest masterpieces.

~ Peter

Hyde Park Adventures

The Colonel's Lost Vault

An Article by Sophie Lions

How much is art worth? To the right people, a lot. Now, imagine, if you will, a vault filled with stolen artwork. The world's greatest stories, painted in oil, stolen from the world and hidden away. Crates stacked in a small warehouse sized space, each filled with the most valuable works in human history. How much would that be worth? A life? Or even hundreds of lives? A price too great to measure.

This was my most recent journey: to discover the truth as to whether such a place, filled with immeasurable wealth, truly existed, and if so, return it's lost and stolen contents to the world. You can imagine my surprise when I did indeed learn there was such a place. But what I uncovered during my journey was even more surprising: the story of one man and his selfless humanity.

Behind every work of art is someone trying to connect with the world. Someone sharing their own experiences and dreams, as well as their own story. Same goes for the curator of these stolen treasures, Peter Wagner, in his own way. Through his collection and the clues he left behind—written in his own words—he shared with me his tale. A German Nazi Colonel, who ended the war as a martyr. An angel among demons, protecting the world's most cherished works from the Nazi's selfish shroud. While the Nazi's brutalized and propagandazied both Germany's heart, Wagner risked both his life and his own humanity to see that Germany and the world had a future. Wagner's story took him, and me, on a journey of beauty and self-discovery: from Athens' blue-crowned hills—among caves guarding his secret behind the gates of hell itself—filled with steaming vents and devils dressed in men's clothing to the vineyards of Florence, home to a 14th century prison guarded by knights who loyally protected his secret in stone. A journey which led me all the way to his hometown, peacefully resting along the shores of a lake painted with more colors than a palette can hold. And what I learned was that he was a hero seeking redemption. One we should celebrate. For with his sacrifice, he protected something more valuable than art: he defended people's lives.

Wagner understood that art is never made for just one individual. Not for any one king, a lone Pope, or a rogue dictator seeking to rule without mercy. Art is made for all of us, for the world as a whole. And when a group of people had their world taken from them, he chose to give that part of the world back in return, hoping to repay even a small portion of that debt.

So, while I regretfully never found Wagner's lost art collection, I can confirm that those works are safe and where they rightfully deserve to be. And perhaps, just maybe, one day they shall be returned to us all. But only when the time is right. When the shudder of gunfire and the horns of war fall silent, then we'll see them again. To quote the great collector himself:

"Let them remain hidden. As someone once told me, art isn't about the colors we see on a canvas, nor the shapes that we carve in stone. They are people's lives: the world's greatest masterpieces."

Until our next adventur.

Sophie Lions

Epilogue
LONDON, ENGLAND

HEARING THE GENTLE piano and cello players perform the evening's serenade, Oz sat at his table overlooking the Thames River as it sparkled in the twilight with the endless riverboats. He was dressed in his finest white collared shirt and waistcoat, looking to fit in with the crowd among the high-priced establishment. London's Friday nightlife had come, and all that was missing was his guest of honor. He checked his watch and sighed, seeing another ten minutes had passed.

Oz drank his water in his solitude. He heard someone approach him to his right. As he diverted his attention, he choked on his water.

Sophie stood before him, dressed in a burgundy evening gown and heels. Her hair was pulled back into a curled bun with her bangs draping either side of her makeup-complemented complexion. She slung her purse over the chair across from Oz and sat down gracefully.

Oz's heart beat against his chest out of nervousness, unable to recognize his longtime friend and colleague. "You look…"

"Like a barbarian in stilettos?" Sophie replied. "Yeah, I feel like it. Don't rub it in. Took me an hour just to get my hair to stay the way it is."

"No, you look... incredible."

Sophie paused as she sat, visually caught off-guard by his compliment. She sat down and pulled the napkin from the table before draping it across her lap. She picked up the menu and began reading it. "'Figured I'd try to look more presentable for once."

Oz snickered, taking a look at the menu. "Thank you."

Sophie smiled at him and winked. "You've always been there for me, Wizard. 'Was the least I could do for you."

Oz smiled back, looking back down at his menu. "If it helps, don't think of this as a date. Think of it as a celebration of your latest story and continuous employment."

Sophie chuckled.

The two of them sat reading their menus in silence as the waiter approached the table. Oz ordered a bottle of wine to share as Sophie continued to analyze her menu as though he was about to test her on its contents. He requested another moment from the waiter as Sophie bit at her index finger anxiously.

As the ambiance of the restaurant once more filled their conversation, Sophie finally put her menu down, appearing as though she was ready to crawl out of her own skin. "God, I've never been used to this. Even when I was little. Honestly, I think this is the longest I've sat still in a while without someone pointing a gun at me.

Oz lowered his menu. "Would it help if we discussed something else besides the date?"

"Yes, please," Sophie replied, drinking her water.

Oz dug through his mind, trying to think of a question to ask. "How was Germany? Did you ever square your debts with Bjorn?"

Sophie laughed boisterously causing the tables around them to stare. She set her water glass down. "Oh! It's been squared. More like buried would be a better way to phrase it."

"And how was Corbin?"

"Corbin's swell. Send you his regards by the way," Sophie replied, eating a slice of bread from the basket on the table.

"And what about you?"

"What do you mean?" Sophie asked, chewing her bread.

"I mean, how are you? After everything with Bjorn and seeing Corbin? I know you don't get much time to sit still, so how are you doing?"

Sophie swallowed. She sat idle for a moment with almost a torn and perplexed look in her eyes. She placed her bread down on the plate before her and cleaned her hands as though she had something important to say.

"Nazer's back…" she muttered.

The waiter reapproached the table with their wine. The two of them sat in silence with their eyes locked, waiting for the waiter to leave. Oz could see the lingering fear in Sophie's eyes. The waiter stepped away from the table as Sophie took a drink of her wine. Oz watched her place her wine glass back down; the same hand with two digits missing shaking subtly, uncontrollably.

"You saw him?" Oz asked.

Sophie shook her head, keeping her attention on the table. "I don't know what he wants, but he's out there looking for me."

Oz took a drink of his wine, feeling the tension at the table becoming unsettling. He placed his wine glass back down and cleared his throat. "Well, he'll have to go through a lot of people who love you first: Corbin, Izzie, me…"

Sophie stared up at him in surprise.

Oz looked away from her, picking up his wine again nervously. "Oh, and Marco," he said, drinking his wine.

They both laughed.

Oz set his glass back down. "To hell with him. There's no way he'll find you in a city this big. Besides, I have just the thing to take your mind off of him."

Oz reached into his pocket. He pulled out a folded sheet of paper and handed it over to her across the table. "I was gonna wait until after dinner, but now seems like a good time."

"What's this?" Sophie asked, unfolding the page.

"Did some reading up on your 'Earl of Pembroke,' William Marshal II, while you were away in Germany. Not much on him, but our clue about the knights of the red cross did help. I found that among a set of documents written by one Guillaume de Chartres—

grand master of the Knight Templar—in 1218. One that thankfully wasn't found at their headquarters during the fall of their order and burned with everything else."

Sophie began reading the document. "It's in French."

Oz nodded. "Just read."

Oz watched her intrigued expression with a giddy smile as he drank his wine.

Sophie muttered the document out loud as she read. "'On a foggy and rainy morning, we brought the Earl of Pembroke ashore. To the north we rode, under French escort, towards Paris to speak with the Bishop, Pierre de La Chapelle. There, they spoke in the sight of God, before the Rose window, of changes being made to the cathedral to house William's offering.'"

Oz waited for her to connect the dots.

"Mud inlets!" Sophie said with growing excitement. "Normandy! William Marshall *did* take the jewels to France! He must have brought them with him when he met with the French king after King John's death. Which means—"

"He entrusted them to the Bishop of Paris there, under guard by the Knight Templar. And not just anywhere. The same place where that document was found."

They both spoke in unison. "Notre Dame."

Sophie and Oz both smiled with excitement.

Sophie quickly hurried up from the table and removed her shoes.

She ran through the restaurant, only to stop and run back for her purse. She kissed Oz on the lips, catching him off guard.

Oz sat stunned for a moment with his eyes closed. He opened his eyes to find her dashing towards the main entrance, weaving her way around waiters and tables. "Wait, where are you going?"

"Where do you think!?" Sophie shouted back.

Oz sighed and picked up his wine glass, finding himself alone at the table once again. "France."

For More Worldy Adventures Visit
TSWieland.com

Thank you!

Made in the USA
Monee, IL
08 July 2022

0d0f1ac8-a3ad-4262-a2f3-ef3b4f2ff4f5R01